A. M. Donelan

Flora Adair or Love Works Wonders

Vol. I

A. M. Donelan

Flora Adair or Love Works Wonders
Vol. I

ISBN/EAN: 9783337272777

Printed in Europe, USA, Canada, Australia, Japan

Cover: Foto ©Andreas Hilbeck / pixelio.de

More available books at **www.hansebooks.com**

FLORA ADAIR;

OR,

Love works Wonders.

BY A. M. DONELAN.

"IN FUNICULIS ADAM TRAHAM EOS, IN VINCULIS CHARITATIS."
Osee xi. 4.

IN TWO VOLUMES.

VOL. I.

LONDON:
CHAPMAN AND HALL, 193, PICCADILLY.
1867.

FLORA ADAIR.

CHAPTER I.

In Rome, on a bright sunny morning in the
month of March, 186–, two ladies were seated in
a drawing-room, the windows of which looked
upon the Corso. Mother and daughter they evidently were ; and, as they play a prominent part
in this story, we may be permitted to devote a
short time to describing them.

As a mark of respect to age, we shall give the
elder lady precedence. Although she was dressed
in black, and seated at a table working, one could
judge that her figure was tall and elegant. In her
youth she had been a great beauty; yet it could
not be said that strong traces of that beauty still
lingered over those thin, worn features, for " sor-
rows, nor few, nor light," had set their mark
upon them. But neither time nor grief had de-
stroyed the calm, gentle expression of that countenance, ever ready to light up with a cheerful

smile and look happy in the happiness of others. Her character may be expressed in a single word —devotedness. As daughter, sister, wife, and mother, her whole life had been one almost unbroken act of self-sacrifice. Most of those whom she loved had been taken from her while she was still in the bloom of life; her children alone remained. The two elder—a son and a daughter—were married, and therefore, in some degree, lost to her, so that Flora, her second daughter, was the only one really left; and in this, her youngest child, was centred Mrs. Adair's every hope and thought. Their affection was mutual: Flora Adair believed herself to be blessed indeed in her mother.

And now let us turn to the young lady. We are obliged to confess that, although she is considered to be like her mother, it is a resemblance not boasting of much physical beauty. A sad drawback this, doubtless, to a heroine; but, according to the old saying, " what can't be cured must be endured." Her figure, however, was really good; she was about the middle height, with tiny hands and feet, a broad forehead, blue eyes—fairly large and dark—a small but well-formed nose, round cheeks, a large mouth, with a tolerably good, but an over-crowded, range of teeth; a complexion far from bright or clear, and a profusion of dark brown hair brushed off her forehead, and twisted round the back of her head in thick plaits. Such is our heroine's picture— not a very attractive one, it may be said, and of this no one was more fully conscious than Flora Adair herself.

As to her character, she was generally looked upon as cold, and somewhat haughty, yet she was really rather indifferent than haughty; but how often is indifference of manner called haughtiness in the world! Her seeming coldness in a great measure came from a shrinking dread of forcing herself upon others. It is true she cared but little for society, and found a young lady's life weary and objectless; her constant thought was how to make the hours go faster. Had any one asked her why she found them so long, she would probably have borrowed her answer from Shakespeare, and have said—

"Not having that, which, having, makes them short."

Something of all this could be seen in her listless air, as she sat there near the window, not reading, but with a book in her hand, gazing out vacantly, as if to ask, "How shall I get through to-day? Will it be anything more interesting than usual?" Better, perhaps, had it not been so, some would say—better had the blank been left unfilled, as she was now but negatively unhappy, the unhappiness arising from her own disposition, ever yearning for something more, something deeper, than she had yet known; and also because she had not yet learned that "the first principle of wisdom is to be satisfied with that which is;" or "in the state in which she was therewith to be content."

Which is the better lot :—a short spell of deep happiness and after misery, or an even life, unmarked by great joy or great sorrow? Flora Adair would answer, "Give me, were it only for a short time, intense happiness, at any cost; no price is too great for it, or it would be worth nothing!" So that had the choice been offered to her she would have taken the very lot which was destined for her.

There was another member of their little circle, a young lady of about Flora's age, named Lucy Martin, who was travelling with the Adairs, and who was absent for a few days on a visit to some friends at Albano : as she shortly afterwards returned home, it is needless to describe her more fully.

Mrs. Adair looked at her watch, and said, "Half-past ten, Flora; and the Eltons are to call for us at eleven. We had better get ready."

Flora followed her mother out of the room,

letting her book fall, rather than placing it, upon the table.

Soon after, the carriage came, and away they drove with their friends to Frascati, where they were to have a croquet match, and an *al-fresco* dinner given by Mrs. Elton. Their party now consisted of that lady herself, her son and younger daughter, and the Adairs. At the place of rendezvous—the Villa Torlonia—they were to meet the rest of their friends.

It was a soft, balmy day, such as, in the middle of March, can only be enjoyed in Italy; the hot, bright sun tempered by the fresh breeze of early spring, and the air perfumed by the fragrance of the wild flowers, which so abound in southern lands. Out of the Porta San Giovanni and along the Via Tusculum lies the road to Frascati, bounded on one side by the Alban hills, and on the other by the desert Campagna.

The desultory conversation which was carried on during the drive consisted of the usual subjects talked of among strangers in Rome, and during Lent:—"How do you like Rome? What have you seen? Have you obtained tickets for all the ceremonies of Holy Week?" The horrors of crushing at these ceremonies—histories told of ladies having had their veils torn off, their prayer-books dashed from their hands, and, as a climax, fainting—as, on a memorable occasion, when a stalwart English lady called out to the crowd ruthlessly pressing upon a falling victim, "Take her up—take her up! for if she is killed we shall all be shut out from the Cena!"

In the course of the drive, Helena Elton said suddenly to Flora, "Have you happened to meet with a Mr. Earnscliffe who is here now?"

"No. What of him? Is he anything out of the common?"

"Rather," rejoined Miss Helena, who slightly indulged in mild slang, and generally answered in a prolonged, emphasised manner, "rather," when she meant to say "very much," "exceedingly," &c.

"Then tell me something of him. What is he like?" asked Flora.

"Like something very tall, strong, handsome, and aristocratic in appearance; in manner, proud and distant, certainly not a lady-worshipper."

"And very rich," interposed Mrs. Elton. "I knew his parents most intimately, but they both died when he was quite a child, and I had lost sight of the family altogether, until by chance we met him abroad a short time ago. Earnscliffe Court is a magnificent place."

"A capital speculation, Helena," said Flora, with a smile. "Do you enter the lists? As you seem to think the conquest a difficult one, it might be worth a struggle."

"Oh! he is not in my line at all—I should be afraid of him; but if you think so much of the prize you should enter the lists yourself."

"No, no, Helena, I am not so foolish as to risk a defeat for what I do not value; besides, I am neither pretty nor fascinating. How, then, could I catch this modern Childe Harold, as you describe him? Moreover, I hate a *bon parti*. I shall never marry, unless I meet with one whom I can admire and love beyond all the world!"

The conversation did not seem to please Mrs. Elton, who cut it short by saying, "It is all very well to read about desperate love in novels; but, believe me—and I have seen a great deal of the world—marriages based upon calm respect and affection are far happier than your ardent love matches. You will understand this, dear child, when you are a little older."

Helena shrugged her shoulders, and murmured in an under tone, meant only for Flora's ear, "Oh, have I not heard enough of all this!"

"Well, Mrs. Elton," replied Flora, "I am not such a child after all! I am more than one-and-twenty, and can vouch for it that *I* will never have anything to say to a marriage based upon 'calm respect and affection!'"

Mrs. Adair—who had remained silent, quietly amused at this animated discussion—now thought that it was going a little too far, and managed to change the conversation.

Shortly afterwards they arrived at the entrance to the Villa Torlonia, where they alighted, and the coachman drove to the hotel in Frascati to await their order to return.

The villa is but a stone's-throw from the town: a magnificent terrace leads to the large, rambling, white building, in which one could well imagine half-a-dozen families living with separate households. The view from the front is grand indeed. Beneath the windows, and across the high road before them, is the Casino, with its pretty gardens; beyond this, and far below, stretches out the great Campagna, and Rome, with her countless domes and steeples gleaming in the sun.

The grounds of the villa are, in their style, very beautiful and extensive, although to our English eyes somewhat stiff and formal, cut up as they are by broad avenues, with their majestic lines of trees. Across the centre, and leading from the grand terrace, a wide opening shows an artificial grotto, cascade, and basin; a flight of covered steps on either side of the abundant stream of falling water winds under this cascade, and leads to a terrace above, from behind which spreads out a beautiful bosquet, the bounds of which are entirely hidden by thick foliage. The outer walls of these steps are so overgrown by luxuriant vegetation as to be completely masked, so that, on approaching, these apertures look like entrances to subterranean caverns.

This picturesque cascade was the place of rendezvous; towards it, therefore, our friends were proceeding, when Charles Elton, who had for a moment or two been watching a figure moving among the trees, exclaimed, " By Jove, there's Earnscliffe ! "

"How delightful !" rejoined Mrs. Elton. "Now he cannot avoid making one of our party. Go quickly, Charles, and overtake him : we will follow."

Charles soon captured the retreating Mr. Earnscliffe, who had just seen the Eltons, and was making a desperate, but vain, effort to escape. He could not pretend that he did not hear Charles, so with a tolerably good grace he turned and surrendered.

" Where on earth were you going so fast? " said Charles, nearly out of breath. " Here is my mother, who is determined on making you join our party ! "

." Indeed ! " accompanied by anything but a look of pleasure.

Mrs. Elton advanced to meet him with out-stretched hands. "How charming to find you here, Mr. Earnscliffe; you cannot well refuse to join us, see the croquet, and partake of a cold dinner. I would have written to invite you, but that I so feared a refusal, feeling certain that you would not think our croquet party worth the loss of a day from Rome's immortal ruins. I do so wish I could prevail upon you to accompany us to some of them; how delightful it would be to have *such* a guide!"

"Pray be undeceived, Mrs. Elton; I should be but a very poor guide for you; believe me, 'Murray' would be much more instructive, and would enable you to talk far more learnedly about those things than I could."

Was there not a covert sneer in those words? The lady, however, did not see it, or appeared not to do so. As a possible husband for one of her daughters, many things must be pardoned in him which would not be passed over in a poor younger son. She replied with a smile, "Well, we can arrange that at some other time; for the present, having caught you here, we may of course count upon your remaining with us." Taking his answer for granted, she continued, "Allow me to present my friends, Mrs. and Miss Adair." Mr. Earns-cliffe bowed to the Adairs, shook hands with

Helena, and then walked on with Mrs. Elton towards the cascade.

Mrs. Elton opened the conversation with that very original question, " How do you like Rome, Mr. Earnscliffe ?"

" In what way do you mean ?—as she was once, the mistress of the world, and her people a nation of kings ; or as she is now, the decrepid representative of all the superstitions of bygone ages ?"

Mrs. Elton laughed approvingly ; but Flora, who was walking close behind with Charles Elton, said, in a slightly subdued tone, " See what prejudice will do ! I *do* wonder how persons, otherwise noble and generous, can say such things simply for the pleasure of abusing what they do not understand, and therefore dislike ! "

" Oh ! Miss Adair, he might have heard you," exclaimed Charles Elton.

" *N'importe!*" said Flora, with an impatient shrug of her shoulders.

Almost at the same moment, Mr. Earnscliffe, who, notwithstanding Mrs. Elton's efforts to drown Flora's voice, had heard every word, turned and bowed to her, saying, with rather a scornful smile, " Bravo, Miss Adair, you are quite an apostle, and I, according to you, am something very like a simpleton ! "

" I did not say that," she answered, blushing ;

"it would have been rude and untrue ; but, were you to think of it, I am sure you will admit that what I *did* say is true."

He smiled, returned to Mrs. Elton, and said, "Adair !—a Scotch name ?"

"An Irish name, also ; my friends are Irish."

"Indeed, one might have guessed it, from the spirit of the young lady's observations."

"Mamma," interrupted Helena, "there they are all at the cascade waiting for us ; and I see Thomas, too, with the croquet boxes."

"Well, my dear, we are going to them ; don't be impatient."

This injunction was given in vain. Helena had already darted off to her friends at the cascade. They consisted of Mr. and Mrs. Penton, —both young ; the lady, tall, slight, and dark, —very elegant, but apparently haughty, and evidently accustomed to be admired ; the gentleman, a large and rather an unwieldy figure, with a sandy complexion, and a heavy, although good expression of countenance ; Mary Elton, Helena's sister, and somewhat like her, but in manner as grave and sedate as the other was gay and thoughtless ; Mr. Mainwaring, and Mr. Caulfield,— the latter, a good-looking, bright, laughing Irishman ; the former, an Englishman, and particularly grave and solemn.

Helena was received with marked pleasure. Her great liveliness made her a general favourite. She was soon in deep conversation with Mary and the gentlemen about the selection of the croquet ground, while the Pentons turned to greet the others who had just come up.

Mrs. Elton announced, in a delighted tone, that they had been fortunate enough to meet and capture Mr. Earnscliffe. " What an addition to our party, is it not, Mary?" turning to her eldest daughter.

"Yes," Mary replied, quickly; "we are all, I am sure, very happy to see Mr. Earnscliffe. Does he condescend to play croquet?"

" I have never played," said he ; " but I have seen people knocking balls about with things like long-handled mallets. That is croquet, I believe?"

" Oh, Mr. Earnscliffe," exclaimed Helena, " what a description to give of playing croquet ! But whatever you may think of it, I find it very jolly fun, and mean to lose no time before setting to work."

"To play, you mean, Miss Elton !" said a voice behind her ; and on turning round she found that Mr. Caulfield was the corrector, whereupon she at once gaily attacked him.

" I never heard of such audacity, Mr. Caulfield ; you, a Hibernian, to venture to correct me, a true

Briton, in the use of my own language! Take
care that you don't get a defeat at croquet for
this!"

"I am sure it will not be *your* fault, Miss
Elton, if I do not"—in an aside, meant only for
her ear—"But have you not conquered already,
though not, perhaps, at croquet?"

She got a little red, and said quickly, "This is
all waste of time! Mary, you said you had seen
a place that would do beautifully for us; so, lead
on. I will go and see that Thomas has all the
things right."

Mary did as she was desired, while her sprightly
sister, followed by Mr. Caulfield, ran back to the
servant to see that all was in order.

Helena and her companion were enjoying themselves greatly, if loud laughter is a sign of enjoyment. At length they came running after the
others to a broad grassy alley, bordered and over-
hung by wide-spreading trees. This was the
place which Mary had spoken of, and, fortunately,
it met with Helena's approval. "Oh, yes, Mary,
this will do, capitally," she said; "and there is
shade, too, under these trees. Mark out the
ground, place the arches and the balls, and give
me a croquet-stick!"

"Yes, miss," replied Thomas, who seemed
quite an adept at arranging the playground.

Having done this to his young mistress's satisfaction, he approached Mrs. Elton and asked where the dinner was to be laid.

"It is true, we have not chosen where we shall dine. Caroline," to Mrs. Adair, "will you come with me and seek a nice place for our repast, while the young people begin their game? We can trust them to Mrs. Penton's chaperoning for a few moments, although she is too young and too pretty for such a post."

Mrs. Penton laughed, and said, "You may very safely trust them to me, and I will give you a good account of my stewardship when you return. So you may go in peace."

Mr. Caulfield, who helped Helena to arrange the game, now struck his "mallet," as Mr. Earnscliffe had named it, three times on one of the balls in order to attract attention; and called out, "Who will play? Will you, Mrs. Penton?"

"Not just yet. I will sit down and look on for the present; later, perhaps, I may take a turn."

"Then the players are, the Misses Elton, Miss Adair, Penton, Mainwaring, Elton?"

"Nay," interrupted Charles, "I am quite unable to play to-day."

"Mr. Earnscliffe?" continued Mr. Caulfield, inquiringly.

"I know nothing of the game, and I should not like to make my first essay among such proficients as, I presume, you all are."

"Then there only remains my humble self to make up the party. Now for the division; you ladies should draw lots for choosing sides."

"I dare say Flora is as willing as I am to yield this to Helena," said Mary. "If so, we need not take the trouble of drawing lots."

Flora smiled assent, when Helena exclaimed, "Very green of you both. However, it is your affair, not mine; and as I am decidedly the gainer by it, I ought not to object. First, then, I choose Flora; secondly, Mr. Mainwaring. I leave Mary to manage Mr. Penton and Mr. Caulfield; no easy matter, I can answer for it, with regard to the latter gentleman."

"How cruel not to choose me as one of your subjects," he said in a light tone, yet looking a little annoyed.

"Choose you for a subject! Not for worlds. I shall delight in croqueting you; and this, of course, I could not do if you were on my side. But as my enemy, you shall be well croqueted!" and as her foot rested upon one of the balls near her, she looked laughingly at him, and struck the ball lightly with her "mallet."

The elder ladies now returned; the gentlemen

placed stools for them near to Mrs. Penton; and, after some jesting about the conduct of her charge during their absence, the game commenced.

For a considerable time the contest continued with varied success, Helena and Mr. Caulfield seeming to think more of croqueting each other than of anything else, so that they were frequently called to order by their respective sides. Flora had become quite animated, and intent on victory, if only to disappoint Mr. Penton, who said, when they were beginning, " Oh ! our party is certain to win, two gentlemen and a lady against two ladies and one gentleman. I really think we might give them odds ! " a suggestion which was indignantly spurned by the players of the opposite side, who declared that skill and not strength was the thing required, and, therefore, they had not the slightest fear of losing. Flora devoted all her energies to making good the boast, and she was well seconded by Mr. Mainwaring, whose steady, cautious game counteracted Helena's wild, though at times brilliant, play.

Towards the end of the game the excitement grew very great; four had gained the goal, and all now turned on Mr. Caulfield and Helena; she had only the last arch to make, and he had two

arches, but it was his turn to play; so, if he
could manage to send his ball straight through
the two arches, and on to the starting-point, the
game would be his. His ball was badly placed,
however, in a diagonal line from the first arch, so
that it would require great skill to make it pass
through that and go straight to the other; yet
he sometimes made very skilful hits, and it was
a moment of intense interest to his adversaries.
He struck the ball; but, instead of sending it
through the first arch, it grazed the side of it
and stopped short. This gave Helena a fair
opportunity for trying to croquet him; the
safe play was not to do it, but to make the
last arch at once and ensure the game, yet it
was a strong temptation—how charming for
Helena to send his ball far away and distance
him! On the other hand, it was of course possible that she might not croquet him well, and
then the chances were that he would win. She
looked at her partners as if to ask permission to
risk the game.

"Very well," said Flora, smiling; "on your
head be it if we lose!"

"How can you give your sanction to such
recklessness, Miss Adair?" exclaimed Mr. Mainwaring. "Pray, Miss Elton, consider for a moment; if you will play rationally we are sure to

win, but if you persist in croqueting we shall probably lose—at least we should deserve it."

"Just the contrary! 'Nothing venture nothing win.' Oh! how can a *man* be so cautious? It is a blessing for you, Mr. Mainwaring, that you are not a lover of mine, or I should play such pranks to rouse you into something like rashness as would 'make the angels weep.' Hurrah, then, for daring and a good croquet! Now, Mr. Caulfield!" and with an ominous shake of the head she raised her "mallet" to strike, amidst much laughter at her attack upon poor Mr. Mainwaring, who, although he did his best to join in the merriment at his own expense, evidently winced under it. Down came the mallet with a sharp ring upon her own ball, on which her foot was firmly planted, and away bounded the other to the very end of the last line of arches.

"Bravo! bravo, Miss Elton!" arose from all sides, as she stood looking triumphantly at Mr. Mainwaring, and saying, "Now, Mr. Caution, I shall not only win the game for you, but distance one of our adversaries!"

"Not so fast, if you please, Miss Helena," interposed Mr. Caulfield. "I might save my distance yet."

"Might! but you are not equal to it, fair sir; only *do* play quickly, I am all impatience to hear

our side proclaimed victorious, after Mr. Penton's
contemptuous boast that *his* side could afford to
give us odds, because, forsooth, it numbers two of
the precious male sex, and ours has only one of
them! But, to the proof; we are losing time!"

Mr. Caulfield made a good attempt at saving
his distance, but he failed; so Helena came in in
full triumph, amidst loud acclamations.

Mrs. Elton immediately proposed that they
should take a stroll before their repast, which
was ordered for two o'clock. If they were to
drive back by Grotto Ferrata, she said, they must
start, at latest, by four.

"But," objected Helena, "we have had but
one game of croquet; and Mrs. Penton and Mr.
Earnscliffe have not played at all! Poor Charles
cannot; so it is not a matter of any interest for
him."

"As for me, Helena, foregoing a game will not
render me *tout à fait desolée;* and I think I may
answer too for Mr. Earnscliffe." He bowed, and
Mrs. Penton continued, "So it would be a pity to
lose the beautiful drive by Grotto Ferrata for the
sake of another round of croquet. It is much
better to follow Mrs. Elton's suggestion."

The young lady saw that there was nothing to
be done but to submit, whilst her mother said,
"Come, Helena, let Thomas carry away those

things. We are going to walk." And they all
went on, excepting Helena, Flora, and Mr. Caulfield; the two latter waiting for Helena, as she
lingered, looking, with an expression of comic
resignation, at Thomas "bagging the balls," as
she expressed it; then, turning away, she said
with a sigh, "It is too bad not to give poor crest-
fallen Mr. Caulfield a chance of revenge!"

"Shure and niver mind, cushla machree," he
answered, imitating the brogue of the Irish pea-
santry. "I'll have it some other time. Whin
did you iver know an Irishman be bate in ginerosity?"

"May I ask, Mr. Caulfield, if you Irish call
revenge 'ginerosity?'" she exclaimed in a mocking tone; then she added, more seriously, "Please
to let us get on quickly, or we shall lose our
friends; and oh, Flora, what a lecture we
should get for separating ourselves from the
rest!"

The party was soon overtaken; and Flora observed, to her great amusement, that Mrs. Elton
had succeeded in getting Mary and Mr. Earnscliffe together.

For about half-an-hour they wandered about
the grounds, when Mrs. Elton led the way to
their *al fresco* banqueting-hall—a grassy plateau,
so surrounded by trees as to be shaded from the

afternoon sun; and here the servants had laid
out the dinner.

They had spread a tablecloth, fastened down
by pegs; in the centre were baskets of flowers
and fruits, surrounded by tempting sweet dishes,
and next by the more substantial delicacies. Mrs.
Elton had planned this pic-nic, priding herself
justly on her catering for these occasions. In
this case her task was comparatively an easy one,
as Spillman—the Gunter of Rome—had a branch
establishment at Frascati, whence the feast was
supplied.

" Really this is quite a banquet of pleasure ! "
said Mrs. Penton; "all the delicacies of a grand
dinner, without its heat, boredom, and ceremony.
We certainly owe you a vote of thanks, Mrs.
Elton ! "

" Well," replied Mrs. Elton, with a complacent
smile, " I do think that Spillman has carried out
my orders very fairly; and the most acceptable
vote of thanks you can award me is to let me see
you do justice to the repast; so let us begin at
once; the ground must serve for seats. I told
Thomas to bring all the shawls from the carriages in case any one should like to make
cushions of them."

For some time the principal sound to be heard
was the clatter of knives and forks. Gradually

this grew fainter, and was succeeded by the clatter of tongues. Champagne was freely quaffed, healths were drunk, and much laughter was excited by Mr. Caulfield, who rose and made a speech,—such as only an Irishman could make, with credit to himself—concluding it by asserting that his highest ambition was to be permitted the honour of proposing a toast to Miss Helena Elton, as the queen of croquet players, and by expressing a hope that she would return thanks for the toast herself. He remained standing, with his glass in his hand; and when the laughter had subsided a little, Helena, looking round the table, said, "I appeal to you all : can a gentleman refuse to act as a lady's deputy in returning thanks, if she requests him to do so for her?"

The answer was unanimous : "Certainly not?"

"Then, Mr. Caulfield," said she, with a graceful bow to him, "I hope you will do me the favour to return thanks for the toast which is about to be drunk in my honour!"

With one accord the gentlemen rose, applauding her, and claiming the toast. Mr. Caulfield made a profound inclination to Helena, and after a few more flowery words, proposed the toast, proclaiming her "the queen of croquet players and repartee." It was drunk with great enthu-

siasm; and all sat down, not excepting Mr. Caulfield, who seemed quite unconscious of the
wondering looks directed towards him. After
a few moments, however, he stood up again, and
commenced with the utmost gravity :—

" Ladies and gentlemen,—I rise to return
thanks to the gentleman who gave the last toast,
which we all drank with such unusual pleasure.
Miss Helena Elton has done me the honour of
calling upon me to act as her deputy on this occasion, an honour I so highly appreciate that I consider myself more favoured by fortune than any
gentleman in this worshipful company, save the
one who had the happiness of proposing a toast so
admirably adapted to my fair client." He was
interrupted by calls of "hear, hear," "bravo,"
and much laughter; and after continuing for
some time in an amusing strain, he sat down
"amidst loud applause."

To Mrs. Elton it seemed as if the hilarity would
never end. At length she said, " I am very
sorry to interrupt your enjoyment, but we must
think of getting home. And see how the day has
changed! I do not think it will be wise to extend
our drive by Grotto Ferrata."

But the younger portion of the company would
not hear of any danger from change of weather;
true, there was a black cloud in the direction of

the town, but it would probably drift away, they said, and, at all events, there would only be a shower, which, as Helena (who was in wild spirits) declared, would but add to the beauty of their drive through the fine old wood of Grotto Ferrata. The green of the trees would look so bright and fresh, sparkling with rain-drops. She could not conceive any necessity for haste, or for shortening their drive home. Mrs. Elton persisted in thinking that there was immediate danger of rain, and suggested that they should seek refuge in the cascade steps, where, at least, they would find shelter. In this, too, she was over-ruled; all consented, however, to have the carriages ordered. There was a little more drinking of wine, eating of fruit, laughing, and merry talk, when, suddenly, a large drop of rain fell upon the table-cloth, followed by another and another, dropping slowly and heavily,

> " One by one,
> Like the first of a thunder-shower."

The gentlemen started to their feet, helped up the ladies, urging them to run quickly to the cascade steps, as it was evident that there was heavy rain approaching.

Helena looked a little discomfited as she caught her mother's reproachful glance fixed upon her; but she carried it off with a laugh, and " Well !

it will only be a shower. You'll see that I shall be right after all!"

"Come, come," called out Mr. Penton; "you ladies must wrap yourselves up in whatever shawls there are, and get to shelter as fast as possible, or you will be drenched with rain. In the meantime, I will go to the hotel and send any other wrappings that I can find. You will be sure to take cold if you sit there upon those damp steps."

"Why can't you send one of Spillman's men, George?" said his wife.

"My dear, don't you see that they have already as much as they can possibly do to get those things away before the storm comes on?"

"Oh, as you like, my dear George; I only wished to save you trouble," languidly replied Mrs. Penton.

As they hastened to the cascade, the large drops fell faster and faster; then they suddenly ceased. The quickness with which thunder-storms come on in southern climes is proverbial. Less than an hour before, the sun was shining brightly in an azure sky, and a light breeze gave freshness to the air. Now, that azure sky was all overcast; the air was heavy and sultry; there was a dead stillness all around; and the very leaves of the trees seemed to be weighed down, drooping under some unseen pressure. It was indeed the lull before the storm.

Hardly had they got into shelter, and Mr. Penton, accompanied by Charles Elton, had started for the hotel, when there arose a hurricane of wind,—whistling, tearing through the trees, waving the largest and strongest of them in its wild grasp, like the merest reeds; whirling into clouds the gravel of the walks, and rushing with unchecked fury through the covered passages wherein our party had taken refuge. Then, back again it came with unabated vigour; and across the black, lowering sky darted a vivid flash of lightning, followed almost instantaneously by a clap of thunder which seemed to burst over the cascade.

It is curious to watch how differently a violent thunder-storm affects people, and ladies in particular. Many make themselves quite foolish on such occasions, indulging in the most silly demonstrations of terror, clinging to each other, hiding their faces, uttering little shrieks to manifest their fears; others, although evidently frightened, have the good sense to remain quiet, and, if they are pious, begin to pray; others, again, seem to take delight in it,—it excites them,—they watch its course with riveted attention, and become lost, so to say, in admiration of its grand yet awful

beauty; looking as if they would fain say, with
the poet,

> " Let me be
> A sharer in thy fierce and far delight,
> A portion of the tempest and of thee ! "

Among our friends there were examples of the
three classes. Mrs. Penton and Helena were of
the first; Mrs. Elton, Mrs. Adair, and Mary, of
the second; and Flora, of the third. She left the
rest, and mounted to the opening at the top,
where she stood leaning against the wall, watching the storm. The lightning flashed, the thunder
rolled and burst over her, and there she stood
alone for some time, until she was startled by a
voice close behind her, saying—

"Miss Adair is, I see, not only an apostle, but
also a braver of storms; quite free from feminine
weakness both in speech and action."

She looked round and saw Mr. Earnscliffe,
whose words seemed to jar upon her ear; yet
there was nothing in them at which she could
take offence, so she answered—

"I do not think I am a coward in any sense of
the word, and I would brave the storm were there
any reason for doing so; but now there is none,
and standing here is not braving it. Why you
say 'braver of storms,' I know not. I merely
came here because it is pleasanter to feel the wind

blowing against one and see the vivid lightning than to sit below on a damp step in a dark passage, listening to senseless exclamations of fear."

"In which you do not share?"

"Certainly not."

"Well then, was I not right in calling you a braver of storms?"

At this moment the sky opened and sent forth a bright forked streak of light, which darted in a serpent-like form through the air, and struck straight into the ground beneath them; with it came the deafening thunder, and, as it died away rumbling in the distance, he said, looking fixedly at her—

"Are you still quite free from fear?"

"From fear—yes; but it was a grand, a solemn sight,—one that none could witness without feeling their own littleness and helplessness; yet we know that no harm can reach us without the consent of Him who rules the storms."

"Yet these storms are very dangerous!" he replied.

"Visible danger does but bring the idea of death more forcibly before us, therefore it always seems to me that all should preserve their calmness in moments like these; not Christians only, but even fatalists,—those because they know that they must submit to the will of God and should make the only preparation then in their power; these, because they think it vain to cry out against fate. It is said that every one finds it difficult to part with life, but I do not believe it. I am sure it is often more difficult to be resigned to live than to be resigned to die!"

"It is!" was the emphatic answer; but as Flora turned to look at him, she saw his lip curling with the same contemptuous smile which she had seen in the morning, and, getting very red, she said—

"Now you are ridiculing me; how foolish it was of me to speak in this way, and to a man! We never know when you are talking seriously, or only drawing us out in order to laugh at us."

"This is not half so difficult for you as it is for us to know when women are true or false," he retorted quickly; but, seeing her look of wonder, he at once added—

"Pardon me. I did not mean to offend you; experience teaches us hard lessons! Still I will try to believe with Byron,

" That two, or one, are almost what they seem,
That goodness is no dream, and happiness no name."

"We have got into rather a gloomy train of conversation," said Flora. "Let us change it to something else, or to silence if you prefer it."

He *did* remain silent, but the expression of his face was so changed, so softened, that Flora wondered why she had ever thought it stern.

The storm appeared to be abating; the rain had almost ceased, but there were still occasional flashes of lightning, and the thunder murmured in the distance; it was evident that the weather was not settled. Mary came up to say that they were to go at once, as the carriages were ready and it was thought better to make no delay, for heavy rain would probably come on again.

Mr. Earnscliff awoke from his fit of abstraction and said—

"Quite right, the sooner we start the better; but first come out and look at the cascade; all is so bright and fresh. It is very delightful after the oppressive sultriness which preceded the storm. We can cross over and go down by the opposite flight of steps."

The girls followed him and stood for a moment looking at the waters falling into the basin underneath. As they were turning away Flora's foot slipped upon the wet moss, and she would have fallen had she not caught hold of Mary's arm, who exclaimed—

"I hope you are not hurt, Flora!"

"What is it?" asked Mr. Earnscliffe, turning back quickly.

"I slipped," replied Flora, "and my ankle pains me slightly. I dare say it will be over in a moment."

"Not a sprain, I hope, Miss Adair," he said, looking anxiously at her; "if so, how shall I forgive myself for being the cause of it? I see you are in pain; pray take my arm, it will give you more support than Miss Elton's."

"There is nothing to forgive or to be annoyed about" (taking his arm); "even if my ankle should be sprained, it is not your fault. I might have slipped anywhere else!"

"Nay, had it not been for me you would not have walked upon stones covered with wet moss; I cannot avoid blaming myself!"

Helena's voice was now heard calling, "Mary! Flora! what can you be about? Mamma is so impatient to be off; we are going, come on quickly!"

Mary turned to Flora: "Can you get down? or will you wait a little, and I or Mr. Earnscliffe will go and tell them?"

"I would rather go at once; and, with Mr. Earnscliffe's kind help, I shall get down the steps very well."

"Then let me really be of some assistance to you; lean heavily on me." And with the greatest care he helped her down the steps.

"Thank you," she said, as they reached the flat ground below; "it was so kind of you to let me lean on you as I did; now, I think, I can get on alone, and need not encumber you any longer." She drew away her arm from his.

"It was anything but an encumbrance, Miss Adair," and he smiled as she had scarcely thought he could smile; "to help you was a most pleasing reparation for the mischief I have caused. Do take my arm again!"

"Yes, I will do so, though not to give you a means of making reparation, since there is nothing to do that for, but because I find that I cannot walk as well as I thought I could. And now let us try to overtake the others."

As soon as they reached the party Helena exclaimed, "Flora, what is the matter? You look so pale!"

"I have sprained my ankle, I believe, and it hurts me a little."

"*Quel malheur!* Then you will not be able to dance to-night. A loss to you gentlemen, I can tell you. Flora was pronounced to be the best dancer at the Wiltons' ball!"

"We are all aware of Miss Adair's superior dancing," rejoined Mr. Caulfield, "except perhaps Mr. Earnscliffe; and, being her countryman, as the painter before a celebrated masterpiece said, *anch' io son pittore !'* I can say, 'I, too, am Irish !'"

"But," said Flora, laughing, "there is a slight difference between the two arts. One of my mistresses at school remarked, on hearing dancing praised, 'Yes, dancing is certainly a great accomplishment; dogs can be taught to do it so well!' We have yet to learn that dogs can be taught to paint."

To poor Flora's great comfort, the gate and the carriages beyond it now came in sight. Mrs. Adair and Mrs. Elton were already seated. As the former saw Flora limping and leaning on Mr. Earnscliffe's arm, she said, "My child, what has happened?" Flora answered that she had hurt her ankle a little, and then she got into the carriage, kindly and skilfully helped by Mr. Earnscliffe, who, as he shook hands with Mrs. Adair, asked permission to call on the next day to inquire after the invalid, which request was of course granted. Mrs. Elton pressed him to come to them in the evening; he refused politely, but firmly; accepting, however, Mrs. Penton's offer of a seat in their carriage back to Rome.

And so ended the croquet party at Frascati.

CHAPTER II.

EASTER TUESDAY had arrived, and all the excitement of Easter in Rome was over. Our
friends had joined in the grand ceremonies of
Holy Week; they had heard the silver trumpets
sound forth the Alleluias on Easter morn, and
on the evening of the same great day they had
looked upon the glorious illumination of *San
Pietro;* on the next day they had seen the *giran-
dola,* or fireworks, on the Pincio; and Easter, with
all its festivities, had become bygone things.

Before we proceed we surely ought to ask how
Flora Adair had got over her accident at Frascati.
On the day after it happened Mr. Earnscliffe
called, as he had said, to inquire for her; and,
considering himself in some degree as the cause
of the mishap, he was quite distressed to find that
it was so serious as to give her a good deal of pain,
and keep her from walking for some time. It
was so tiresome, he said, to be obliged to lie
upon a sofa in such lovely weather—and in Rome,

too! Would that he could do anything to make amends for the mischief he had caused!

He exerted himself to the utmost to amuse and interest her during the time of his visit; and so well did he succeed, that before he left her she had become quite animated, and seemed to have forgotten her ailment. When he stood up to take leave, he said, "I hope, Mrs. Adair, that you will allow me to call again to see how the invalid progresses?"

"Certainly, we shall always be happy to see you, and, now that Flora cannot go out, society is particularly desirable for her. The interest of conversation will make her forget her suffering—for a time, at least."

"Thank you! Then I shall indeed avail myself of your permission; I shall be *so* glad to think that I can in any degree lessen, even for half an hour, the weariness of that imprisonment of which, I must repeat, I feel I am the remote cause."

Thus he went constantly, and Flora found a charm in conversing with him which she had never known before. They often disagreed and looked at things each from a different point of view, yet their *way* of thinking seemed the same; there was sympathy even where they least appeared to agree. As she recovered, and when the excitement of Easter was over, she began to feel the blank caused by the cessation of those long and looked-for visits. There remained nothing to expect from day to day with hope and pleasure. She enjoyed his society as she had never enjoyed that of any other person, and did not at all like the prospect of being obliged to do without it, or indeed without much of it, for the future.

There are women who centre every delight in the object of their affections, and this, to a certain degree, even in friendship ; but in love alone is it fully shown. To love, for such, is to centre everything in the beloved ; they have no fits of great ardour followed by calmness—theirs is one unbroken act of love. Should there be no obstacles to their love, it is to them a source of happiness undreamed of by many, for their world is full. They have attained happiness, as far as it can be attained on earth from earthly things—for the human heart is made for the Infinite, and nothing finite can ever *fully* satisfy it. These do not stop to calculate whether loving another will be for their own advantage; they call that, egotism—the very opposite of love. " *Non amate Dio per voi* " is for them the expression of perfect love ; and is not the love of God the model, ay, and the motor too, of all true human love ? When love is pure and disinterested it wants not its due reward, but it obtains so much the greater recompense the less it seeks.

But should such obstacles arise, should they be separated from the object of their love, their misery is correspondingly great. Like a native of some sunny clime banished in the noonday of life to a northern land, clouded in chilly mists, it is vain to surround him with all that should cheer his heart; vain to strive—how tenderly soever it may be—to beguile his weariness; he pines for the beloved sun of other days, and sighs hopelessly for the glowing brightness of his home. So is the sun of *their* life beclouded,—he who was their sun, he who threw a halo over all, is gone; the chilly mist is ever upon their hearts, and they know in this life something of that terrible torture—the pain of loss.

But another pang is often reserved for them, and it is of all the most bitter; it comes when they have to choose between love and conscience, and when, in obeying the dictates of the latter, they have to bear the reproach of not loving truly, whilst, as they know but too well, they love so fully that few understand or realise it. To feel all this, and yet to be powerless to prove their love, is torture so great that they must indeed be watched over from above if they get safely through the ordeal.

Flora Adair thought and dreamed of the truest love to be found on earth, and without it life seemed to her but a sunless sojourn. Could she but have soared high enough so to love God, without the intervention of any creature, how great would have been her happiness! No struggle, no doubting, no separation possible! To this, however, she felt unequal,—she rested on a less lofty height, yet it was still a *height*, since all love, in order, is homage to God!

Was this great enjoyment of Mr. Earnscliffe's society the dawning of her dream of day? We can only answer that she herself did not so think about it; she only felt that he pleased her more than any other had ever done, and that she wished her ankle had not got well so quickly, that she might still have had the pleasure of meeting him frequently.

To dissipate the weariness which she felt to be stealing upon her, she proposed to her mother and Lucy to go to the Blakes, as Mina Blake had said something about going on that day to the novitiate house of one of the teaching Orders, to see Madame Ely, an old and intimate friend of theirs, who was an inmate of that convent, and had asked if they would like to go also. Flora said that she would be delighted to meet Madame Ely again in order to see if the warm poetic South had softened that apt pupil of the frigid discipline of her Order, or if she were still the same icy being as before in their northern climes. Mrs. Adair agreed to the proposal, but Lucy declined, pleading that she had a pretty novel and would rather stay at home to finish it than go to see such a prim old lady as Flora described Madame Ely to be. Accordingly, Lucy was left to her novel, and Mrs. Adair and Flora set off for the Piazza di Venezia, where the Blakes lived.

Of "the Blakes" there were only the mother and daughter then in Rome, Mr. Blake had not been able to accompany his wife and their only child, Mina, to Italy. Mrs. Blake was very lady-like, clever, and agreeable. Mina and Flora had been school companions and were great friends; there were some traits of similarity between the two girls—both were habitually reserved and un-demonstrative in manner, although enthusiastic enough when they liked any one very much; but they were not easily attracted, and their apparent indifference made them somewhat unpopular.

The arrival of the Adairs was greeted by many expressions of pleasure, especially from Mina, who exclaimed, "Oh, Flora! I am so glad that you have come, because you and Mrs. Adair will, per-haps, join Miss Lecky and me in going to the convent,—you remember I spoke of it the other day. Mamma has got a cold and cannot come, so I was in despair at the prospect of an after-

noon's drive *tête-à-tête* with old Lecky. We are
to go to the Doria Villa afterwards—*do* come."

" I shall be delighted," answered Flora; " and
mamma, will you not come also ? "

Mrs. Adair assented, and Mina said she would
go and get ready, as they were to call at the
hotel for " old Lecky " at four, and it was then
half-past three. She soon returned dressed for
the expedition, and the Adairs took leave of Mrs.
Blake. When they reached the Piazza they
called one of the open carriages which are so
common in Rome, and drove to the Hotel d'
Amerique, where Miss Lecky was staying. She
did not keep them waiting many minutes, so they
reached the convent a little after four.

They were shown into a small square room, the
walls of which were white-washed; rows of cane
chairs and a table in the centre completed its furniture. There was a glass door standing open leading into a garden which looked so fresh and green
in the bright sunshine that Mina said it would be
a blessed change from that little cold, prim room;
she hoped that Madame Ely would ask them to
walk in it, so that they might mount the rising
ground at the back and see from it the celebrated view of Rome. This hope, however, was
not destined to be gratified by Madame Ely, who
made her appearance just as Mina ceased speak-

ing.   She was tall and slight, with finely cut,
sharp features, dark brown piercing eyes, thin
lips, and a firmly closed mouth ; she looked as
rigid as ever, and her manner was as freezing.
Flora saw at a glance that not even Italian suns
had succeeded in melting that block of ice.

She whispered to Mina, " Byron says—

> ' The deepest ice which ever froze,
> Can only o'er the surface close ; '

but I scarcely think he could say so here, as he
would see some which had frozen far beneath the
surface, or else there never was anything to freeze
over : perhaps it is so."

During the conversation with Mrs. Adair,
Madame Ely named a Madame Hird, whom, as it
turned out, Mrs. Adair had known very well.   She
now expressed a wish to see her, which request
was granted, and Madame Hird came down.

She was the very opposite of Madame Ely—
short in stature and of drooping carriage; she had
small, delicate features, soft blue eyes with a most
gentle expression, and, if she also was somewhat
cold, it was merely a conventual coldness,—it
could easily be seen that, in her, the ice had
indeed

> " Only o'er the surface" closed.

She remembered Mrs. Adair quite well, and they

talked of former days and old acquaintances till
Mrs. Adair thought it was time to say adieu, and
she asked Madame Hird if they could take any
commands for her to Paris, or indeed to Ireland,
whither they were eventually going.

"I thank you, no," she answered; but after a
momentary pause she continued, "Yet you could
indeed do me a great service, if it would not be
asking too much. It is to take charge of a little
protégée of mine as far as Paris,—instead of *protégée* I should rather have said one who has been
particularly recommended to my care by a dear
friend, Madame de St. Severan, a countrywoman,
but, as her name proclaims, married to a French-
man, Colonel de St. Severan."

Mrs. Adair said she would be most happy to
oblige her old friend Madame Hird.

"Well, then," answered the latter, "you must
allow me to hand over to you a sketch of my
little charge's history, which Madame de St.
Severan sent to me. You can take it with you
and read it at your leisure; then come again and
tell me if you are still willing to take charge of
Marie. She is the daughter of an Arab chief,—
but all that you will see in Madame de St.
Severan's account of her. I will go and fetch it."

She left the room, but returned quickly with
the packet. Mrs. Adair thanked her for it, said

they would call again in a few days, and then the whole party stood up to take their leave.

When they got to the door, Mrs Adair said, " Come, Flora, we must get home as quickly as possible ; it is already past five."

" Oh, Mrs. Adair," exclaimed Mina, "please not to take Flora away ; let her take a drive with us and spend the evening ; you know mamma is always delighted to have her, and as Miss Lecky lives in your neighbourhood, she can see her home."

" But she has not dined, child, and you have ! "

Mina look imploringly at Flora and glanced with dismay at Miss Lecky. Flora understood the mute appeal, and said—

" Really, mamma, I could not eat any dinner as I made such a very good luncheon, therefore *that* need not keep me from going with Mina ! "

" And we shall have a 'thick tea' when we get home," added Mina ; " so, Mrs. Adair, you will not be so cruel as to refuse to let her come with us ;—but why will you not come also ? "

" Oh ! I am too rational to leave my dinner for a drive ; besides, Lucy would be waiting for us. I must go home, but if my fair daughter chooses to go without her dinner she may do so."

" I thank you *so* much, Mrs. Adair," answered Mina : " but you will let us take you home ? "

"Indeed I can allow no such thing,—it would make you far too late for the Villa Doria. I will say good-bye, now; and, Flora, pray come home in good time."

"You may depend upon my leaving her at home in good time, Mrs. Adair; I never stay out late," said Miss Lecky.

Just then one of the little open carriages passed; Mrs. Adair called it and drove home; the other three ladies then started for the Villa Doria.

But we have not yet presented Miss Lecky to the reader,—she has only been heard of as "old Lecky." It is true she was no longer young or interesting, yet a few words must be said, not of her appearance so much as of her character. She was, then, a desperate saint and a church-haunter, but, at the same time, indefatigable in running about to all the profane sights. In the galleries of painting and statuary she evinced the most rigid modesty in turning away her head and looking down when any undraped figure—of which there is no lack in Italian galleries—caught her eye, and this to the great amusement of the girls, who, whenever they went with her to any of these places, took the greatest delight in pointing out to her on the catalogue objects which were particularly to be observed, and afterwards watching the poor old lady's start of horror

at such representations; being short-sighted,
moreover, she did not see anything until she was
quite near to it. For the rest she was a good-
natured, kind-hearted old creature, yet a little
wearisome withal to our young friends.

As they drove to the Villa Doria the task of
entertaining her fell principally upon Mina, as
her mother's friend and guest. Flora sat silently
enjoying the delicious Italian evening ; she might
have been accused of looking a little abstracted,
as, with eyes apparently fixed on vacancy, she
leaned back in the carriage. Perhaps there were
floating before them visions of other and yet more
delicious evenings, when she lay upon a sofa near
an open window and listened to a voice and words
very different from old Lecky's !

They drove out of the Porta San Pancrazio, a
little distance beyond which are the grounds of
the Doria Pamfili Villa, one of the most extensive
and park-like places to be found on the Continent,
and although somewhat disfigured by avenues,
terraces, and fountains, it is an enchanting spot,
especially in the gorgeous Roman spring-time.

Such it was on the evening when our party
entered its gates. Had they come to see the
fashionable world it was rather late ; already the
carriages were disappearing, for the sun was
declining rapidly towards its setting in the west,

and the Romans are far too careful of their
health to brave the dangerous half-hour which, it
is said, precedes and follows sunset.   Our friends,
however, did not come to see the *monde*, and the
lateness of the hour only enhanced the beauty of
the grounds.   As for the health question, the
young ladies simply ignored it, and Miss Lecky
probably did not know anything about it, or *she*
would not have been so recklessly indifferent to it
as her companions were.

One of the chief objects of interest is the
Columbarium.   Perhaps, for the advantage of
our readers who have not been to Rome and have
not studied Murray, we ought to say that Columbarium is a name given to certain sepulchral
buildings from their likeness to a modern pigeon-
house with its tiers of little niches ; and in these
were deposited in former days urns containing the
ashes of the dead, whose names are inscribed on
marble tablets above.   In one of the *Columbaria*
on the Appian Way there is a curious record
placed - by a lady over the ashes of a favourite
dog ; his portrait accompanies the inscription,
and he is designated as the delight—" *delicium*"—
of his mistress ! . . .

The *Columbarium* in the grounds of the Villa
Doria consists of one large chamber and several
smaller ones ; it contains a great number of urns,

but few inscriptions, and none of any great
interest, so the inspection of it detained our
friends only for a few minutes.   They then drove
to the monument erected by Prince Doria to the
memory of the French who fell there in the year
1849, when General Oudinot forced Garibaldi and
his Republicans from the Casino and grounds,
where they had taken up a strong position.   It is
situated at the end of one of the great avenues of
evergreen oaks, and is an octagonal temple, supported by four columns of white marble, on which
is placed a statue of the Blessed Virgin, and on
the pedestal are the names of those who fell in
defence of the Villa. This is a beautiful object seen
from the other end of the avenue,—the white
marble contrasting so well with the dark green of
the majestic oaks.

It was now high time for them to think of
returning, as the gates of the villa were about to be
closed ; but the evening was still so lovely that
Mina declared it would be a sin to go home so
soon.   Miss Lecky agreed with her, and asked if
there were any church which they could see on
their way back.   Mina answered, " Yes, *Santa
Sabina ;* we shall pass close to the *Bocca della
Verità*, which is very near to it ; one of the
fathers of the Dominican convent is my cousin,
so I can ask to see him."

Miss Lecky said that she would be delighted to go, as she had never seen that church. Mina whispered to Flora that she would not see much of it, unless she had cat's eyes and could see in the dark; but it was a good joke to storm the convent. after the *Ave Maria*, and astonish the monks by the sight of three women at that hour.

Accordingly they drove to Santa Sabina, or rather, to the foot of Mount Aventine, on the summit of which it stands. The driver begged them to walk up as "the hill was so steep," and, the light fading, he was afraid that his horses might stumble and fall on their way down; so they got out and went up on foot, the carriage waiting below for them.

On reaching the convent they rang at the door, which was quickly opened by a lay-brother, who looked wonder-struck on seeing the three ladies. Mina ignored the look of surprise, and calmly asked if she could see "*il Padre* Osmondo." The lay-brother said he would inquire, and showed them into the parlour.

It was already so dark that they could see but indistinctly, and suddenly it appeared to dawn upon Miss Lecky that it was somewhat of an unseemly hour for a visit to a monastery. Mina and Flora could hardly suppress their laughter at the thought that the old lady should only then have

arrived at the knowledge of that long evident
fact.

Just then the door opened, and in came Father
Osmond. He shook hands with Mina, who introduced her friends, and laughingly apologised for
the lateness of their visit, saying that as they
were passing at the foot of the hill, and Miss
Lecky was so anxious to see the church before
she left Rome, they had ventured to call at that
hour, fearing they would have no other opportunity.

Father Osmond was a tall, fat, good-natured-
looking Irishman, with ruddy cheeks and laughing
blue eyes. He answered, in a rich brogue,
" Shure inough, Miss Blake, I'd niver doubt you
to be me counthry-woman—to come and see a
place in the dark ; but as you are here, I suppose
I must bring you into the church, and thry if a
candle will help you to see Sassoferrato's sweet
Virgin."

" Thank you," replied Mina, as they followed
him to the church door, where he begged them to
wait a moment while he went to get a candle. He
quickly returned, with a lighted one in his hand,
and led them to the chapel where is Sassoferrato's
beautiful Madonna, a picture unsurpassed, perhaps,
in sweetness of expression, by any in Rome.

The scene was indeed a strange one ; the large

dark church, with the glimmer of a small lamp in one of the side chapels the three female figures standing there, staring up at the picture, and the Dominican in his white habit moving the candle from side to side. The girls were keenly alive to it, and the twinkle in Father Osmond's eye showed that he too was not insensible to its absurdity. At last he said—

"Well, Miss Lecky, I think you'd do as well to come some *day* to see the church, for shure you can't judge of anything by this miscrable candlelight."

"You are right," she answered; "I must manage to come some day to see the church, and have a look at this beautiful picture. Now we had better think of getting home."

Father Osmond led the way back to the reception-room, and said he would call the lay-brother to let them out, adding, "Your carriage is at the door, I suppose."

"No," replied Miss Lecky,—the girls did not trust themselves to speak,—"the driver asked us to walk up; the hill, he said, was so very steep for the horses."

"You don't mean to say that you came up by yourselves! Shure thin I don't know how you'll iver git down again! Why this hill is so lonely and dangerous a place after nightfall that one of

the lay-brothers would not go out alone, and you
three ladies are going to walk down alone as late
as this ! No, that can't be ! "

The spirit of mischief must have taken
possession of the two girls, for, as they saw poor
Miss Lecky grow pale with terror, and heard her
exclaim, " Oh ! Father Osmond, what shall we
do ? " they laughed outright.

Father Osmond looked at them with a half-
amused, half-impatient expression, and said, " It
is all very well to laugh, young ladies, but may
be it's the wrong side of your mouth you'd laugh
if you walked down that hill alone to-night.
But that you'll not do. Shure I couldn't sleep
aisy in me bed for thinking of what might happen
to you. I'll go and get somebody to go down
with you." So saying he left the room. Poor
Miss Lecky expressed the most ardent wishes
that they had never left the carriage, and that
they were safe back in it again, and the young
ladies tried to regain a little gravity.

In a few minutes Father Osmond came back
and said that the man who took care of the
garden would take a lantern and see them safe
to the carriage. They thanked Father Osmond
warmly for all his kindness, and as Mina shook
hands with him she begged him in a low voice

to excuse this wild freak of theirs, and forgive all their laughing.

"You're young, me children, you're young, and shure it's not meself that would find fault with you for being merry; long may you remain so;—and now, good-night, and may God bless you both."

They followed Miss Lecky, who was impatiently waiting for them at the door, and trying to make out something of what the man with the lantern was saying, which, as she knew very little Italian, seemed rather a hopeless task; and she looked as much afraid of him as of anything else. In truth, he was rather a formidable-looking personage, with his tall, gaunt figure wrapped up in a long dark cloak, a large slouched hat covering his brows so that nothing of his face could be seen but two fierce black eyes, and a profusion of dark hair. He did indeed look rather bandit-like.

As the girls came out he said, "*Andiamo presto, Signorine,*" and started off at a brisk pace with the lantern. Mina could not resist the temptation of drawing out poor old Lecky's fear of their protector, and giving Flora a sign to follow the lead, she said, "Don't you think, Miss Lecky, that the man looks to be a very suspicious

character? Suppose he was to be an accomplice
of those dangerous people we hear of, and that,
when we are half way down the hill, they should
dart out from some dark corner! He might pretend that he was frightened by their number, and
run away, leaving us in their hands."

"But surely you don't think the fathers would
employ such a person, do you?"

"Of course not, if they knew it," said Flora,
gravely; "but you know Italians are so cunning
that they easily deceive poor monks, and *that*
man certainly is like the descriptions which we
read of bandits."

"Well, do you know," began Miss Lecky, in a
trembling tone, "it struck me as soon as I saw
him, but I did not like to say anything, fearing——"

"What's that!" interrupted Mina, as a low
whistle was heard; "it is the signal perhaps!"

"My God! there they are!" exclaimed the
poor old lady, as she convulsively caught hold of
Flora's arm, "and he is speaking to the leader.
Oh! let us run away!"

Mina laughed aloud, Flora at the same time
trying to keep from following her example,
and to calm poor Miss Lecky's fears by telling
her that it was only a flock of goats, and the
terrible leader a peaceable herdsman, with his

crook, to whom their attendant spoke a few words.

Miss Lecky, as we have already learned, was a good-humoured creature, so she laughed heartily at her own mistake, and said she was so ridiculously short-sighted that she could not distinguish anything at a distance; but how she wished they were safe in the carriage!

The girls felt that it would be carrying a joke to ill-nature to teaze her any more, so they changed their tone, and began to reassure her by telling her that they were nearly at the foot of the hill, and then all cause of fear would be at an end. It was almost too much for them to keep from bursting into fits of laughter at the thought of the poor goats and their herdsman being taken for a party of bandits with their leader.

At length they reached the end of their walk, without any further adventures than passing now and then dark-looking individuals enveloped in cloaks, who stared curiously at them, but went on their way without speaking. The girls, however, *did* afterwards admit that it would not have been pleasant for them to have been alone.

The moment when they came in sight of the carriage Miss Lecky made a rush towards it, and got in. Mina thanked their cavalier and gave him

a couple of pauls, when he took off his hat,
courteously wished them *buon viaggio e filice
notte*, and returned to the convent.

They told the coachman to drive back fast to
the Piazza di Venezia, and when they got home
they found Mrs. Blake expecting them rather
anxiously, as it was so late. As Mina had said, she
appeared delighted to see Flora, and told them
that tea would be ready for them in a moment.

Mina hoped that there was plenty of good
substantial eatables, particularly for poor Flora,
who had not dined; but Flora declared that she
did not deserve to be pitied, since she had enjoyed
the drive far more than she would have enjoyed
dinner.

A little after nine Miss Lecky left Flora at her
home. As soon as she got into the drawing-room
she threw herself into an armchair, and then
proceeded to give an account of their adventures.

CHAPTER III.

WE must now turn our attention to some of our other friends of the croquet party, and especially to one about whom, as we have already seen, Flora Adair's thoughts were not a little occupied, namely, Mr. Earnscliffe, in order to endeavour to learn something of his appearance and his mode of life.

He lived in the Piazza di Trajana, in a handsome and thoroughly Italian apartment on the second floor—or, as it is more properly called, *secondo piano*—of a house situated at the lower end of the Piazza, nearly opposite to the church of Santa Maria di Loretto.

He was seated in an armchair by a table covered with books and writing materials,—to all appearance he had been reading. His tall and strongly-built form seemed made for activity and energy, and in keeping therewith was the well-shaped hand, which rested upon the arm of his chair,—a hand full of vigour, one of those which show at a glance that its support could be trusted to in any trial or danger. His brown, yet almost auburn, hair was brushed off from a high forehead, but one marked with many a line,—too many for a man of six-and-thirty. Byron speaks of

> " Those furrows which the burning share
> Of sorrow ploughs untimely there ; "

and so, perhaps, was it with Mr. Earnscliffe. His large blue eyes had a strangely stern expression in them, "*pour les doux yeux bleus*," but at times, when moved by even a momentary feeling of enthusiasm, there beamed in them a winning softness which looked far more natural to him than that strange sternness. It may be, however, that this was

> " A light of other days."

His slightly aquiline nose, and his somewhat full lips closed firmly over an unbroken and even range of strong teeth, and his firm and resolute mouth betokened an ardent, passionate nature. A beard and moustache, of nearly the same colour as his hair, covered the lower part of his face, which was naturally fair, but somewhat bronzed by southern suns.

He was dressed in a dark morning suit, without any *recherche ;* but in a peasant's costume there would have been that same air of ease and high breeding which so strikingly distinguished him,— that distinction of nature which no outward adornment of wealth or fashion, or even birth with all its advantages, could give. "It is the soul," says the great Christian doctor and philosopher, "which is the form of the body and which gives its beauty to it."

We have heard from Mrs. Elton that Mr. Earnscliffe was rich. Why then did he live in this unfashionable quarter? Probably because it *was* unfashionable, and out of the way of his sight-seeing, gaiety-hunting country people, who congregate about the Corso and the Piazza di Spagna; probably also because in the Piazza di Trajana, where the houses look down upon the remains of that once magnificent Forum and the unrivalled column which still stands there, he lived in some degree in the Rome of old, "the mistress of the world, whose people were a nation of kings," as he had said on that day at Frascati, and not in the modern Rome, which to his clouded vision appeared so despicable.

If the pride of human reason, which was so strong in him, would have permitted him to endeavour to pierce that cloud, he would have seen how much more glorious is her diadem now than it then was. Then her sovereignty rested

on material force alone,—she was the capital of
the peoples whom she had conquered for her
Cæsars by the force of arms, and her government
was the lower one—the government of *power;*
now her sovereignty is a moral sovereignty,—she
is the capital of Christendom, of the nations
which she has won to God by the power of per-
suasion, and her government is the highest of all
—the government of *love!* But these things
were hidden from Mr. Earnscliffe,—he " did not
believe, and therefore he could not understand."

Upon the table beside him lay Nibbi's " *Roma
Antica e Moderna,*" " *Les Catacombes de Rome,*"
by Louis Perret, an open volume of Plato,
Bulwer's " Zanoni " and " Godolphin." It was a
small but somewhat miscellaneous collection, and
formed a fair index to the mind of him who sat
in the armchair. There were few men who had
read or thought more than he had done in his own
way; but the more he read and the more he
thought, the more baseless everything seemed to
him. At times he would sit with an open volume
beside him, and, ceasing to read, bitterly ask himself what he gained by all his study and thought?
It only isolated him, he would say, from the
generality of people, and left him tossing without
a rudder upon the unstable waters of human
opinion, to which there seemed to be no attain-

able shore. . . . Yet the shore was close to him, only he *would* not see it.

There had just risen up before him a vision of years long past and gone, when he dreamed of love, of the unutterable delight of conferring happiness upon another; and for a moment his blue eyes regained their natural soft expression— but for a moment only; the next it had passed away; and throwing his head back impatiently, as if he would shake off

" Those spectres whom no exorcism can bind,"

he exclaimed, "What nonsense all this is! Do I not know by experience the hollowness of love? The best of women are but the best of actresses— for they are all so more or less—and would I sigh again for aught so worthless? A thousand times, no. I made my choice long ago; I determined to be self-sufficing, true and virtuous for my own sake, and to prove what man can be of himself alone! Ay, Plato," and he drew the book towards him, "thou art my best friend, my only master! But even thou dost not teach enough! Yet come, thou canst teach me more than any other!" And, with the old stern look in his face, he began to read again.

Will his proud spirit of self-reliance, his iron will, ever be humbled? Will he ever learn to kiss the rod under which he writhes? If so, it must indeed be after a deadly struggle with his mortal enemy, himself.

He did not go much into society, and rather avoided that of ladies, although he could make himself most pleasing to them when he chose to do so, as indeed he had proved in regard to Flora Adair. His sense of justice was unusually strong, and therefore it was that he had broken through his rule of rarely visiting by going so often to the Adairs; he considered it as a sort of moral debt to render the time of Flora's imprisonment as little wearisome as possible, having been, as he said, the remote cause of her accident. As that obligation was now over, he tried to persuade himself that he was delighted at it; yet many things which had happened during their conversations were constantly recurring to him; he wished he had said this, or that,—something, in short, which he had not said. He thought, moreover, that he should like to be able to study Flora Adair more closely, but merely to find her out, as no doubt she was an actress like the rest of her sex. He was generous too, ever ready to give money to relieve others, and, notwithstanding his assumed stoicism, his tell-tale eyes would light up with a passing glow whenever he felt that he had been the means of doing good to a suffering

creature, or given any pleasure to others. To his
servants he was a kind master, although habitually
reserved and distant, but never to them was he
proud and scornful, as he often was to his equals.
For the rest, his character must develop itself.
We shall not now be astonished at acts of apparent
inconsistency caused by that perpetual warfare
between the two natures, the real and the acquired. Thus flashes of the enthusiastic spirit of
his youth would every now and then dart athwart
the sombre hues of the philosopher and fatalist of
later years.

On this day there certainly seemed to be something very wrong with Mr. Earnscliffe, for he
could not as usual, by the mere force of his will,
fix his attention to the book before him. Closing
it with a jerk, he said to himself, "What on earth
has come over me? What has called up so many
memories which I thought buried for ever—
memories of days when I was not the cold lonely
being I now am? Have I not found out the
hollowness of all things? Have I not sought in
vain for proofs even of the Creator's goodness,
about which one hears so much cant? I can see
only human beings endowed with sensitive powers,
and thrown into the world for the greater part
to be tortured, and all left without any certain
guide, the sport of their own wayward minds!

And then, indeed, people talk about the consolations of religion ! What are those consolations ? What is religion ? A helpless human being in the bright morning of this deceptive life is suddenly struck down by a blow which not only strikes at him, but at his faith in all goodness and truth ; he turns to religion and asks for its consolations, and religion turns out to be a collection of rules and maxims laid down by one or more men of different sects, who call themselves ministers of God, and its consolations are certain texts of Scripture interpreted by them as they please, each giving a different meaning, whilst they are united in nothing save in hating and attacking the oldest and most dominant of their creeds : and this perhaps is the best feature about them, as it proves that even they have an instinctive horror of deceit and superstition. *A propos*, I wonder how Flora Adair believes in it; for although she too is an actress, she is capable of thinking. However, I believe it is supposed to be right for ladies to be religious. Ah! that's it, is it ? Yet she *did* seem to speak from conviction at Frascati. I wish I could unravel her! She would be rather a new and interesting study,—she takes a different *rôle* from young ladies in general. I don't know that it would be a bad plan to try to unearth her,—it

would be something new to think about, at all
events; so, young lady, if you come in my way I
shall try to find out all the *dessous les cartes*. As
for religions, I am surely not going to fall back to
thinking about them and seeking that *ignis fatuus*,
certainty! Reason is the only power which I can
recognise, and Plato is Reason's highest, noblest
disciple. How is it, then, that to-day I cannot
find in him food to satisfy—nay, he never *satisfies*
—but to stay the mind's craving? Well, it
seems to be an unsolvable riddle. I only know
that I cannot solve it; so, for dream-land! Bulwer
is a good magician, and however unreal may be
the visions which he conjures up, it is a relief to
forget one's self in them even for a time."

He threw himself back into his chair and took
up "Godolphin," which he opened at about the
middle of the volume. His eyes grew bright,
and a slight colour came into his face as he read.
Was it his only goddess, Reason, which thus
moved him? We will leave it to those of our
readers who know "Godolphin,"—and who does
not?—to answer the question for themselves.

Having discovered as much of Mr. Earnscliffe
as we can now see, we will transport ourselves to
a more fashionable quarter—to the Via Babuino—
where the Eltons lived.

Their apartment differed essentially from Mr.

Earnscliffe's ; his was Italian, theirs was English
in everything,—an English servant opened the
door and ushered visitors into a handsome drawing-room luxuriously furnished *à l'Anglaise,* with
a rich soft carpet, couches, and lounging chairs of
various kinds.   Mrs. Elton was still in her room;
being an invalid, she seldom made her appearance
much before one o'clock, and it had but just
struck twelve.

Mary Elton was seated at a table, writing;
her younger sister, Helena, lolling rather grace-
fully on a sofa, with a novel in her hand, from
which, however, her thoughts seemed to wander
not a little, and her restless eyes were fixed
oftener on her sister than on the page before her.
She seemed to be meditating—if such a word
could ever be applied *justly* to one who was so
thoughtless and impulsive—something in regard
to Mary, and she shrugged her shoulders impatiently as she watched the incessant motion of
her sister's pen and her close attention to what
she was doing.

We must not pass over in silence the appearance of these two young ladies, who were said,
indeed, to be very much admired.   Mary's figure
was tall, rather full and stately ; she moved
quietly and with a certain degree of dignity ;
while Helena was not much above the middle

height, and slighter than her sister; there was
a careless grace, too, in her quick, restless movements, which was very attractive. Never were
there greater contrasts, in appearance as in all the
rest, than these two sisters. They had both red—
some called it auburn—hair, but in truth it was
scarcely auburn; both had brilliantly fair com-
plexions and hazel eyes, but there the resemblance
ceased. Mary's eyes were large and round; they
looked at one with a calm, *steady* gaze; they
could burn at times, and when they did, it was
with no mere flash, but a fierce steady flame.
Helena's were smaller and more almond-shaped,—
sparkling, dancing, laughing eyes they were indeed! Mary had a broad and rather high forehead, a straight, almost Grecian, nose and a well-
cut but large mouth. Helena's forehead was low
and very narrow, her nose was slightly *retroussé*,
and her mouth small, with red pouting lips. The
expression of one of these faces was constantly
changing; that of the other was habitually calm
and thoughtful,—a face which changed but
seldom, but when it did change it was no April
sunshine, or cloud, or summer storm that passed
over it.

Helena could bear the monotonous scratching
of Mary's pen no longer, and exclaimed, "For
goodness' sake, Mary, do stop writing, and give

up looking so intensely interested in that stupid
letter to our saint of an aunt! I know it must
bore you dreadfully!"

"Because you are bored yourself, Helena; is it
not so? But mamma wishes this letter to go to-
day, so I *must* write it, in any case."

"Yes, of course, you dear delightful child;
but there is plenty of time, and I want you to
talk to me now. Tell me, are you coming to the
Catacombs this afternoon? You know that we
have tickets, and can join a party of which
Cardinal de Reisac is to be the cicerone."

"The Catacombs? No! What could have put
such an idea into your head? Surely you are not
thinking of going?"

"Surely I am, though!"

"And, in the name of all that is wonderful,
for what? You would not tell me that such a
madcap as you are can care to go poking about
in those damp underground passages, listening to
an old Cardinal's fabulous legends of this Roman
nonsense? A little poetic association with the
past is very telling for them, no doubt; but you
are never going for all this, Helena?"

"No, not I! But, my precious matter-of-fact
sister, can you not imagine any one going to the
Catacombs for any other motive than that of seeing
them and listening to tiresome old histories?

'Poking about in those damp underground passages,' as you most irreverently designate visiting the last home of the saints, the persecuted, the martyrs!'"

Mary could not help smiling as Helena went on with mock gravity. "Venturing to repeat your profane mode of speaking, my dear Mary, I beg to say that 'poking about in those damp underground passages' might be made very pleasant indeed, and one might hear there something far more agreeable than the twaddling of a reverend monsignore."

"Pray be sensible, if you can, Helena. I suppose you have discovered that Mr. Caulfield is to be of the party, and that is, no doubt, your motive for going."

"With your usual wisdom you have divined it, O 'most potent, grave, and reverend' lady!"

"How silly you are! But I am sure I don't know why you have told me your motive for going, since you know it is one of which I cannot approve. It would be mistaken kindness, indeed, were I to encourage you in this wild fancy which you have taken for Mr. Caulfield. You will not be allowed to marry him, therefore all these meetings will but make you unhappy!"

"Most admirably reasoned! Only you seem to ignore the existence of that tender passion called love, which is not remarkable for its obedience to reason, as far as I know. I love Harry Caulfield, so the mischief—if mischief it be—is done: therefore, whether I am allowed to marry him or not, it is too late to think of saving me from unhappiness by preventing me from seeing him. Now listen to me, Mary, and I will be as serious as you like; I repeat I love him,—not perhaps in the way that Flora Adair——" (a strange expression passed over Mary's face as this name was uttered; Helena's quick eye caught it, but she continued without making any observation) " and her friend Mina Blake talk about,—a feeling into which everything is merged, concentrated into the one thought, can I make him happy? How amused I have been when listening to them; you know they say that a woman's happiness consists not in the least in doing what *she* likes, but in the happiness of the man she loves! Where they learnt such notions I cannot conceive!"

"Nor can I see what their ideas on the subject can have to do with your reasons for making me your confidant, which was what I wished to know."

"Nothing on earth, most lawyer-like of young ladies; but I could not help telling you *en passant* how Flora and her friend talk about love." Had Helena really no other motive for bringing in Flora's name?

Mary shrugged her shoulders impatiently, and said, " To the point, Helena, if you please."

"Shure now, you wouldn't be for hurrying and flusthering a poor young crature!" answered Helena, with provoking trifling; but, seeing that Mary looked really annoyed, she added in a more sober tone, " Well, I said I would be serious, and so I will; please, Mary, do have a little patience with me. My reasons, then, are threefold: first, I wanted a confidant; secondly, I chose you because I know that, after all, you are fond of your madcap sister, and can help her so much if you choose to do so; thirdly, I could repay your kindness by telling you something which you would be glad to hear."

"Helena!" interrupted Mary, whilst an angry flush spread itself over her face.

" Nay, Mary, hear me out; I did not mean to speak of this as a bribe; I know you too well to imagine that you would be induced to help me to a little enjoyment for the sake of any self-gratification; for that I depend on your affection; yet, as I said before, it is pleasant to feel that I can repay you; or, if you will not help me, you shall have my information gratis."

" I don't in the least know what you mean, Helena," rejoined Mary, in her coldest manner.

" Of course not, you never knew a young lady

who was considered a model of sense, held up as a
pattern to an incorrigibly wild younger sister,
who was always at some mischief or other,
flirting—what not? Well, this young lady did
really seem to be a model one, and an immovable rock of sense; to possess those treasures, a
well-regulated mind, and a heart which, like a
good watch, but ticked slow or fast according to
the regulator; and to have far too much dignity,
self-respect, proper pride, and all the rest of it,
ever to care the least for any man until he had
formally proposed, and was accepted with the full
approbation of her family; when—would you
believe it, Mary?—all——"

"Nonsense, Helena, I shall not stay to hear
any more of this." Mary stood up looking flushed
and angry. "Let me go, please," she continued,
as Helena held her dress; but Helena held on,
saying—

"Mary, you must sit down again, and let me
say what I have to say, or I shall be obliged to
describe the model young lady to somebody else,
and see if they can recognise the original." She
put her arms round her sister's waist, and, pulling
her down upon the sofa, seated herself on the
ground at her feet; then she went on, "When
you interrupted me, Mary, I was just going to
ask you if you could believe it, that all of a

sudden this compound of dignity, self-respect, and maidenly reserve fell in love with a man who didn't care a pin for her"—Mary winced—"and this was not all: she became furiously jealous of a young lady friend who did seem to interest him, a supposed woman-hater, not a little. A few glances and unheeded words betrayed it all to the giddy girl, who immediately felt a new well of love spring up in her heart for that apparently immovable sister, whom she had discovered to be something more than the well-regulated time-piece she had before seemed to be. She saw her suffer silently; she saw tears, all unbidden, start into her eyes; she longed to throw her arms round her, and win her to tell her pain, and thus lessen its sting; to help her, perhaps, and give her hope. Mary, my sister, let me comfort you as well as I can; further secresy is useless,—I have seen it all. Love makes us wondrously keen-sighted. Had I not known something of the little god's wiles myself, I might not have been so sharp. Confide in me, Mary; I am generally thoughtless, it is true, and talk at random, but I can be silent as the grave where I love, and I love my sister."

Poor Mary could bear it no longer; the slowly-gathering tears fell, at last, as Helena looked up fondly and pleadingly at her. And the sisters changed *rôles:* the calm reserved Mary sobbed passionately, and Helena endeavoured to soothe and comfort her.

Mary Elton was not one who—young-lady-like —"enjoyed a good cry;" tears were rather a pain than a relief to her, and seldom were they forced from her save by a sudden shock, such as her sister's discovery, and the laying bare of the secret which she believed to be hidden deep in the recesses of her own heart. After a few minutes her sobs ceased, and she became calmer; drawing back a little from Helena's arms, she said, coldly—

"You have stolen into my confidence, Helena, so I have no power to give or to refuse it!"

"Oh, Mary!" and Helena's tone told how much her sister's coldness pained her.

Mary felt it, and suddenly bending over her, she kissed her fondly, saying, "Foolish child, do not think that I am not grateful for all your affection, or that I do not return it. Ah, Helena, you don't know how I love your frank, impulsive nature, and how I envy you your light-heartedness, your power of forgetting, in the enjoyment of the hour, all pain and sorrow; but I cannot be tender now; tenderness would unnerve me, would break down the barrier of self-restraint. Child, you don't know what it is when we habitually calm people burst the bonds of the so-called principles which had before guided us; all seems to give way around us, and the passion by which we are possessed becomes fearful. Yes, you are right,—I do love this man, who cares not for me, and I hate her who, though it be for a moment, seems to interest him; and dear, surpassingly dear as he is to me, I would rather see him dead than loving and beloved by her. I would plunge into the fiercest fire that ever raged to tear her from him!"

She paused and sat with her head erect, and her teeth clenched, glaring before her as if, in imagination at least, she saw her yet unconscious rival by his side. This burst of passion so amazed Helena that she could not utter a word, and before she had recovered from her astonishment Mary continued in a calmer tone, "I trust you fully, Helena, and shall gratefully—yes, I have fallen low enough for that—gratefully accept any help you can give me. But all this time I have not answered your question as to whether I will forward *your* wishes as to Mr. Caulfield. First tell me clearly how the case stands, and what you wish me to do."

" The case stands thus, Mary : Mr. Caulfield has asked me over and over again to let him speak to mamma, but were he to do so I should probably only be forbidden to see him, and I love him too dearly to let him risk the refusal which I know he would get. So, as I have already told you, it is too late to think of sparing me pain by preventing my meeting him; it would but take away from me all the happiness I can now have—that of seeing him occasionally. What I want you to do, Mary, is to help me in this, and still further, to try to incline mamma more favourably towards him, and you have great influence with her. If you will do this I will promise not to marry him for a year, at all events, without her consent; but if you drive me to desperation, if you deprive me of the delight of being with him sometimes, I cannot answer for myself."

Helena had grown serious enough, and her voice and manner borrowed some of her sister's determination, as she continued, "And as for mamma's rich favourite, Mr. Mainwaring, nothing on earth could induce me to marry him! It is all very well for calm, quiet people to marry from respect and esteem, as they call it, but were I to do it, I know I should run away before a year had gone by. Mary, you would not like to see me wretched, and I am sure that you would do more to save me from being so than any one else, therefore have I asked you to help me now, and you will?" Helena laid her head upon her sister's knee, and her arm tightened its clasp around her waist.

Mary remained silent for a moment or two; then she said, " Yes, I will help you, poor child, as far as I can, for I see that in your bright sunny way you do love Mr. Caulfield. The cold, calculating code under which we have been schooled could never be yours. I, being of a less easily excited nature, accepted what I was told, and I was fast becoming what you described as the model young lady. I met Mr. Earnscliffe, and thought of him first as eligible, in obedience to what I knew were mamma's wishes; but suddenly I found that something, the existence of which I dreamed not of, had taken possession of me, and mastered me. What had become of all the trite rules and maxims of which I had heard so much, and which until then I had obeyed? They were all swept away by that rush of feeling which forced upon me the conviction of their emptiness and falsehood, that there was no real principle in any of them; the reaction carried all before it, and left nothing but this wild reckless passion, goaded as it is by the mortification of loving unloved. . . But he *shall* love me, or, at least, he shall not be another's!"

Again she had become excited, and Helena seemed half frightened at her vehemence; but the next moment she added, with a complete change of manner, "Enough of myself. Thank heaven you are not like me, Helena! Did you not ask me to go somewhere with you to-day?"

"Yes, to the Catacombs; if you come, mamma will not think it necessary to send my aunt to guard me. We can go with Mrs. Penton; I half promised her that we would join her, and she said she would call for us at two o'clock if I sent her word that we wished to go; so, if you consent, I will send to her now."

"As you like!"

Helena accepted the somewhat ungracious assent, and stood up to ring for the servant; as she reseated herself on the ground by Mary, one of her old malicious little smiles played over her face. Was she thinking that perhaps she could change Mary's indifference into eagerness, equal to if not greater than her own?

The servant appeared at the door, and was told to go to Mrs. Penton's, and say that the Misses Elton would be ready for her at the appointed hour.

As soon as the door was closed Helena said, "Can you not be natural, Mary, and say that you are dying to hear the information which I said I could give you, and which you would be glad to

know? I am sure you are, only you are too
dignified to say so."

"Too dignified! why, child, that word and I
have parted company for ever. Was it dignified,
think you, to betray such a secret as mine?
When and how did you guess it?"

"At Frascati, during that thunder-storm, when
I was so frightened. You remember that I hid
my face in your lap; suddenly I felt you tremble,
and, not seeing any lightning, I looked up at you
to learn the cause. Mr. Earnscliffe was gone, but
his voice could be heard speaking to Flora Adair,
and your eyes were fixed in the direction from
which the voice came. Their expression was so
strange that I kept looking at you in wonder.
Then came a flash of lightning; you covered up
your face with your hands, and kept them there
long after the flash had passed. When you did
at last take them down, your eyes were red, and I
felt sure that hot tears had been standing in them,
tears which only your strong will had kept from
falling; you looked so inexpressibly sad and
sorrowful as you turned away and leaned your
head upon your hand, that it came to me at once,
'Mary loves that man!' Since then I have watched
you, noticed your eyes flashing when you heard
of his attention to Flora during her illness, and

now, this very day, how irritable you became
when I spoke of her ideas of love. How I have
pitied you, sister, and wanted to be allowed to
comfort you!"

"Fool that I have been! I thought myself
less demonstrative."

"You *are* undemonstrative, surely, Mary, and
I should never have guessed anything of this but
for that trembling at Frascati. Had you even
trembled opportunely, when there was a flash of
lightning, I should have supposed it was on that
account. But, Mary, is it not better so?—better
to talk to me of it sometimes, than for ever to
brood over it alone? And you know that you can
trust me; you have even said so."

"That I can, and do, Helena; forgive me if I
seem ungenerous. As I said before, it is a sort
of barrier with which I am obliged to fence in my
heart, in order to enable me to keep up appear-
ances; but, believe me, I am most grateful for all
your affection, even when I may the least appear
to value it."

Helena caressed her hand as she said, "Listen
to my news. There is somebody else going to the
Catacombs, besides Mr. Caulfield."

"Of course there is; I did not suppose that
Mrs. Penton, ourselves, and that redoubtable
gentleman were to compose the whole party."

" Well, if you choose to be obtuse, Mary, and then a wee bit impatient, I suppose I had better speak as plainly as possible. Mr. Earnscliffe is going ! "

" Mr. Earnscliffe ! " Mary's indifference had vanished. " How do you know it ? He hates parties of that kind ; he likes going to such places alone, or merely with another man."

" All the same, he *is* going to-day. Harry was by when some grand personage, meaning to compliment him, introduced him to the Cardinal, who asked him if he would like to join their party to the Catacombs to-day. Harry says that Mr. Earnscliffe did not look enchanted at the good Cardinal's condescension, yet he bowed acceptance, probably because he knew that it would be a breach of etiquette to refuse a prince of the Church. Now, is not that news worth hearing ? What a reward for your goodness in consenting to go for my sake ! But I have other news for you, and which you will like still better, as it may be of lasting advantage to you : Harry told me that that rich Mr. Lyne is going to marry Flora Adair ! "

" Ah, Helena ! is it true ? " exclaimed Mary, eagerly.

" If I were to answer as I think myself, I would say, no. She evidently does not care for him, so

it could only be as a *bon parti* that she would
accept him, and that is not like Flora. Harry
says, however, that Mr. Lyne is quite certain of
success."

"Well, you know, Helena, that it would be the
height of folly for her to reject him; she has no
provision whatever; everything dies with her
mother, and a petted darling as she has been
could never bear the life of a governess. Penniless
girls cannot afford to refuse such an offer as Mr.
Lyne's, merely because they do not love in the
desperate way of which, you say, Flora talks.
How hard we try to persuade ourselves that that
which we wish to be true is true."

"I can scarcely think Flora false."

"No, not false; I am sure she thought all
that she said when you heard her speak; but that
was in the abstract; when it comes to a question
of choosing between wealth and position, and
poverty and humiliation, what girl would rather
take the latter than marry a man whom she does
not love intensely? If Mr. Lyne was strikingly
plain, ungentlemanly, or disagreeable in any way,
it might be so; but, as it is, there are numbers of
girls with fortunes who would be very glad to
get the chance. What signifies the probabilities,
however, if Mr. Lyne is sure of her? And of

course he could not be so without some reason. How does Mr. Caulfield know it?"

"From Mr. Lyne himself; he likes Harry very much, and talks to him quite confidentially, and Harry innocently told it to me as a piece of good fortune for our friend. He thinks Mr. Lyne an excellent fellow, and Flora a most lucky girl. They are of the same religion too, so that is a great point in his favour."

"Everything is in his favour," answered Mary, quickly; "but I hear mamma coming, Helena; are there any traces of tears upon my face?"

"None to speak of, none that will be observed if you sit with your back to the light; the place where you were sitting before will do perfectly."

Mary quickly changed her place to the writing-table, and Mrs. Elton's entrance put a stop to all further conversation on the subject about which the young ladies had been discussing so eagerly.

Mrs. Elton was handsomely and appropriately dressed, for a person of her age, although, perhaps, a little too much in the extreme of fashion. Her hair, or, at least, that part of it which her *coiffure* of ribbon and lace allowed to be seen, was of a lightish brown colour, and braided over a high, broad forehead, like Mary's. She had bright— but coldly bright—brown eyes, a straight nose,

aud thin drawn lips; her habitual expression was
placid and determined, and it must be acknowledged that, for a lady of fifty-five, she was
remarkably *bien conservée*, although she had
altered a good deal of late, and at times looked
much worn. As to character, she was a strange
mixture. We have heard what her ideas on
marriage were, yet she herself married a comparatively poor barrister, against the consent of
all her family. Every worldly thing prospered
with them; he succeeded in his profession, and she
was left large sums of money by her relations, so
that eventually they became very rich. She was
a devoted wife; and when, after they had been
married about fifteen years, her husband died, her
grief was deep but undemonstrative. Thus she
became a widow at seven or eight and thirty, and
being wealthy, good-looking, and elegant, she did
not want for suitors, but none of them could tempt
her to be faithless to her husband's memory,
although, after the usual time for mourning, she
wore colours again, dressed richly, and seemed to
study the becoming. She never—widow-fashion
—made any professions of not marrying again;
but she did it not. She would speak of her
husband calmly, but her cold, bright eyes would
fill with tears as she named "William;" and in
speaking of her daughters, of her dread of their

falling a prey to fortune-hunters, she would betray deep emotion; and yet, notwithstanding all this, she was, as we have seen, a determined enemy to love-marriages, and was sternly immovable towards Helena's predilection for Mr. Caulfield, merely because he had not a large fortune. Nevertheless Mrs. Elton's life proved that her only object on earth was her children's happiness, however enigmatical it may appear to be.

"You don't look well to-day, mamma," said Mary, as Mrs. Elton seated herself close to the fire, although one would have thought that fire in the room even was quite unnecessary.

"Nor do I feel very well," replied Mrs. Elton; "but luncheon and a drive afterwards will, I dare say, do me good. Your aunt is coming at two."

"I'm glad of that, as you will, perhaps, spare Helena and me to go the Catacombs with Mrs. Penton. She asked Helena several days ago, but that giddy child forgot to tell of it until to-day; and now she wants me to go with her, as she says you do not always like her to go alone with Mrs. Penton."

"Helena is quite right; Mrs. Penton is too young and too handsome for a chaperone, particularly to one so thoughtless as Helena. You are far steadier than either of them, and I can very well spare you to-day ;—indeed, if you did not go, I would ask your Aunt Alicia to accompany Helena. But of course it is pleasanter for her to have you."

"R-a-t-h-e-r, I should say," observed that young lady.

"Well, then, it is just one," said Mary, looking at the clock on the mantelpiece ; "we lunch at half-past one, and Mrs. Penton is to call for us at two, so I will go and get ready."

Perhaps Mary was very glad of an excuse to get away, but Helena exclaimed, "Mary, you don't mean to say that you count upon taking half an hour to get ready, half an hour for luncheon, so as to be prepared to stand on the step of the door at two waiting for Mrs. Penton. How awfully punctual you are to be sure ; if you had not me as a counterpoise it would be quite dreadful ; you would be the terror of all your acquaintance !"

"On the contrary, Helena, it would be well if you would follow your sister's example in that as in everything else."

"Indeed !" and Helena gave a sly glance at Mary as the latter left the room. Mary blushed slightly, and closing the door quickly, went into her own room ; but instead of getting ready, she threw herself into an armchair before the dress-

ing-table, speaking to herself in an undertone—
" Follow her sister's example; indeed, God forbid !
I do wish that mamma would let her marry
Mr. Caulfield and be happy ; it is enough that one
of us should be miserable ! Mamma, doubtless,
has nothing to do with my unhappiness, save in
having tried to make me what Helena calls a
well-regulated timepiece, and in having taught
me to look upon every rich man as a possible
husband. But she must never know my secret ;
it would drive me mad to hear her talk and reason
calmly on this wild love which is consuming me.
Lena has discovered it, but no one else ever shall ;
none other must know that I have loved him, until
he is mine. Flora Adair, would that you had not
crossed my path ! I liked—I like you still, but
stand in my way you shall not. I do not think
that he really cares for you yet, but he certainly
likes you better than any other woman ; therefore
you must be lowered in his estimation, and I
have the means now in my hands."

An expression of disgust settled upon her face
as she spoke these words. Having heretofore
been true and honourable, she hated herself for
thus acting towards one whom she liked, and
whom she had called her friend ; but the master-
passion must be gratified at any cost. " Yes,"
she continued, " I have the means in my own

hands, although it is base and mean to resort to
it.   I hardly believe that what I have heard is
true, but it has been told to me, and it shall serve
my purpose now.   Mr. Earnscliffe shall hear from
me to-day that Flora Adair is going to sell herself
to Mr. Lyne, and, thinking as he does about
women, he will seize upon it at once, and so will
be dispelled that sort of latent unacknowledged
idea, which I *felt* he had, that she is something
different from and superior to the generality of
women.   I will try to induce him to come to our
ball on Friday.   He will see them there together,
and will probably inquire no further.   I shall
have gained one victory, I shall have got her out
of his way; for the rest, God knows how it will
end!   Why, why am I not what I was taught to
be, a well-dressed automaton, a stone, anything
but what I am?   What bitter mortification it is
to feel that I love this man so much that I can
stoop to do what my nature abhors, and even plan
and scheme in order to gain his love! . . ."

She lay back in the chair with closed eyes, and
so remained for a few minutes, then, starting up,
she exclaimed, "This will not do, I must be calm
and ready before luncheon or Lena will give me
no peace."   Again she looked at her watch and
found that it wanted but five minutes to the time.
Then she set about dressing as quickly as possible,

first bathing her face with cold water to remove
any traces of emotion which might still remain.

The luncheon bell rang a moment or two afterwards; she descended to the dining-room, where
she found her mother and sister already seated at
table. As she entered Helena expressed a hope
that Mary was "got up" to her own satisfaction,
as she certainly had been long enough about it!

CHAPTER IV.

As soon as luncheon was over Helena went to dress, and Mrs. Elton and Mary returned to the drawing-room; the latter seated herself in the window, and gazed out abstractedly, until Mrs. Elton said, "What has bewitched Helena, that she should want to go to the Catacombs? They are not much in her line."

Mary answered as near to the truth as she could do without betraying confidence: "Not the least in the world; but if she likes the people who form the party, it does as well as anything else."

"Then it is for the people that she is going, and not for the Catacombs? I thought there must be some such motive. Mr. Caulfield will not be there, I hope. Helena flirts far too much with him. I do not know how far it has gone, but I have told her that there must be an end of it. I would never allow her to accept him! He is not rich enough to marry a girl of her position

and fortune, yet she goes on encouraging him
and preventing that most eligible Mr. Mainwaring from coming forward, although he evidently likes her."

"But, mamma, are Lena's feelings not to be
taken into any account? Perhaps she does not
like Mr. Mainwaring, and does like Mr. Caulfield."

"She should check that liking then, when I
tell her that I disapprove of it."

"Surely, mamma, the liking may be a stronger
one than can be checked so easily, merely because
you do not think him rich enough; that is hardly
a sufficient reason to induce us to give up one
whom we love."

"Love, Mary? I am amazed at you! Have I
not always impressed on your mind that a girl
properly brought up should never allow herself
to love any man until she is regularly engaged to
him; and that, too, with the consent of her
friends?"

"Nonsense!" exclaimed Mary; then, blushing
at her own vehemence and rudeness, she added
quietly, "I beg your pardon, mamma, for speaking so hastily. You know that I am not romantic,
but one cannot love or be indifferent at word of
command. At first you only laughed at Lena
and Mr. Caulfield; now you tell her to give him

up all at once, merely because he has not a very
large rent-roll : if you can give her a *good* reason,
I am sure she will try to obey you ! "

" I really can scarcely believe that it is you
who are speaking, Mary—you who, as I thought,
understood how completely a girl should have all
her feelings under control"—Mary smiled bitterly—" and that the happiest marriages are
those formed upon equality of position and fortune, accompanied by mutual respect and calm
esteem !   I should be very sorry indeed to advo-
cate that a girl should marry a person whom she
disliked ; but she ought not to take unreasonable
dislikes.   If a man be good, gentlemanly, and in
every way suited to her, is she to dislike and
refuse to marry him because, forsooth, she has
taken a passing fancy to some ineligible person ?
And *you*, Mary, defend this !   What has come
over you ?   I suppose that you, too, imagine
yourself to be in love with some poor esquire,
who, in reality, loves your fortune rather than
any other thing ? "

Mary looked her mother full in the face as she
answered, with heightened colour, " I do not love
any poor esquire, nor does any poor esquire love
me.   Lena is more fortunate, if she loves and is
beloved : you need not fear for me, I shall never
seek to obtain your consent to marry a poor man."

She said this in an odd, determined tone, and then continued pleadingly, "But if Lena really cares for Mr. Caulfield, let her be happy in her own way, mamma. He is not rich, it is true, but he has quite enough for a gentleman's condition, and for happiness; and with her fortune there is no reason why she should marry for money."

"I can't say how much you amaze me, Mary; though you do possess a remnant of sense for *yourself.*"

"Sense!" replied Mary immediately. "Yes, indeed; but——here is Mrs. Penton! I must call Lena."

"And pray, Mary, if Mr. Caulfield should be one of the party, do not let her be much with him."

Mary left the room without answering; but as she closed the door she murmured to herself, "No, I cannot be a kill-joy!" Then she called out, "Come, Lena, here is the carriage"—a loud ringing of the bell having announced that Mrs. Penton was waiting.

Lena came out of her room busily occupied in getting on a pair of the palest lavender kid gloves: the young lady had small hands, and liked to do them justice.

Mrs. Penton was alone. "Her husband," she said, "had so often seen those places that he did not care to go again;" so away they drove to the Catacomb of St. Calixtus, on the Appian Way.

In the Vigna Ammendola—at the entrance to the Catacomb—our friends loitered for some time waiting for the Cardinal, who, although it was somewhat past the appointed time, had not yet arrived. They found many there before them, but all were strangers except Mr. Caulfield and a Signor Lanzi, both of whom they met near the gate on entering.

Signor Lanzi—as his name denotes—was an Italian, but he had been in England, spoke English with a certain ease, and was particularly fond of showing it off. He was one of Mrs. Penton's most devoted admirers; and, through her, had become rather intimate with Mr. Caulfield and the Eltons.

It must not be supposed that there was anything reprehensible in Mrs. Penton's conduct because we speak of her having admirers. She was what is called a beauty, and was accustomed to be admired and followed. Her husband and herself were on the best of terms, and never seemed to pull in different directions; on the contrary, they appeared fond of one another in a calm sort of way, yet it could not be said that there was anything very ideal in their happiness. It is true, they were not quite a type of union in

thought and feeling ; perhaps neither of them was
capable of such love ; nevertheless, theirs was not
a lot to be despised, and they were quite content
with it, and with each other.

As soon as Mrs. Penton and the Elton girls
appeared at the gate the two young men joined
them, and they took a few turns up and down the
walk leading to the Catacomb. Mary then proposed sitting on the wall near the gate, ".as," she
said, " they would have walking enough underground, and they had better not tire themselves
beforehand ; " and there they waited for the Cardinal's arrival.

In a few minutes the sound of carriages was
heard ; the gate was opened, and in came Cardinal
Reisac, and with him three or four priests. Mrs.
Penton at once went forward and spoke to his
Eminence, being personally acquainted with him.
During this interval the gate opened again, and
at last Mary's watching was rewarded—Mr. Earnscliffe entered. Mary was nearest to the gate, so
he could not avoid speaking to her, and even
walking with her, as the Cardinal quickly moved
on, and all followed him.

Mary felt that she must not lose this opportunity of saying something to excite Mr. Earnscliffe's curiosity about Flora ; he would, she
thought, naturally try to hear more, if he were not

indifferent to her—and it would be a good test;—
so, as they were lighting the tapers, she said, " I
hope we shall not have any falls or spraining of
ankles to-day. Do you remember Miss Adair's
accident at Frascati ? "

" Surely I should be the last to forget it, having
induced you both to go upon the wet, slippery
moss; but she is quite well now, I believe ? "

" Quite well; and, report says, going to be
married to that rich Mr. Lyne."

" Mr. Lyne ! "

" Yes; you know him, don't you ? He is very
rich, very good, quite a saint, indeed; rather
slow, they say; but then poor Flora has no fortune, so it would be an excellent thing for her.
But we must not stand here talking about her, or
we shall be left behind;" and Mary suddenly became most anxious to follow close to the Cardinal.

A flight of steps leads down from the vineyard
into a sort of vestibule, in the walls of which are
numerous graves, and in the spaces between rude
inscriptions, supposed to have been made by pil-
grims who came to visit the last resting-places of
the saints and martyrs. The guide went first
with a large torch, then the Cardinal, the eccle-
siastics, and the lay visitors, each carrying a
light. There were about fifteen in all; so they
formed rather a long procession in the narrow

galleries or passages, where two can hardly walk abreast—not two ladies, certainly, in those days of crinoline.

From the vestibule a long gallery leads to the Chapel of the Popes, and passes by one of the sepulchral chapels which occur at intervals in nearly all these passages. In many of the larger of the crypts or chapels there are altars upon which the Divine Sacrifice was offered during the persecutions of the first centuries, when armed force vainly strove to put down the religion of the Cross inaugurated on Calvary. Long afterwards, when that Cross had established its time-enduring reign in Rome's high places, these crypts were resorted to by the faithful for purposes of devotion, as hallowed places consecrated by the sanctity and martyrdom of those who lay entombed in them.

As soon as the whole party was assembled in the Chapel of the Popes, the Cardinal began to explain the different monuments, and pointed out the graves of the four popes of the third century buried there, according to the inscriptions in Greek characters which are still distinctly to be seen and read by those who understand them.

From the Chapel of the Popes they proceeded to that of St. Cecilia, and thence to the others of less note, the Cardinal explaining the different inscriptions and paintings on the walls of the galleries and chapels.

Perhaps none of these are more interesting than the curious paintings representing the celebration of Mass in those early days of Christianity. The priest turned towards the people with his hands stretched out in blessing; the vestments almost the same as those now used, and numberless details proving the identity of the past with the present. These striking evidences of the early Christian practices had often puzzled Mr. Earnscliffe before. "If such outward ceremonials then existed," he would ask himself, "how can they be a human invention? . . . Human things pass away; even the greatest dynasties of earth run their course and disappear to give place to new orders of things. . . . Was immortality to be found here only?" . . . He could not comprehend it, could not explain or reconcile it to his own mind; but, as he had often done before, he turned aside this train of thought by saying to himself, "It can make no difference how far Christianity in this or that form can be dated; even should it be shown that, as a religion, it was one with that of Moses and the Patriarchs,—a progressive Divine Revelation, first by oral Tradition, then by the written Law of Moses, and now, as they call it, by the Reign of Truth, the dogmas of an Infallible

Church; Christianity itself is but one of many pretenders to the governance of mankind."

In the midst of these contending thoughts his mind turned to Flora Adair, and once more he asked himself, " Can she really believe in all this ?" Then flashed upon him Mary Elton's words, "She is going to be married to that rich Mr. Lyne." Was it true ? He himself had heard her call him "a good-natured bore." He determined to hear more about it, and with this intention he turned to look for Mary Elton, whom he had not seen since they had entered the Catacomb.

Helena, who had candidly acknowledged that she was not going to the Catacombs solely to see them, but to have her eyes gladdened by the sight of a bright, laughing, loving face, and her ears gladdened by the sound of a voice whose tones were music to her, took care to keep in the rear of the party, and condescendingly informed Mr. Caulfield that he might talk to her if he would do so quietly, so as not to attract attention. Sad to say, these irreverent young people only thought of how "jolly" those dark narrow places were, as they found them not at all inconvenient for their pleasant little love passages and whispered conversations. The numerous chapels were certainly rather annoying interruptions, as they were of course obliged to be silent there, and, apparently at least, to attend to the Cardinal's explanations. Yet an ordinary observer could have seen that their eyes were more occupied with each other than with the paintings and monuments so carefully pointed out to them.

As they got back into those "dear" galleries, after visiting one of the chapels, Mr. Caulfield succeeded in getting hold of one of the pretty little hands, about the gloving of which their possessor had been so particular. Perhaps she expected that some such notice might be taken of them; but, be that as it may, Mr. Caulfield had got the little hand prisoner, and pressed it tightly in his own as he said, "Lena,"—he had learned the pet name by which her sister generally called her, and appeared to have a particular affection for it,—"I can't bear this uncertainty any longer; you must let me speak to your dragoness!"

"Harry, you are very impertinent," and the little hand made a feint to get itself free, but it was only a feint. "You must not call mamma my dragoness; I will not allow it, sir; nor must you speak to her unless you want to be off; if you do, rush up early to-morrow morning and request an interview with Mrs. Elton; then formally demand the hand of Miss Helena, her daughter, and be as formally refused. You will be politely begged not to repeat your visit; in other words, you will be forbidden the house ; and when you have ranted a little and finally bowed yourself out, your poor victim, Helena, will be sent for to be coldly lectured on her levity and her flirting propensities, and solemnly commanded by her obedience as a child never to see or speak to you again, save as the merest acquaintance. In fine, a distinct *fiat* would be pronounced against Mr. Caulfield, who does not, perhaps, know how determined a person Mrs. Elton is ; but her daughter does know it, and but too well. If you speak to mamma *we* are done for, Harry."

That "*we*" and that "Harry" sounded very sweetly indeed in Mr. Caulfield's ears, yet he answered indignantly—

"But you don't mean to say that you would submit to all this, Helena ?" . . . He could not afford to call her Lena now, it was not impressive enough. "You are mine by right of conquest, and what authority has your mother to keep you from me ?"

"For shame, Harry ! has a mother no voice in the disposal of her child ? Not that I think a parent should refuse to allow a daughter to marry one whom she loves, unless she had good reason for so doing ; nevertheless, I could scarcely marry

in defiance of her express command. Harry, do
not *brusquer les choses*, and force her to pronounce
that command; have a little patience, and time
may do a great deal. Mary has promised to use
her influence to gain mamma's consent, and she
will facilitate my seeing you as much as she can.
Is she not a darling, Harry?"

"Yes," he replied, but in a much less enthusiastic tone; then he went on eagerly, "It's all
very well for you, Lena, to talk about having
patience, and the wonders that time may work;
you have a pleasant home, and this darling Mary
to pet you; but it is quite otherwise for poor
me. There I am, all alone in an hotel, comfortless
and miserable, and unable to get out of my head
tantalizing visions of the happiness I might enjoy
if I could only have my little cricket with me."
And there was a very sensible pressure of the
imprisoned hand.

"Oh, come now, Harry; it is too absurd to see
you trying to do the romantic. You know very
well that you go everywhere, and enjoy yourself
thoroughly. Who would believe in your sitting
at home conjuring up visions, and becoming
miserable because you cannot realise them! There
is nothing *grandiose* about *us*, you know. Just
imagine our attempting a *grande passion*, and
declaring that out of each other's presence the

world is but a desert to us! No, no, that is not at all in cricket's line, Harry. All the same ——" and her eyes drooped, "I am sure that horrid hotel *is* very dull and lonely."

Perhaps had there been a convenient turning in the passage to separate them for a moment from the rest of the party, that charming little speech might have been rewarded; but fate was not so propitious. The passage appeared interminably long and straight, so there could not be any warmer expression of gratitude than words could give.

After a few moments Helena said again—"Now, Harry, you are to be very good and quiet, and if you are so, I will give you a reward in the shape of an invitation to our ball on this day week; but perhaps that is too far off. A cricket who goes about chirping from hearth to hearth might, you know, forget."

"How wicked you are, Lena!"

"Wicked, am I? Then, master cricket, you shan't have an invitation from me, and if you wait till you get one from Mrs. Elton, you'll wait for ever."

"Then the cricket will appear without one."

"Will he indeed! To be handed out by the servants! But I am going to be serious now, and please to be rational for a few minutes and listen to me. The invitations are only to be sent out to-morrow; mamma was not well enough to permit us to send them before; indeed we were beginning to fear that the ball would not come off at all. It would be vain to expect that mamma would send you an invitation, but Mary shall ask you to-day, and when we return home she can say that she has done so, and mamma will not be able to help it then. How good I am to plan all this for you, considering that it is quite indifferent to me whether you are there or not. I hope you are fully sensible of my disinterested goodness towards you, Mr. Caulfield."

" If I had but the opportunity, would I not make you pay for all this, Lena ! "

She looked up innocently at him, and asked in a most apparently unconscious tone, " How, Harry ? "

What a temptation was that upturned smiling face ! and, with a sigh for the *bonne bouche* which he was obliged to relinquish, he said, " I declare, Lena, it is cruelty to torment a man so; but my time will come——"

She withdrew her hand hurriedly, exclaiming, " Here is a chapel ; now we must be demure," and she followed the others with the air of a little Puritan, which tried Harry's gravity sadly.

A glance from Mary told Helena that she had

flirted enough for that day, and, not being at all dissatisfied with the day's adventure, she determined to obey the glance; accordingly, as they were leaving the chapel, she glided past Harry, and whispered, "Good-bye, cricket; I am going to talk to Mary."

Poor Cricket looked rather woeful at this intelligence; but there was no help for it, so, making a vain attempt to seize her little hand again, he let her glide away from him.

We left Mr. Earnscliffe looking round for Mary Elton, in order to obtain some information about "that Lyne affair;" and, a moment later, Mary heard a voice beside her saying—

"Well, Miss Elton, are you deeply interested in the Catacombs?"

As she listened to those words, she felt as if a sharp knife were cutting away the hope she had begun to cherish, that he was indifferent to Flora Adair; for she felt certain that it was from the desire to hear more of what she had said about Flora and Mr. Lyne that he came to her. There could be no doubt, she thought, that the Catacombs would otherwise have been far more attractive to him than a conversation with her; nevertheless an answer must be given, and she said, "Not particularly so. I have scarcely read or thought enough about the Catacombs to be greatly

interested in them. Indeed, it was to please my
sister that I came to-day."

"Your sister! does she then take greater
interest in these things than you do? I should
hardly have supposed it."

His tone, even more than his words, made her
laugh,—the idea of Helena's being interested in
the Catacombs for their own sake, was certainly
very amusing; so she replied—

"Well, no; Lena is not particularly devoted
to antiquarian researches, but she thought it
would be a pleasant party, and begged me so
earnestly to accompany her that I did not like to
refuse."

"Ah! I understand."

A silence ensued, while Mary thought, "Poor
man! he does not know how to get at the subject
which he is so longing to talk about; he thinks it
beneath him to let any one see that he could feel
curiosity about a young lady's proceedings, and I
have a great mind to make him pay for his
dignity, and not help him over the dilemma.
This I could do, but that it would defeat my own
purpose of crushing any incipient fancy which he
may have taken to Flora. Yet how mean it is!
Were I but sure that she is really going to marry
Mr. Lyne, I should not feel so false as I do now.
But what is the use of all this self-reproach? If

I am to do it at all there must be no looking back; yet would it not be better to give it up altogether, and let things take their natural course? Yes, it would indeed be truer, nobler, better to do so; but——"

The silence continued, and she walked on like one in a dream; yet there was not much of dreaming in the hard struggle which was going on within her between her better nature and passion. The former had almost triumphed; she felt it was too base to try to rob another—one, too, whom she liked—of a man's love; for, with the quickness of jealousy, she *felt* that he loved Flora, even unknown to himself. But, whilst good and evil thus hung in the balance, there occurred one of those chances which so often seem to decide a question. She was suddenly roused from her reverie by Mr. Earnscliffe's laying his hand upon her arm and saying—

"Miss Elton, do you not see the flight of steps before you? What a fall you might have had!"

She drew back with a start and looked at him—the good angel was vanquished. That touch upon her arm—that voice—that countenance, to which circumstances lent a momentary interest in her favour, were more than she could withstand. She murmured to herself, "No, I cannot give him up—I will die rather than see him another's." Then

she calmly answered, " Thank you, Mr. Earnscliffe; had it not been for you I might indeed
have had a bad fall, so *you* have saved me."

Had he done so? Did it not rather appear to
be the contrary? A moment before good was in
the ascendant; had she not been thus saved from
a fall good might have triumphed, but that saving
seemed to give the palm to evil.

When they had descended those steps Mary
said, " Now, Mr. Earnscliffe, I am going to ask a
favour of you; and one which, I hope, you will
not refuse to grant."

He had quite resumed his cold indifferent
manner as he answered—

" Let me hear the request, for I can make no
guess as to what I can possibly have it in my
power to grant or refuse you."

" Undoubtedly it is in your power to grant it;
whether you *will* do so is another matter. We
are to have some friends with us on Friday, this
day week, and mamma would be so pleased if you
will come also."

" Friday?—let me see——"

" Do not try to improvise an engagement, or
say, ' Parties are not much in my way.' I know
that it is so; but surely for once you might condescend to come; particularly as we are going
away on the following Monday, so that—by us, at

least—you could not be importuned any more.
We shall have some good music, of which I know
that you are fond." And now to throw out her
bait without letting it appear that she thought it
was one: "And—only I suppose you would not
care about that—you would have an opportunity
of seeing Flora Adair perfectly recovered from
her sprain, for our evening is to wind up with a
dance, and, as you heard at Frascati, she is a
great dancer. Mr. Lyne will also be there, so we
shall see how he plays the lover's part."

She had watched him narrowly while she spoke,
and saw by the change of his countenance that
the bait had taken, and so she was not deceived
as to the motive of his accepting when he replied—

"Asked thus as a favour and a farewell, I cannot do otherwise than say in the recognised form,
'I shall be most happy to accept Mrs. Elton's
kind invitation.'"

"Very well, then, it is agreed that you will
come. Of course you will receive a formal invitation, but you need not answer it, as I shall tell
mamma that you have already accepted. And
now, Mr. Earnscliffe, as you are almost an *habitué*
of these underground regions, perhaps you can
tell me if we have nearly *done* them?"

"Well, I have not been paying much attention,
but from the time we have been here"—looking

at his watch—"I should say yes. I see we are coming to a chapel, probably that of St. Cornelius, which is generally the last."

It was the chapel of St. Cornelius, as he had said, and there it was that Helena received the glance from Mary, which she rightly understood to be an intimation that her flirting had better come to an end for that day. When they were once more in the passage, Helena succeeded in getting close to her sister and whispered, "You are an angel, Mary!"

"Don't be silly, Lena," answered Mary, almost roughly. Perhaps the being called an angel just then, when she knew how much the reverse of it she was, irritated her.

"But you are indeed an angel, and I know you will carry your angelic sisterly charity a little farther by asking Harry to our ball; then, when you tell mamma that you *have* asked him, it will be too late for her to object. You will ask him, Mary, will you not?"

"Yes," was the curt reply; and she added, "And now do be quiet; surely you have talked enough to-day."

"Not nearly enough, you dear *dame Sagesse*. I am quite ready to begin again."

"Then I beg you will not do so; and be pleased, Lena, to give up that absurd habit of calling me such names as angel and *Sagesse*—you ought to know how inapplicable those terms are to me, and they annoy me."

Helena began a warm denial of this, but Mary interrupted her by saying, "That's enough, Lena; do cease talking—my head aches. Thank goodness, I see the daylight, so I suppose we shall soon get into the open air again!"

No wonder that her head ached and that she longed for rest, even for the rest of lying back silently in the carriage.

A few minutes more and they were in the vineyard, enjoying the warm rays of the sun, which still shone brightly in the clear blue sky.

Mrs. Penton, having kissed the Cardinal's ring, received his blessing, and thanked him for all his kindness, bade him farewell, and turning to her own party, said—

"Will either of you three gentlemen take the vacant seat in the carriage? We are going to take a turn on the Pincio." She looked at Mr. Earnscliffe, but he answered—

"Thank you, Mrs. Penton; I think I must have a walk in this clear fresh air, after the darkness and damp of the Catacombs."

"Then Signor Lanzi, may we hope that *he* will escort us?"

"To escort la Signora Penton is alway de most

high honour for me; but I did ride here, also la signora must have de goodness to allow me to accompany her on horse."

Mrs. Penton bowed, and smiled slightly as she said, "Well, Mr. Caulfield, I left you for the last as you are the youngest; what say you to coming with us?"

"That I shall be delighted to go with you, Mrs. Penton."

"With my company, rather, *non è vero*, Mr. Caulfield? And now let us start; it is late enough as it is."

Mr. Earnscliffe accompanied them to the carriage; and, as he took leave of Mary, she said, "Remember Friday night." He bowed, and, raising his hat, left them.

Mary immediately turned, and asked Mr. Caulfield and Signor Lanzi for the same night. They accepted; and Signor Lanzi having mounted his horse, the party proceeded to the Pincio, and thence to their respective homes.

CHAPTER V.

Flora's mind was filled with interest in the young lady of whom Madame Hird had spoken. On the morning after their visit to the Villa Ianthe she read all the papers which Madame Hird had given them about their little *protégée*. They consisted, first, of a letter from Madame de St. Severan; next, of the manuscript containing Marie's history. They were as follows:—

"Although, dear Madame Hird, we have lost sight of each other for many years, and you would not recognise, under my present name, the Caroline Murray of our merry school days, yet I am sure that you, like myself, remember those days. I venture, therefore, to ask you to interest yourself in a young lady who will soon be an inmate of your convent, and who is dear to me because she is so to my husband.

"For some time I have been in correspondence with your superioress, and have obtained permission for our little friend to be received at the

Villa Ianthe, and placed especially under your care. We are very anxious that she should spend a few months in a convent in Europe before making her *entrée* into the *beau monde* of Paris, and knowing that you are in Rome, I have made every exertion to have her confided to your care; and in this I have fortunately succeeded. Will you, then, dear friend, kindly undertake this charge, and direct her studies ?

" A good priest will protect her from Algiers to Rome. As I am writing to you I know that I need not say, be very kind to her. She is, by all accounts, a most affectionate little creature, and is now in great grief at being separated from the guardians of her childhood.

" I have compiled a little sketch of her history, which I now send you. The first part of it is drawn from my husband's account of his African experience; the rest from the joint accounts of Marie and the good nuns who had charge of her . . . ."

Here the remainder of the letter was torn off, not relating, as Flora supposed, to the little Arab girl. She next took up the manuscript, which ran thus :—

" After the battle in the plain of Cheliff, where the Duc d'Aumale and his little army so bravely captured Abd-el-Kader's encampment, many of

the officers left their tents in the evening and
wandered over the scene of their late conflict.
Among them was Colonel, then Captain de St.
Severan. He had strayed to some distance beyond the rest, following the direction which the
fugitives had taken, and was about to return,
when, standing for a moment gazing back upon
the battle-field, he was startled by the sound of
a half-smothered cry. A few paces before him
lay the body of an Arab; he approached it, and
as he shook the cloak which nearly covered it,
the cry was repeated. Within the folds of the
bernous there was a little child, whose large black
eyes were wide open with fright, and little hands
stretched out, as if to ward off some coming
danger. With no slight effort he drew the child
from the dead Arab, and tried to quiet its cries
by caresses and marks of endearment. After
taking it up in his arms he returned to his tent,
and sent for one of the camp women, to whom he
related his adventures, adding that he had determined to adopt the child as his own, and
confiding it to her care.

"Having been wounded in one of the later
skirmishes, Captain de St. Severan was sent back
to Algiers with a detachment of troops, when he
took care that the woman to whom he had en-
trusted the little foundling was to accompany

them. The child was a little girl of about two
or three years old, and was christened Marie.
Day by day she became a greater darling—the
pet, indeed, of the whole brigade—and was in
danger of being completely spoiled, when her
protector was ordered again on active service.
Of course, he could not take little Marie with him,
so he yielded to the advice of his lady friends,
and, stipulating that she should learn her father's
language, placed her under the good guardianship
of the French nuns at Algiers.

"It so happened that he never returned to
Algiers, save to pass through it almost in a dying
state on his way home. After a long and tedious
illness in Paris, which left great depression of
spirits upon him, a friend, Mr. Molyneux, induced
him to accept an invitation to the family seat of
Mr. Molyneux's father in England, and try there
the invigorating tonic of English country life.
At this house I met him, and the sequel of that
meeting was, that a few months afterwards I
became Madame de St. Severan.

"I need scarcely say that I heard many stories
of Algiers, and of Marie. We had agreed to send
for her as soon as we should get to France, but,
on our arrival in Paris, my husband was offered
an important post in one of the colonies, and
thought he could not well refuse it without re-

tiring from the army, which he did not wish to
do, therefore he consented to go ; in consequence,
Marie was left at the convent in Algiers. We
remained away nearly ten years, and only returned to Paris last winter, when we wrote at once
to request that Marie should be sent to us; being
doubly anxious to have her, as we had, alas ! lost
our own dear ones. But the answer received
from the superioress caused us the greatest pain
and anxiety. She said, that shortly before our
last letter arrived Marie had been missed one
evening from prayers at church, when it was
found that she had obtained permission to walk
in the grounds, as she was suffering from headache, and that, on search being made for her, a
door in the garden was discovered to have been
forced open from without, and a scarf, which had
been worn by Marie, found on the ground there.
These, with other facts, left no doubt that she
had been carried off by some Arabs, who had
before been seen about the place.

" Three months passed without any tidings of
poor Marie. At length a letter came containing
the joyful news that she had been safely restored
to the convent, and was suffering only from
weakness and exhaustion.

" Marie's account of what occurred tells us that,
having obtained permission, she went out alone

and sought shade and repose in a summer-house at the far end of the grounds—a favourite retreat of hers. She supposes that she had been asleep, when she was roused by feeling something thrown over her head and twisted tightly across her mouth, so that she could not speak or scream. She was then carried for a short distance, placed upon a horse by some one, who got up behind her and galloped away. Save the rapid movement through the air, Marie remembers nothing until she found herself lying on a bed of moss in what appeared to her to be a rocky cavern. As she awoke the bright rays of the sun were pouring in upon her, and for a moment she thought she must have dreamed some fearful dream. An old man in a white *bernous* then entered the cavern, and all the terrible reality was revealed to her. He came and bent over her, when she exclaimed, 'Oh, sir, take me back! What injury have I ever done you that you should steal me away from all those whom I love? Only take me back and you shall have as much money as you like.'

"'Money!' he sorrowfully repeated. 'Can money buy me back my beautiful, my brave children whom the hateful Roumi killed? Can money make the old man young again, and give him new sons to perpetuate his race?'

"'I pity you very much, sir; but what have I

to do with your misfortunes? Why revenge
upon a poor weak girl like me the death of those
who were dear to you?'

"'What have you to do with my misfortunes?
Are you not the child of my firstborn, his only
one? Did they not tear you from his dead body,
to which you clung with all your baby strength?
Did I not see it all? Yes; lying wounded at
some distance from my brave boy, your cries
roused me from the almost death swoon into
which I had fallen, and I saw you taken away
from him. I vowed then to the Prophet, that if
I recovered from my wounds, my life should be
spent in trying to rescue you from our enemies,
that you might become the mother of a race of
strong warriors to struggle against those hated
usurpers. During all those weary years I never
flagged for an hour, and repeated failures did but
urge me to new exertions. At last the great
Prophet rewarded my fidelity by giving you up
to me, and now you cry and pray to be taken
back to your father's murderers, and ask what
you have to do with my misfortunes? Child, I
have told you.'

"He stopped as if exhausted by his own vehemence, and gazed at her in seeming anger. Poor
Marie could not repress the shudder which crept
over her as her eyes rested on her grandsire.

Visions of what her fate would be with him, and
still worse as the slave—for what else is an
Arab's wife?—of an infidel husband, rose up
vividly before her eyes and filled her with horror.

"At length the old man went out, and Marie,
being left alone, rose from her rude couch, and
kneeling, she drew forth her silver crucifix—it
was Colonel de St. Severan's parting gift—and
prayed earnestly to Him who had died for her,
that He would save her now from worse than
death, and restore her to the care of His true
followers. Hearing a step she rose, and carefully
hiding the precious crucifix, she stood waiting to
see what would happen next. She had come to
the conclusion that the best chance of escape
was to endeavour to win the old man's heart, and,
as he entered with cakes and fruits which he had
brought for her on the previous night, she thanked
him and began to eat. This seemed to please
him greatly.

"As soon as she had finished he said, ' Now we
must start again, for we have a long ride to take
before we reach the tribe.' He gave her an old
cloak, and told her to draw its hood over her
head; then he desired her to wait for a few
moments in the cavern while he got the horse
ready. Again he went away and left poor Marie
alone. Her heart began to sink. That night

they were to reach the tribe. What hope was there now for her.

"Journeying on, the old man tried to amuse her by talking of the handsome young chief whom he wished her to marry. Then he related stories of the brave deeds of her ancestors, and of her father especially. He told her that her mother was a Frenchwoman whom the Arabs had taken captive, and whom his son fell in love with and married. He spoke much, too, about the great honour which his son had done her in making her his wife, and about her ingratitude to him, and said that she fretted and pined until she lost all her beauty, got ill, and died shortly before the battle on the river Tanguin.

"At last, after a long and, to Marie, a terrible day's ride, they came to the encampment. As soon as they got to the entrance of the circle of tents they were surrounded by the men of the tribe; the women stared, but remained at their occupations. Many questions were asked of the old man, but, before he answered any of them, he lifted Marie almost tenderly from the horse; she could scarcely stand, and terrified by all those strange faces which crowded round her, she clung to him for support and protection. At this moment a witch-like looking women came and asked, ' Is this the lost child of thy brave son, Ben Arbi?'

"' It is, Masaouda,' he replied; ' help her to my tent and take care of her; she is weary, and, as I fear, ill ? '

" The old woman obeyed, and as soon as they got into the tent Marie saw a seat, and fell upon it with a moan of pain. Masaouda knelt down beside her, felt her hands, her forehead, and cheeks, and then left her to repose.

" Marie was alone, but she could not rest; all that Ben Arbi had said to her about the chief whom he wished her to marry haunted her, and when at last sleep stole upon her, fantastic and horrible forms seemed to crowd around, driving her to despair. This, she says, is the last thing that she remembers of that night.

" When next she awoke to consciousness it was broad day-light, and she saw Ben Arbi and Masaouda sitting at the door of the tent. She felt strangely weak, and closed her eyes almost as soon as she opened them, yet not before Ben Arbi had seen that one returning ray. Approaching her, he asked in a low anxious tone—

"' Does my child know me ? '

" Again she looked up for a moment; he saw that she had recognised him, and exclaimed—

"' Allah be praised ! She may live now ! '

" By degrees Ben Arbi's presence and Masaouda's recalled her sad history to her. Soon she was able to connect all the links of that chain so coiled around her. One day as she lay with closed eyes thinking over her forlorn condition she heard Masaouda and Ben Arbi talking together. From their conversation she learned that she had been more than three weeks ill, and that at one time they had almost despaired of her recovery. He spoke much of his anxiety that she should get well quickly, as war was menacing, and he wished her to be married before it broke out, otherwise it might be impossible for some time.

"How Marie's heart bounded as she heard these words! And how she prayed that God would not permit her to get well until this, for her, blessed war should have begun! She determined to speak as little as possible and to avoid giving any signs of returning strength. Accordingly, day after day she resisted all the efforts made to rouse her, and refused much of the nourishing things which they constantly brought to her, and thus she endeavoured to retard this dreaded recovery. Nevertheless, she felt that she *was* rapidly improving, and every day it became more difficult to repress the natural restlessness of convalescence.

"Time passed on slowly, and nothing more was said of the war; she was beginning to lose hope, when one evening she heard Masaouda come into the tent with Ben Arbi, who was questioning her eagerly about his child's health; he asked if it would be possible for her to be married in a week from that time, as the war had been determined upon, and the chiefs would depart. 'It is impossible,' the old woman answered; 'the child is too ill, and a relapse would probably cause her death.' Ben Arbi sighed deeply, but made no reply; while Marie felt that she could have fallen at Masaouda's feet and have blessed her for speaking these words. She knew, however, that she must remain silent, and from the depths of her heart she sent up a fervent thanksgiving to God. She was not yet saved, but this was a respite, and whilst it lasted might not her friends find and rescue her? It was a renewal of hope, and that is almost a renewal of life.

"At length the happy day arrived when the greater portion of the tribe set out for the scene of war, and from that day forward Marie improved rapidly. She devoted herself completely to Ben Arbi, vaguely hoping that if she could make him very fond of her she might perhaps be able to induce him to take her back to Algiers. She succeeded to her heart's content in exciting his tender affection for her, but he would not hear a word about taking her back, and appeared to be as intent as ever upon her marrying.

"Marie observed that his strength seemed to decline, and he himself said frequently that the old man's course was nearly run, and that if he could live to see his child married the object of his life would be gained, and he would be glad to sleep in peace with his brave sons.

"About two months from the time when the chiefs set out for the war, the survivors returned in triumph, and, with pride and joy lighting up his countenance, Ben Arbi told Marie that her husband elect was waiting to see her. She fell upon her knees, and clinging to him, besought him not to force her to marry, if he would not see her die of grief, as her poor mother had died. He sternly repulsed her, and left the tent in anger. It was a rude shock to Marie's hopes, and now, for the first time, she felt despair.

"Passively she submitted; she heard them agree that her marriage should take place in a few days, and even this did not rouse her. Ben Arbi tried to caress her and win her from this deep sadness, but she shook off his hand roughly, as she exclaimed, ' Do not touch me,—do not add hypocrisy to your cruelty. Is it not enough for you to force me to do that which will be to me a living death, without making false professions of affection for me? As you killed my mother, so

will you kill me!' She stopped her ears and
would not listen to a word from him.

"A few days before the fatal one named for
Marie's wedding, Ben Arbi said that he must go
to visit some holy shrine, to which there was then
a great pilgrimage, but that he would be back on
the day of the wedding. They were to be
married, as is the Arab custom, in the evening.

"Early on the morning of this eventful day
an old man tottered across the encampment and
entered Ben Arbi's tent. Marie was already out,
and was sitting at a little distance from it in a
state of mute despair, yet she recognised her
grandfather's form, and followed him into the
tent. He had fallen upon the ground, and was
lying there moaning as if in mortal agony. A
feeling of sickness came over Marie as she looked
at him, and she leaned against the side of the
tent for support.

"At this moment the whole camp seemed
roused, and were gathering round the tent, and he
to whom she was betrothed implored her to come
to him, saying that they must lose no time in
departing from a place which was cursed by the
plague.

"'What!' she cried; 'you would leave the
old man here to die alone? Go; I will remain
with him!'

"'Are you mad, girl!' exclaimed her betrothed. 'Come before you are yourself infected
—before you have touched him!'

"He advanced a little way into the tent and
took hold of her arm, but she shook him off, and
springing to her grandfather's side, she laid her
hand upon him and said—

"'Now come and take me away if you will, but
with me take this fell disease!'

"One and all they stood as if spell-bound,
gazing at her; then slowly and silently they
withdrew.

"At last, Marie, and the sufferer by whose side
she knelt, heard the heavy tramping of men and
flocks, as the caravan moved away from the presence of the plague-stricken. Marie turned and
kissed the old man's forehead.

"That kiss seemed to thrill through him. He
raised himself up, and looking intently at her, he
exclaimed—

"'My child!—I have never wrought thee
aught but evil. I stole thee from those who
were dear and kind to thee. I spurned thy
prayers and tears, entreating to be taken back to
them; and even this very day I was about to force
thee into a marriage against thy inclinations.
Nevertheless, in my hour of need and misery
thou remainest with me, whom all others have

abandoned! Child, who taught thee to act thus?'

"'Grandfather, it was the lesson which our God came down from heaven to teach us. He died to save those who most cruelly injured him. His doctrine and example are summed up in this one sentence—"Love thy God above all things, and thy neighbour as thyself!" And it was He who said, "Inasmuch as ye have done it unto the least of these, my brethren, ye have done it unto me!" And I have only done to you as I would that you should have done to me were I struck with this terrible disease, whilst I know that in thus attending to you I am ministering to Him.'

"The old man bowed his head, and said, 'Thy God shall be my·God! The religion that could make thee act as thou hast done must be divine. Child, make me what thou art.'

"Marie clasped her hands together in deep but silent thankfulness; then she exclaimed, 'Would that some one were here to teach you; yet I can baptize you and make you a Christian. Oh, how happy you have made me! I can even thank you now for having stolen me from my dear convent!'

"'Do not say thou canst not teach me, child; for thou hast taught me so great a lesson that nothing could surpass it. Make me what thou art, and I shall die in peace. But what is to become of thee, my poor child! If thou shouldst survive this danger they will claim thee, and thou wilt not escape them. Would that thou wert in safety with thy Christian friends!'

"Marie trembled; yet a moment after she smiled brightly, and said, 'Fear not for me, grandfather; God is with us, and He will protect me. I no longer fear for myself; but say, are we far from Algiers?'

"'Not more than a good day's journey on foot. I brought thee by a longer route, in order to elude pursuit. But what does that avail; there is no one to send thither!'

"'It is all in the hands of God, and all will be well; do not let us think any more about me, but about yourself.' And when she had done all she could to soothe him, she sat down beside him and talked to him about the loving Saviour, whose follower he wished to become; and related to him as much as she could remember of the touching Gospel histories.

"Towards evening he fell into a light sleep, then Marie went out to breathe the fresh air, and was thinking of the happiness it would be to her if she could send for the dear old chaplain of the convent, who would baptize her grandfather, and,

if he lived, find means to have him as well as herself removed to Algiers. Whilst she was musing,
a sound of footsteps fell upon her ear, and looking up, she saw coming towards her a poor, half-
witted boy, to whom she had been kind, and who
seemed to have taken an ardent fancy for her.
He was leading a goat; and, as soon as he saw
her, he hastened to her, and said he had brought
the goat for her that she might have some milk
to drink.

"Marie took his hand, and pressing it within
her own, thanked him warmly for thus thinking
of her. The boy blushed, and laughed sillily;
then he asked if he could do anything for her.

"'Yes,' she answered quickly; 'if you would
go to Algiers, and bring back something—some
medicine—for my grandfather, I shall love you so
much.' The boy assented gladly; and then she
asked him to wait until she had obtained the necessary instructions.

"Finding Ben Arbi asleep, Marie had to wait
some time before she could speak to him; then
she told him that God had sent them in the poor
boy a messenger to Algiers, and asked him if he
knew any Arab there to whom she could entrust
a message to the convent. The old man thought
for a few moments, and said he knew one who
was under great obligations to him, and in whom

he could trust. 'Then all is well,' she answered ; 'only tell me how I am to describe the place where we are?' She had her little pocket-book still with her ; and what a treasure it proved to her now, since it gave her the means of communicating with her friends !

"The old man having given her the necessary directions, dictated a few lines to the Arab, to desire him to give the messenger a little phial containing a certain cordial, and above all to lose no time in conveying Marie's packet to its destination.

"When all this was done, and the messenger had departed, Ben Arbi seemed inclined to sleep again, and she began her night-watch; a lonely one indeed would it have been had not the bright star of hope shone through all its gloom.

"Slowly passed the hours until the next day, when, about noon, the faithful messenger appeared again. He gave her the phial, and told her that the Arab desired him to say that Ben Arbi's wishes should be executed. Marie could have cried for joy, and her gratitude to the poor boy was far greater than she could express. It was necessary, however, to send him away; and this cost her a severe pang, as she thought of when he would return and find the place deserted by them.

"Every feeling was, however, soon merged
in an intense longing for the arrival of the good
chaplain. Her grandfather was sinking rapidly,
and she began to think that Père de la Roche
would not be there in time to baptize him ; and
how she shuddered at the thought of being left
there alone with the dead. Evening came, and
twilight waned into night, but no Père de la
Roche ; and poor Marie's heart began to droop
again. Perhaps he had not received the note, and,
if so, what was she to do ? She almost shrieked
aloud as she thought of her probably forlorn condition, for she felt sure that her grandfather had
not long to live,—he had said so more than once ;
and during the whole day he had been tormenting
himself about what was to become of her if no
one came from Algiers.

"The old man had fallen asleep; the bright
light of the moon showed Marie that his eyes
were closed. In her anxious hope she went out
of the tent and climbed up a tree which stood
near, to gaze across that vast plain ; but nothing
appeared. She then determined to descend, and
baptize her grandfather herself as soon as he
awoke. One last yearning look, however, brought
before her something which made her heart throb
almost aloud. It was but a small spot; but it
seemed to move, and to draw nearer to her. At

last she could see that it was a man on horseback. There was no Arab dress ; it must be, it was Père de la Roche ! She almost sprang from the tree, and ran towards him.

" Père de la Roche and Marie hastened to the tent, and Marie went in to announce the glad tidings. The old man was lying with his eyes wide open, and looked at Marie fondly and sadly as she entered ; but when she told him that Père de la Roche had arrived, his countenance lit up, and he exclaimed, ' Then thou art happy. I can now die in peace, and thou wilt go back to those whom thou lovest ! But go, child, and send him to me quickly, for my course is nearly run.' Marie went out and led Père de la Roche into the tent. She left him there, and waited without for him.

" She was roused by the good father, whose hand lightly shook her. ' Come, my child,' said he ; ' thy grandfather would see thee again before he dies. He is now a Christian, and will be with his God before many minutes have passed. Ah ! what a great work thy faith has wrought !'

" Hardly were Ben Arbi's eyes closed in his happy death, when the sound of horses caused Marie once more to tremble. Père de la Roche reassured her by saying that it was probably a detachment of cavalry from Algiers, sent to guard their safe return. Taking her by the hand, he led her out of the tent, and there she saw again the beloved French uniforms. This second shock of joy, and the death scene she had just witnessed, were too much for her. She sank down quite overcome; and they laid her upon the long grass, where they left her to slumber, whilst they hurriedly performed the last rites to Ben Arbi.

"When all was done, they gently awoke her; and placing her on horseback, they returned to Algiers. Poor Marie was carried exhausted into the convent just as the bell was tolling for matins. The nuns came gathering round their lost child, now restored to them, to their great joy."

CHAPTER VI.

THE Adairs were doubly anxious to know Marie
and to have her with them, after reading the
papers which Madame Hird had given them;
moreover, she would, they thought, so well supply
Lucy's place, and be a companion to Flora.

Accordingly, when the day arrived which had
been fixed for Lucy's departure, and they had
confided her to the care of the friends with whom
she was to travel to England, they determined to
drive straight to the convent. They got into an
open carriage, but the driver looked wonders
when he was told that their destination was the
Villa Ianthe, on the Lungara—a long distance
indeed from the Piazza dei Termini. He tried to
console himself, however, by driving as slowly as
possible, being too truly Italian to trouble himself
as to whether, in so doing, he lost other fares or
not. What true Italian does not prefer the *dolce
far niente* to gain? Fortunately it was a matter
of indifference to the Adairs; they were not pressed

for time, and that slow motion through the soft, hazy air of Rome was far from disagreeable, so they let him *gang his ain gate.*

Even their slow pace brought them, at length, to the convent, and once more they were shown into the little square room, with its prim air— that room which not even the sun of Italy could cheer or warm.

Madame Hird came down quickly, and when the usual greetings were over, and they were all seated, Mrs. Adair gave back the papers, and said, "These have interested us so much that we are longing to make the acquaintance of the little heroine, and to have her with us. When can she come? We leave Rome on Tuesday week, and should like it to be as soon as possible, that she may get accustomed to us before we set out on our journey."

"You can see her now, if you wish," replied Madame Hird, "but the Superioress will say when she can go to you. I had a letter from Madame de St. Severan yesterday; she is greatly pleased to hear that Marie is to travel with you, and that you intend to make some *détour;* a little travelling with you and your daughter will, she thinks, be of great advantage to Marie. I wrote to her of you from what I knew of you in former days, and of Mademoiselle I said, that as far as I could judge⬤ a visit, she would be an admirable companion for my young charge."

" We are most grateful for your good opinion," answered Mrs. Adair, " and shall do our best to merit it, by making Marie as happy as we can while she is with us."

" I have no doubt that she will be very happy, and the new and varied scenes which she will visit with you will delight her. I will go and tell her that you wish to see her,—she may be a little shy at first, as she is so unaccustomed to meet strangers."

" Very naturally, poor child ; but she will soon get over that with us, I trust."

" Then I will go to announce your visit."

After a short time Madame Hird returned, with a tall, and rather an imposing-looking nun, whom she introduced as " Madame la Supérieure."

The lady was French, but she spoke English tolerably well, and at once addressed Mrs. Adair in that language.

" Mademoiselle Marie will have the honour to salute you in a few instants. Madame Hird tells me that you have the goodness to permit her to make the voyage to Paris with you, and that you desire to know when she can go *chez vous*. It is to-day Friday ; shall we then say Monday next ? Madame de St. Severan has sent me a sum of

money, which she prayed me to give you, should
it be decided that Mademoiselle Marie was to
travel with you; it is for her voyage. Shall I
give it to you now, or when you come for her on
Monday?"

"Then, if you please, since I can have a receipt
ready to give you. You know, Madame, that it
is better to do these things *en règle;* it prevents
misunderstandings."

"Just as you like. At what hour will you come
on Monday?"

"Would five o'clock suit you, Madame?"

"It is equal to me, and Marie shall be ready
for you at that hour. I am astonished that she
has not come down to be presented to you. And
now that all our arrangements are made, I will
ask you to give me permission to retire, as I am
very much occupied. I will send Marie to you at
once. Adieu, Madame,—adieu, Mademoiselle."
And making a formal curtsey to each of them,
she left the room.

Flora drew a long breath as the door closed,
and had not Madame Hird remained in the
room, we should probably have heard her utter
a fervent " *Deo gratias!* " Madame Hird smiled
slightly and said, " Marie will get a reprimand
for dilatoriness, but in reality it is timidity

which has prevented her from coming sooner. I hear a step,—I will go and meet the poor child ; she would never have courage to come in herself."

She went into the passage and returned immediately, leading in a young lady dressed in a black silk frock. She was very short, but she had a well-formed, plump figure, large liquid black eyes, full red lips, a clear olive complexion covered with blushes, and black hair curling round her head in short curls. A pretty little creature she certainly was, and she looked so innocent and clinging that from the first moment it was hardly possible not to be fond of her.

Madame Hird presented her to Mrs. Adair and said, "This is the lady who is so kind as to take charge of you to Paris, Marie ; and to whom I am sure you will be very grateful."

Marie made a shy curtsey and muttered something in French; but Mrs. Adair took her hand and kissed her, saying, "Oh, this is quite too formal; . . . we must be friends, Marie—or must I call you Mademoiselle?"

"*Oh non, Madame,*" and she blushed more than ever.

Flora now came and kissed her also, as she said, "Come and talk to me, Marie." She drew her to

the window and made her sit down beside her.
Meanwhile Madame Hird devoted herself to Mrs.
Adair, and they wisely left the young people to
themselves.

"You must not be shy with me, Marie; I do
not appear very terrible, do I?"

"*Mais non, Mademoiselle,*" answered Marie,
with a smile.

"Well then, you must call me Flora, and not
Mademoiselle.   I call you Marie."

"*Quel joli nom vous avez.*"

"You like it!—then you must show me that
you do by using it.   But you speak English they
say; I see that you understand it well."

"*Oui, je le comprends très bien, Made——*"

Flora looked at her and shook her head.   Marie
smiled, hesitated for a moment, and then said,
coyly, "*Flore.*"

"Wonderful!" exclaimed Flora, "there is a victory already gained!   But you were going to say—

"*Mais je ne le parle pas bien, et j'ai peur de
vous.*"

Marie turned, and for the first time looked up
fully in Flora's face.

"But you are not much afraid of me, Marie,
after all?"

"*Mais vous, vous parlez Français,—c'est très
heureux pour moi!*"

" Well, I must say that I do not quite see that, Marie; perhaps you can explain it to me?"

" *Oui, et très bien même. Je n'aime pas à parler une langue étrangère avec vous, parceque j'ai peur de vous, mais vous n'avez pas peur de moi!*" And she laughed merrily, as if she thought it an absurd idea that any one could be afraid of her. It made Flora laugh also, and the laughing seemed to set Marie more at her ease,—very soon all fear of the formidable Flora appeared to have vanished.

After some little time Mrs. Adair said, " I am glad, Marie, to see that you and Flora are becoming friends."

" *Oui, Madame, et je n'ai plus peur d'elle!*"

" So I perceive, nor must you be afraid of me, either. Now we must leave you, but only until Monday. Flora has told you, I suppose, that the Superioress has given you leave to come to us then."

" *Oui, Madame, et ce sera un bonheur pour moi de faire ce voyage avec vous et avec Mademoiselle votre fille!*"

" I hope you may find it so. Good-bye, then, for a few days." She kissed her, and then turned to bid Madame Hird adieu.

" Only four o'clock ! It is too early for us to go home," said Flora, looking up from her watch as they got into the street.

"Is there anything near that we have not seen?"

"The Farnese Palazzo is quite close, but if the king and queen are not away it is only shown to visitors on Sundays at five in the evening."

"Let us try, at all events; they may perhaps be absent."

As the two ladies turned off the Lungara into the *Via del Ponte*, they met Mr. Lyne coming down the *Via delle Fornaci*.

"Mrs. Adair! who would have thought of seeing you here?" and he shook hands with her and with Flora.

"We are returning from the Villa Ianthe," answered Mrs. Adair.

"And I," rejoined Mr. Lyne, "from the beautiful Fontana Paolina. Are you going to walk home?"

"Yes; or rather we are going first to the Palazzo Farnese to try if we can see it. Flora says it is quite near."

"So it is, and I think you *can* see it. I know that the royal family were absent yesterday, and they may not have returned. May I have the pleasure of accompanying you, Mrs. Adair?"

He addressed Mrs. Adair, but he looked at Flora, who replied, "Well, I suppose you may, as

I dare say your coming will not prevent our seeing the pictures."

" I should think not," added Mrs. Adair, smiling. So they went on together.

Ah ! Flora, could you have known the past events of the day before, or the coming ones of that day, how different would have been your answer when Mr. Lyne asked to accompany you to the Farnese Palace !

Mr. Lyne was about the middle height and rather slight ; he had regular, well-cut features, brown eyes, and dark hair. He was certainly gentleman-like in appearance, and was generally called handsome, being so, indeed, to those who think more of form than of expression ; not that his expression was wanting in goodness or even in intelligence, but it was devoid of animation or energy. He was essentially what is called a good young man,—one who fulfilled every duty with the greatest exactitude, who always did just what was expected of him. His ideas and conversation on most subjects were just, calm, and deliberate, but never original, and he was perfectly guiltless of ever allowing himself to be carried away by feeling or enthusiasm. No one ever heard of his doing a startling act of kindness, self-devotion, or generosity; but on the other hand he was invariably kind in a general way, a sincere friend, too, and moderately generous.

We have heard that he was going to be married to Flora Adair, or at least that he intended to propose for her, and felt no doubt about being accepted. This was true, and his courtship and love were quite in keeping with the other features of his character. As his mother was French, and he had been brought up chiefly in France, he had acquired much of the French ideas about marriage. The Adairs were old friends of his family; so much so, indeed, that Mrs. Adair always called him George; and he was aware that a marriage between him and Flora would be agreeable to his own and to her friends. It was just the connection which his parents wished for, but he was not a person ready to marry any girl who was pointed out to him as eligible; on the contrary, he was determined never to marry any one whom he did not *like* very much. If he could like one an alliance with whom would please his family, he thought it would be a most desirable thing, and therefore he cultivated an intimate acquaintance with the Adairs.

Flora, strange to say, did inspire him with a feeling as nearly akin to love as it was in his nature to feel, and she treated him with a friendly, cordial manner, as the son of a very old friend of

her mother's, never for a moment supposing that
he could think of wishing to marry her, feeling,
as she did, that their characters were too essentially different for anything like union between
them. Thus she innocently encouraged him to
believe that she liked him, and he did not understand the different symptoms of love and liking,
otherwise her friendly but indifferent manner
would have driven him to despair. Her real
opinion of him was that he was a good-natured
"bore," very obliging, gentlemanly, and quite
capable of taking his place creditably in conversation ; better informed, indeed, than the majority
of those around him, but tiresome withal. And
this was the man whom Mary Elton had told
Mr. Earnscliffe that she was going to marry !

When they got to the palazzo they found—as
Mr. Lyne had said—that the royal family had
not returned. They were told that the *custode*
had gone upstairs a moment before with a gentleman. They hurried on and overtook them just as
the door of the gallery was opened. The gentleman turned to let them pass before him,—it was
Mr. Earnscliffe !

The unexpected meeting of those whom we
esteem greatly is a delicious sensation, and this
Flora then felt. Had she known all that had

passed between Mary and Mr. Earnscliffe, how different would have been her feelings !

The Adairs were in advance when Mr. Earnscliffe turned, and his expression seemed to light up a little as he saw them, but it grew dark again as he caught sight of their companion, and he appeared to be in one of his haughtiest moods as he shook hands with them and Mr. Lyne.

"This is a fortunate day for me," said the latter; "as I was returning from a walk to the Fontana Paolina, I met Mrs. and Miss Adair, who kindly permitted me to accompany them here, and now we meet you who are such a connoisseur in painting, our visit will be doubly instructive."

"I believe the *custode* undertakes to point out everything of note," replied Mr. Earnscliffe, stiffly. "It is usually so when one goes round with visitors in such places. But we are keeping the man waiting." He motioned him on, and they all followed.

It would have been too harsh had he not asked Flora if she felt perfectly recovered from her sprain; and in formal politeness Mr. Earnscliffe was scrupulously exact; so he said in a cold tone, " I hope, Miss Adair, that you do not feel any lingering inconvenience from your sprain ? "

"None in the least, I thank you, as you will

see by my dancing at Mrs. Elton's on Friday
night. Helena told me that we were to have the
pleasure of meeting you there."

" Yes, I promised Miss Elton to go ; she said it
was a farewell."

"So it is; they leave Rome on the Monday
after. We met them yesterday evening on the
Pincio after their visit to the Catacombs."

" Indeed !" He turned away, and seemed intent
upon looking at the frescoes and listening to the
guide's remarks about them.

Flora was gazing abstractedly at Domenichino's
Deliverance of Prometheus, as she leaned back
against the wall opposite. She could not rid
herself of the chill which she felt from the
moment that Mr. Earnscliffe had shaken hands
with her, and yet had she been asked why, she
could not have given a very clear answer. But
who does not know that vague sensation of unhappiness which the manner of one dear to us
sometimes causes us to feel, although there may
not be any positive or, at least, any definable
change in it such as an indifferent person could
see ?

How well she remembered what Mr. Earnscliffe
had said to her about this Farnese Palazzo. All
that he had told her of its founder, Alessandro
Farnese, afterwards Paul III. ; of its architecture,

of its frescoes; how it had descended to the royal family of Naples, and eventually become their refuge and dwelling-place in exile. But how different he was on this day. He hardly noticed or spoke to her, save those few words of ordinary civility about her accident. She thought it was too provoking of him to be so changeable, but the next moment she felt indignant against herself for harbouring even a suspicion against him, and thought it was but natural that a clever man like him should not care greatly to talk in such a place to one like herself. When she was a prisoner it was otherwise; then he thought himself in some measure bound to try to amuse her; but that was all past, and his manner to her now was just what she ought to have expected.

Nevertheless, Flora wished that they had not come there then. Suddenly it struck her that it was all that tiresome Mr. Lyne's fault; if he had not met them and said that the king and queen were away, perhaps they might not have come.

The *custode* seemed at length to think that they had spent sufficient time in admiring the frescoes, and he led them into the two large halls looking on the Piazza, where there are a few remnants of the fine collection of statues which this palace once contained. Mr. Lyne appeared to be much struck with the gigantic group hewn out of the stone taken from the basilica of Constantine, and representing Alessandro Farnese crowned by Victory. He was most anxious to hear all about Moschino, whose work it is, and expressed his wonder that he had never heard of it before.

Mr. Lyne will, doubtless, be considered to be a very strange lover, since he was so occupied with the statues whilst in the company of his beloved; but it should be remembered that Mr. Lyne never allowed himself to be carried away by feeling, that he always did the right thing at the right time; and he considered that in visiting celebrated places and galleries of art the object was to learn as much as he could; afterwards he could afford to please himself, and be devoted to the lady of his choice. At last his questionings came to an end, and the guide, seeing that the rest of the party were quite ready to go, moved towards the door.

Would Mr. Earnscliffe walk home with them? This was a question upon which Flora had been pondering for the last ten minutes, and she would have given a great deal to have had it satisfactorily answered. When they got into the Piazza she said, " Mamma, we can return by the Gesù, and inquire for our friend there who has been so ill."

" That was a happy thought, Flora. I am delighted to call to-day, as I fear that to-morrow we may not have time to do so. Do we say good-bye to you here, Mr. Earnscliffe?"

"No, as far as the Corso my way is the same as yours," he replied, after a moment's hesitation.

"Then come, George," said Mrs. Adair, turning to Mr. Lyne; "let us lead, and you must be my guide, for I do not know the way."

They went on, and Mr. Earnscliffe and Flora followed. She wondered whether he would now talk to her as he used to do, or remain in his silent mood. She need not to have feared; he was far too well bred to make a lady feel any such *gène* while walking with him, but she hoped in vain that he would be the same towards her as he had been three weeks before.

He spoke of the topics of the day, of the ceremonies of Holy Week, and of the Easter rejoicings. It was very dull work; and when she saw that he was determined not to glide into their former intercourse, she gave up making any effort to sustain the conversation. She knew that he took no pleasure in speaking of ceremonies and illuminations, and as *she* certainly did not, why, she thought, should she bore him or herself with such things?

Nor was he slow to discover that she did not care to continue their conversation, and, as is so often the case, he fixed upon a wrong motive as the cause of her silence. He supposed that she was thinking of the change which was about to take place in her life. He did not see how different his own manner was to her, but concluded that all he had seen on that day was proof of what Mary Elton had told him; and Flora's seeming indifference towards Mr. Lyne only made him think still less kindly of her, as it showed that she had not the grace even to pretend that she loved him, although she was ready to marry him.

What a run of ill-luck there was against Flora on that day! Everything seemed to confirm what he had heard; yet how different was the reality!

When they reached the Gesù, she said, " I suppose you have had a very dull walk. I know I was very silent, but you must feel that it was *your* fault. I saw that you did not care to talk. . . . Here we are, however, at our destination, so good-bye."

She held out her hand, and as he took it he answered, " I do not quite understand what you mean ? "

Flora smiled, turned away, and went up the steps as Mrs. Adair and Mr. Lyne wished him good-day. He stood for a moment until he saw them go into the convent, and then walked slowly away murmuring to himself, " What could she have meant by saying, 'You must feel that it was *your* fault?' . . . The look, too, which accompanied those words seemed to ask some question. . . . But what is all this to me?"

He quickened his pace, and soon arrived at his apartments in the Piazza di Trajana.

CHAPTER VII.

On Friday morning—the morning of the Eltons' *soirée*—Marie Arbi, who had been with the Adairs since the Monday before, was in a state of great excitement, mingled with no little terror, about her first ball. Flora could but laugh at the timid fears of the world's novice, for she knew that her prettiness and simplicity would amply cover any want of self-possession, and, indeed, render her doubly attractive.

One moment Marie was in ecstasies of delight with her dress and wreath; the next she would rush into the drawing-room to Flora and ask a score of questions. Then she would declare that she knew she should be horribly *gauche*, and looked half ready to cry over her anticipated awkwardness. But a word from Flora about her toilette would set her off again into a rapture of admiration, and, with all a Frenchwoman's delight in the details of dress, she would descant on each particular of it. All this made Flora think of her own first ball, and of how comparatively indifferent she was about it, although she really was fond of dancing; but she had never possessed any of that almost childish gaiety which characterised Marie.

A few minutes before nine o'clock the important business of dressing was satisfactorily completed, and the young ladies went into the drawing-room to Mrs. Adair, who was already dressed. Both the girls were in white. Marie's dress was trimmed with lily of the valley and pink convolvulus; she wore a wreath to match this trimming, and necklace and earrings of topaz. Flora's was looped up with bunches of scarlet geraniums, and a spray or two of the same flowers gleamed through the masses of her hair; she wore a band of pearls round her neck, and earrings to correspond. Marie was, according to all rule, by far the prettier of the two, as she stood there with her black eyes dancing merrily, and her full red lips parted in eager expectation; her short plump figure harmonised, too, so well with the child-like expression of her face. Flora looked well also, and her slighter and more delicately formed figure gave to her a grace which was quite her own.

"I hear the carriage!" Flora exclaimed, "so let us put on our cloaks. Mrs. Elton said that the music was to begin exactly at nine, and it is striking that now ; so we shall not be too early at all events."

At the door of the brilliantly lighted saloon they were received by Mrs. Elton and Mary. Did the latter feel a qualm of conscience as she greeted Flora, after she had been plotting so against her ? No change of countenance betrayed any such feeling. She looked as usual, calm and dignified, as she motioned to her to pass on, saying, " A little farther on in the room you will meet Charles and Helena, who will find seats for you."

The entrance of the Adair party was followed by that of Mr. and Mrs. Penton. She looked queen-like in her training dress of black velvet, which well displayed her majestic bearing; and the smallness of her head was rendered especially remarkable by the way in which her hair was dressed. It was combed back plainly from her forehead, plaited up tightly at the back, and surmounted by a magnificent tiara of pearls. Her fair round-faced husband looked the character of a gentleman farmer quite as well as she did that of a queen. Immediately afterwards came a number of gentlemen, and among them were Signor Lanzi, Mr. Mainwaring, Mr. Caulfield, Mr. Lyne, and Mr. Earnscliffe.

The music-room, which was rather small, was

quite full, and the room next to it nearly so, when Helena went to ask her mother if she wished the music to begin. On her way, however, she discreetly managed to pass close to Mr. Caulfield, and to exchange a few words with him. He cast a questioning glance towards the place where Mrs. Elton stood, as if to ask if there was any hope of her looking favourably on him. Helena shook her head and turned away. In a few moments she returned with her mother and Mary, and the music began.

There were but short intervals between the pieces, so by a little after ten, as the last notes of one of Beethoven's sonatas died away, they were answered from the other end of the room by the inspiriting tones of the Overland Mail Galop. This was a special favourite of Helena's, and she had asked the leader of the band to commence with it; accordingly a few bars of it were played; then there was a pause in order to give the couples time to form.

What a scene of confusion there was at that moment! The girls looking anxiously to see if the *right* one was coming to them; the gentlemen rushing about seeking for those to whom they were, or wished to be, engaged. Gradually the ladies and their partners paired off into the dancing-room, so that single couples could easily be distinguished.

Mr. Lyne, in his usual deliberate way, waited until the first rush was over, and then he went up to Flora and asked for the honour of her hand for this galop.

"I am not engaged," she answered; "but you will oblige me very much if you will dance with my friend instead of with me. She is a little shy, as it is her first ball, so it would be pleasant for her to begin by dancing with one whom she has met before. You will do this, will you not?" and she looked up smilingly at him.

"I would do much more than that to oblige Miss Adair," replied Mr. Lyne, and he offered his arm to Marie. She hesitated to accept Flora's partner, but the latter insisted.

As they went into the dancing-room Flora looked after them with an expression of amusement at Mr. Lyne's answer, which she supposed was meant to be very complimentary, but which was in reality just the contrary; implying as it did, that to give up a dance with her was a very slight sacrifice indeed.

Meanwhile Mary and Helena Elton went about to see if all their friends had partners. They did not adopt the fashionable style of leaving people to get on as well as they can whether they know any one or not.

Mr. Caulfield was watching Helena with long-ing eyes. She had told him that she could not give him the first dance, so he felt half inclined to do the *doloroso*, by not dancing it at all, and he really thought that he could have refrained had the band played anything but that "Over-land Mail." To stand still during such a galop was more than nature could bear, so as he saw Helena going towards Flora with a man "in tow," as he expressed it, to be introduced to her, he hastened in the same direction, and said in a low voice as he passed her, "Well, if I can't have you, I'll have the best dancer in the room," and the next minute he was making his bow to Flora.

"Why did you not say, 'Miss Adair, I want you to dance with me *faute de mieux?*'" she said laughingly, as she took his arm.

"By Jove, Miss Adair, I would rather have you for a partner than *almost* any one in the room; you do go the pace to such perfection!"

She blushed as she felt how humbling it was to be told by Mr. Caulfield that he had chosen her for such a reason; but she knew that he meant it as a very great compliment, and therefore she thought it was unreasonable to be annoyed at it, so she answered lightly, "Well, let us begin."

Mary had asked Mr. Earnscliffe if he would allow her to get him a partner, but he replied, "Thank you, I very seldom dance; especially these dances." He bowed, turned away, and joined some gentlemen who were talking in another part of the room. Mary looked annoyed, and murmured to herself, "He might at least have asked me to dance a quadrille, if only from mere politeness. Ah! I see that I shall never succeed, but, at least, I need no longer to fear a rival in Flora Adair. My plan is working well," and a sinister expression came into her eyes as Flora passed with Mr. Caulfield.

The dancing continued with unflagging spirit until supper was announced, and even then it ceased only because the musicians went away to take some refreshments. Helena, however, considered that it would be too sad to lose such a delightful opportunity of dancing and flirting with Mr. Caulfield, so she managed to induce some obliging lady to sit down to the piano and play a valse. In a moment his arm was round her waist and away they twirled, enjoying intensely the pleasure of stealing a march on the "dragoness," as Mr. Caulfield irreverently persisted in calling Mrs. Elton. Their example was at once followed by all the lovers of dancing, who always prefer the supper dances to any others.

Marie seemed to have got over her shyness, and was quite a focus of attraction; her *naïveté*, and even her blunders in English, attracted every one, and she became a general favourite.

"Time flies when it should linger most," and Mr. Caulfield thought that this was the truest of all things, as Mary came to tell them that the people were coming back from supper. There was a deep recess in one of the rooms, in which was an ottoman. Here they had seated them·selves, and were making plans for bright hours to come. For the moment they appeared to have forgotten the existence of a "dragoness" who might possibly prevent the realisation of visions so fair, but it was forcibly called to their recollection by Mary, who exclaimed, "Helena, how can you be so imprudent? In another moment mamma would have caught you!"

"Not while I have such a dear, thoughtful prig of a sister to guard me," replied Helena, as she jumped up and kissed her; then waving her hand to Mr. Caulfield, she glided away humming, "*Addio del passato bei sogni sorridenti.*" A few minutes afterwards she was seen walking into the supper-room leaning on Mr. Mainwaring, and looking as demure as possible.

To Mary's surprise and delight Mr. Earnscliffe came and asked her to dance the next quadrille

with him. As she took his arm she saw Mr.
Lyne and Flora Adair coming towards them, and
said, "Let us ask them to form part of our
set."

He bowed and led her to them, but he did not
speak. Mary said, "I am so glad that I chanced
to see you, Flora; will you be our *vis-à-vis?*"
The stereotyped answer, "With pleasure," was
given, and they took the places opposite to each
other. How often in the world are these two
words uttered mechanically and untruly.

Mary was looking unusually pleased and animated. Not so was Flora. She felt puzzled
about Mr. Lyne. His marked attention to her
during the whole evening, and his—for him—
devoted manner, made her wonder if so wild an
idea as his imagining himself in love with her
could have got into his head; but she rejected
such a supposition as absurd, and persuaded herself that his increasing attention to her might be
the effect of champagne, which would quickly
wear off, and that it would be best to treat it
lightly, so she tried to appear gay and amused.
She little knew how closely she was watched, and
how false an interpretation was given to whatever
she did.

In taking the usual promenade after the dance,
they passed the recess where Mary found Helena

and Mr. Caulfield after supper.   Pointing to the
seat, Mr. Lyne said to her—

"Will you rest here a little, Miss Adair?"

"Thank you; I would rather rejoin mamma."

"Nay, Miss Adair, I beg you to grant me a
few moments."

She did not ·see how she could well refuse, so
she allowed him to take her to the ottoman. She
seated herself, and he took the place beside her.
How she wished to say to him, "If you are going
to propose to me, I pray you not to do so, and it
will save us both pain."   But of course she could
say nothing of the kind, and must leave him to
take his own course; she had already done all
that she could to avoid the threatened conversation.   He did not keep her long in suspense, but
plainly and directly asked her to be his wife.

"Oh, Mr. Lyne!" she answered, "I am so
sorry that this should have occurred; for although
I feel deeply gratified by your preference, I would
much rather not have had that gratification than
be obliged, as I am, to inflict the pain of a refusal
upon you."

"Pray hear me for a moment, Miss Adair," he
exclaimed, eagerly, "before you give so decided
an answer.   Your mother has given her full
approbation to my suit, and my family would be
enchanted to receive you among them; for myself,

I can truly say that I have the highest possible respect and admiration for you, and you have always appeared to like me. I would do everything to make you happy—agree to anything you could desire. What obstacle, then, is there to your marrying me?"

She looked at him in amazement, and was on the point of giving him rather a sharp answer; but remembering that more or less a refusal must give him pain, she felt that it would be unwomanly not to make hers as gentle as she could; therefore she determined to restrain herself, and after a little hesitation she said—

"There is one grand objection, Mr. Lyne. I feel no love for you, and I could not do you the wrong of marrying you without loving."

"Oh! if that's all, I'll forgive you the wrong. I will try to win your love, and I am too sensible to want that sort of romantic love about which some people rave. Indeed, I do not think it in the least necessary to the happiness of marriage."

This was too much for Flora; she forgot all her good resolutions, and retorted with heightened colour, "I dare say *you* do not; you probably think, as I have heard good people in France say, that *l'amour n'est rien dans le mariage, c'est une affection—un dévouement chrétien, qui doit exister entre les époux, et cet amour ne vient qu'après le mariage.* Perhaps you would be satisfied with that sort of thing!"

No sooner had the words escaped her than she felt heartily ashamed of herself, and she added, humbly, "Forgive me; I have been rude and ungrateful. I have no excuse to offer save that I was carried away by momentary excitement. This is a subject upon which I feel very strongly, and I cannot, as I know many estimable people do, look upon marriage as a sort of half religious, half social duty, for which suitable position and fortune, without any prominent incompatibility of disposition, are the only requisites. If I have ever misled you as to my sentiments towards you, believe me, Mr. Lyne, that it was unintentional. I never thought of you in any other way than as a friend, and, until this evening, I never imagined that you otherwise regarded me—surely we are too unsuited to each other for anything more."

" Yes, I do feel now that we *are* unsuited to each other; yet I never admired you more than I do at this moment. As to your having misled me, the fault, if any, was all my own. I might have seen how reluctant you were to grant me these few minutes, and yet I would persevere, so you are perfectly free from blame. Whatever pain you may have caused me I freely forgive. Remember also, Miss Adair, that should you

ever want a friend you will find a true one in
me."

" Of that I am sure."

He looked gratified, pressed her hand, and
murmured, " God bless you!" and then left her.

Flora felt so unhappy that it was difficult for
her to prevent the tears which stood in her eyes
from falling. She had fortunately refused to
engage herself for the dance which was now
beginning, pleading a wish to rest before the
cotillon which was to follow it, so she had a little
time to recover herself.

This conversation was not long in passing, yet,
short as it was, Mr. Earnscliffe had observed it,—
he saw the parting, and the tears in her eyes
afterwards, yet he never doubted that she had
accepted Mr. Lyne, and he thought to himself,
" What! even in the first moments, is she bewail-
ing the sale which she has made of herself, and
the wrong she is doing to him? I suppose she is
not quite hardened as yet in her *rôle*, and that
it costs her a few tears to act it—soon enough it
will become a second nature to her! . . . . What
soulless things women are! And I was once so
silly as to worship them; but I was cured of that
folly long ago. This is only another proof of
their worthlessness; and that, too, in one of whom
I felt half inclined to believe better things. How

she excited my curiosity as we walked home the other day from the Farnese Palace! I could not comprehend her. . . . . Well, at all events I will go and say good-bye to her, since we may perhaps never meet again."

As soon as he got close to where she was sitting he said, "I am come to bid you farewell, Miss Adair. I leave Rome to-morrow."

She started as she heard his voice, for she had been leaning her head upon her hand, and had not seen him approach, and now, as he took the vacant place beside her, she looked rather confused, and felt very much at a loss for something to say, so she repeated, " Leaving Rome to-morrow ?"

" Yes, I am going to the neighbourhood of Naples; it is so beautiful there in spring."

" I should imagine so; spring is beautiful everywhere, and in Southern Italy it must be doubly so."

He did not answer, and, to break the silence, she added, " We go in the very opposite direction —northwards. I am longing to see Venice."

" But you do not go immediately," he rejoined; looking at her inquiringly, " you remain here some time longer, and then you begin *your* travels?" he laid a slight stress on *your*.

" No, we go at once. What should we remain here for when all our friends are gone? New scenes give variety, and—for the time at least—interest."

Her tone was sad and listless as she said this, and again he fixed his full blue eyes on her face with a meditative and a questioning gaze. She wondered what he meant by looking at her thus, as if he would read her very thoughts, and feeling that it was most unpleasant to be gazed at in this way, she exclaimed, " Mr. Earnscliffe!"

He was on the point of saying, "And Mr. Lyne goes with you, of course?" when the sound of his name, uttered by Flora, arrested his words: had they been spoken, he must have discovered his mistake; but, alas! they were not, and she continued, " Will you take me to mamma?"

This annoyed him, yet he stood up at once and offered her his arm. As they went she said, " I must thank you once more and for the last time, as we say good-bye to-night, for all your kindness to me when my ankle was sprained,—it was so good-natured of you to condescend to come and lighten my close imprisonment. I cannot say how grateful I feel to you."

" There is no cause for gratitude, Miss Adair; I did nothing for you beyond what I was bound in justice to do." It was now her turn to feel annoyed. " Besides, I enjoyed those hours very much."

" Wonderful! I thought you hated women too much to derive pleasure from their society?"

· "Hate them, Miss Adair!—ah! I should do anything but that if I could only trust them. How different this life would be if they were only true! if they were not, as the best of them are— even those to whom it costs a pang to act so— ever ready to sell themselves for wealth and position."

Flora became scarlet. Mr. Earnscliffe noted that vivid flush, and considered it to be caused by consciousness of guilt, whilst in reality it was from a sense of injured innocence. A few minutes before she had been called upon to decide between wealth and possible dependence and humiliation— humiliation in the eyes of the world—and she had chosen the latter; but it was useless as a proof of the falseness of that sweeping accusation—in honour she was bound not to speak of it. She waited until the rush of excited feeling had subsided a little, and then said quietly—

" I *know* that you are wrong, Mr. Earnscliffe— we are not *all* ready to sell ourselves; there are many women who would refuse any man, no matter what advantages he could offer them, if they did not really love him."

His eyes flashed and he exclaimed, " You!" but he stopped suddenly, changed his tone, and added in his usual cold, polite manner, " Here is Mrs. Adair; but I see that she is speaking to some one, so I will not interrupt her; and now allow me to wish you *Addio, e felice viaggio!*"

He held her hand for a moment, whilst he looked at her again with one of those searching glances which had annoyed her before. Mrs. Adair turned round just as he left her, and said, " Why, Flora, how tired you look! Here is Marie as fresh and gay as ever!"

The gentlemen now came to claim them for the cotillon. Marie was engaged to dance with Charles Elton, and Flora with Mr. Caulfield; but Mrs. Adair said to him, " I really think that Flora ought not to dance any more, she appears to be so tired."

Flora saw Mr. Caulfield's look of annoyance, and answered with a smile — although it was rather a weary one if the truth must be told — " Not so much so, mamma, that I cannot fulfil my engagement," and she took Mr. Caulfield's arm.

At last the cotillon came to an end, and it was with a feeling of relief at not being obliged to talk or dance any more that Flora followed her mother down the stairs and got into their carriage, Marie declaring that she wished the ball was going to begin again.

CHAPTER VIII.

THE Eltons' ball, that ball to which our friends
Flora Adair, Marie Arbi, and the two Elton girls
had looked forward with so much eagerness, was
over. Had it brought them pleasure or pain? To
Helena and Marie it had brought pleasure; but
to Flora and Mary, pain. Mary felt that, although she had succeeded in prejudicing Mr.
Earnscliffe against Flora, she had not advanced
one step towards winning his admiration for herself; and when Helena congratulated her on his
having danced with her—that being an honour
which he did not often confer on any one—
she answered bitterly, "You mistake, Helena;
Mr. Earnscliffe danced with his hostess's eldest
daughter, and not with Mary Elton!"

Yet the more the attainment of the object upon
which she had set her heart seemed remote, the
more wildly did she long for it. To gain Mr.
Earnscliffe's love, or even to hinder another from
possessing it, she would stoop to any, even the

most unworthy, means. Hers was a powerful passion, but it was a passion for evil rather than for good ; it was not a passion of devotedness but of selfishness ; she would sacrifice his happiness to her love, and not her love to his happiness. Evidently she did not know that a woman's happiness consists " in another's love become her own." The song of Solomon represents the love of the Saviour and His Church under the type of human love ;—the Christian marriage ceremony says, " Let a woman be subject to her husband in all things, as the Church is subject to Christ ; " and Saint Paul tells " wives " to " be subject to their husbands as unto God ! " It is in such sub-mission, and in such alone, that a woman's happi-ness consists. Short-sighted people call this bondage, but it is that bondage in which alone is true liberty ! . . . To serve truly is indeed to reign !

" What ? " we hear young ladies, ay, and old ones too, exclaim—" Are we never to do what we like,— never to think of pleasing ourselves ? A curious notion of happiness indeed ! " Never-theless it is the only true one. Woman was created to be " a help meet for man ; " her ministry in the world is one of love, and she can never be really happy save in fulfilling the end for which she was created. A mere preference,

accompanied by calm affection and esteem, will
never enable a woman to be to her husband what
the Church is to her Lord.   It must be a feeling
such as Leibnitz speaks of when he says, " To
love, is to place our happiness in the happiness of
another ;"—and as an illustrious French writer
beautifully describes it, so beautifully that we
would not venture to translate it, and must be
pardoned for quoting somewhat at length in a
foreign tongue—" L'amour ne s'arrête pas à
l'acte de choix, il exige le dévouement à l'être
choisi.   Choisir, c'est préférer un être à tous les
autres ; se dévouer, c'est le préférer à soi-même.
Le dévouement, c'est l'immolation de soi à l'objet
aimé.   Quiconque ne va pas jusque là n'aime
pas.   La préférence toute seule n'implique en
effet qu'un goût de l'âme qui a besoin de
s'epancher dans la cause d'où il sort, goût honor-
able et prècieux sans doute, mais qui se bornant
là n'aboutit qu'à se rechercher soi-même dans
un autre que soi.   Si beaucoup d'affections
s'arrêtent à ce point, c'est que beaucoup d'affections ne sont qu'un egoïsme deguisé, on eprouve
un attrait, on s'y abandonne, on croit aimer, on a
peut-être des lueurs de l'amour veritable, mais
l'heure du dévouement arrivée, on reconnait à
l'impuissance du sacrifice la vanité du sentiment
qui nous préoccupait sans nous posséder."

When a woman loves, she creates happiness, so to say, for herself and for those around her, and obtains so much the greater recompense the less she seeks it. In this submission she is immeasurably more free than if she had no law but that of her own will, just as a true Christian is more free than those who follow their own opinions, for " where the law is, there is liberty."

All this was indeed a sealed fountain to Mary Elton ; her idea of happiness was not centred in " another's happiness become her own," but in the triumph of her own unbridled will. Yet she was rather to be pitied than blamed. The too popular code, alas ! now-a-days is, that anything like real ardent feeling is to be ruthlessly crushed down. In this she was educated, and, being of a less impulsive disposition than her sister, she succumbed more to this training. She was like a vigorous young tree whose owner willed that it should grow in a particular form, quite regardless of the one which nature intended it to take, and for this purpose had bound and constrained it with what he thought to be strong bands ; but one day a strange hand cut one of those bands, and at once all the others gave way : the tree then rebounded from its constraint, and took a more natural form, and the trainer found with dismay that it had grown wild and unmanageable. He

had but produced deformity; had he helped to
develop the plant, and not tried to force it from
its natural bent, it would have grown in the beauty
of its own unity: under his hands it had become
a deformed and an unsightly thing!

Such, too, was Mary Elton. Her mother had
tried to swathe her mind and heart in bands of
unnatural propriety and worldliness, and for a
time she seemed to have succeeded. Mr.
Earnscliffe was the strange hand which chanced
to cut one of the bands, and thus caused all the
others to give way; then her natural strength of
feeling burst forth, rank and untrained. Had her
mother carefully directed and not endeavoured to
crush this, it would have made her character as
beautiful as it was strong. Unfortunately Mrs.
Elton had not done so, and the result was, that in
all probability nothing less powerful than that
religion of which Mary knows nothing could show
her the difference between a " disguised egotism,"
in which one only seeks one's self in another,
and love, which is an immolation of one's self to
the beloved object.

We must leave her alone with her gloomy re-
trospections, which were not the less dark and
unpleasing from the partial success which had
attended her planning. She was haunted by
the consciousness of having acted falsely as well

as meanly towards Flora; for she as well as Mr. Earnscliffe had seen the parting between her and Mr. Lyne, and she judged it more truly than he had done. Since then she felt certain—if indeed she ever doubted it—that Mr. Lyne would never be more than a friend to Flora; yet she had done all she could to make Mr. Earnscliffe believe that they were to be married, and she knew that in this she had been successful.

Helena's remembrances of the ball were as bright as Mary's were dark. She dwelt with heartfelt delight on all the enjoyment which it had afforded her, and, as Mary listened to her, her smile grew brighter and more genial than usual. Her protecting affection for her sister was the one virtue amidst many faults—the one feeling from which she could draw unalloyed pleasure.

A contrast not altogether dissimilar might have been witnessed between Flora and Marie. The latter was all animation, and related with infinite zest her adventures of the previous night; while the former spoke but little, and appeared tired and weary. She could not help feeling that she had behaved somewhat unkindly towards Mr. Lyne. She was angry with herself for not having sooner seen that he meant to propose, and that she had not taken care to prevent his doing so;

still, were she in a palace of truth, she would probably have been obliged to confess that it was not the remembrance of the pain which she had inflicted on Mr. Lyne that weighed most heavily upon her spirits, but rather Mr. Earnscliffe's conduct to herself. Save to shake hands with her in the beginning of the evening, he had not approached her until just before the cotillon when his manner and words appeared so unaccountable to her.

We have already said that there is no greater pang than that of being misunderstood by one whom we esteem, and the sharpness of the pang increases with the strength of our affection. Thus Flora felt most bitterly the injustice to herself which Mr. Earnscliffe implied when he said how different it would be if women were not—as even the best of them are—ready to sell themselves to the first man who asks them to marry him, if he can give them wealth or position. It was certainly not a pleasant farewell, and she sighed as she thought that probably she would never know again such pleasure as she had felt in his society. Even the memory of it was more to her than any other actual enjoyment had been; nevertheless she did not deem herself in love. A day after a ball seemed to possess a fatality for Flora; she found this day a very sad one, yet the time may come when, by comparison with others, she may perhaps think it had brought her happiness.

Fortunately for her their approaching departure from Rome, and the preparations necessary for it, did not leave her much time for brooding. As usual, the week after Easter saw Rome thinning rapidly. Some of our acquaintances were going to the south, others to the north : for the former were bound the Eltons, Pentons, Mr. Lyne, Mr. Caulfield and Mr. Earnscliffe, and for the latter the Blakes and the Adairs.

On the Tuesday after the ball, at seven in the morning, a large travelling carriage stood before the door of the Adairs' apartments. It was open, and in it was seated Mrs. Blake. Mina was in the cabriolet, and her uncle, Mr. Vincent Blake, who had joined them a few days before on his way from the East, and who was to return with them to Ireland, was standing on the flags inspecting the packing of the luggage. The Adairs were to complete the party; and as soon as they came down, Mr. Blake hurried them into the carriage with Mrs. Blake—that is, Mrs. Adair and Marie. Flora was to go in the cabriolet with Mina ; and having handed her up, and taken his own seat beside the coachman, he gave the word to start; the whip was flourished, and off they went, the wheels rattling noisily over the pavement to the merry accompaniment of the bells round the horses' necks.

At the Porta del Popolo they were obliged to halt, in order to have their passports examined. Mr. Blake got down, and went into the office. During the delay which this caused, Mina and Flora stood up to take " one last long look " at Rome, that city which, it is said, few—even of those who have suffered there—ever leave without a feeling of regret and a desire to return. It is a strange fascination which Rome possesses even for those who are aliens within her walls! We know how one of the most celebrated of these apostrophises her :—

> "O Rome! my country! city of the soul!
> The orphans of the heart must turn to thee,
> Lone mother of dead empires! and control
> In their shut breasts their petty misery."

If Rome is so dear to those who regard her only as a standing record of a mighty past, what must she be to those to whom she is not merely a

> " Lone mother of dead empires,"

but a living mother of a living world—the heart, the centre, the capital of Christendom itself!

Mina and Flora were fond of Rome for both of these reasons. Flora loved it especially as the scene of the happiest hours she had ever known, and so she could not leave it without a feeling of sadness and a longing to return. How often do we yearn to revisit places where we have been happy, even when all around us has changed!

> " Cari luoghi, io vi trovai
> Ma quei dì non trovo più!"

After a few moments Mr. Blake reappeared with the passports all in order. A *scudo* has a particularly accelerating effect on the movements of Roman officials. At length they bade adieu to Rome, yet not to its memories and associations, for their route lay along the far-famed Flaminian Way.

There is surely no such pleasant travelling for pleasant people as vetturino! When it is through a beautiful country, in fine weather, and with intimate friends, it is truly delightful. The irregular meals, furnished from the contents of capacious baskets, the ever-changing scene, the never-ending variety of flowers and foliage, the newness of all around, the expectation of coming events, the evenings at country inns, where the very "roughing" gives zest to a life so different from the regularity of ordinary existence; the unflagging chatter, the buoyant spirits,—these, yes, and a thousand other charms, tend to make such happy journeys the sunniest of sunny spots in the pilgrimage of life. As for the cabriolet, if a pair of lovers could only get possession of it, it would be the perfection of human enjoyment—a sort of moving elysium. Ah! this is a picture upon which we must not dwell, or we might be teased by importunate wishes to have it realised, and so become dissatisfied with the dull plodding routine of stay-at-home days.

Our new friend, Mr. Blake, was tall, stout, and nearly sixty, but withal strong and healthy in appearance. His fair, florid complexion, large features, and light blue eyes, and, indeed, the whole expression of his countenance, gave strong indications of good-humour and benevolence; nor was there any visible want in it of intellectual power. He proved a most amusing and instructive companion, having travelled over this route more than once before. He pointed out to Mina and Flora the objects of note and of classic interest, quoted scraps from the Latin poets, which he rendered into extempore English for them. The position of Civitta Castellana called forth his loudest praises, and he talked much of the days when it was the proud capital of the Valisci, who dared to contend with Rome herself, even in the days of her warlike glory; and he made them laugh heartily over the story of Camillus and the

schoolmaster. Some years before, Mr. Blake had
spent a few days at Civitta Castellana, exploring
the beautiful neighbourhood with some friends,
and he related many anecdotes of their excursions, declaring that there were few things more
enjoyable than such excursions made in agreeable
company.

The girls assured him that it was not necessary
to impress *that* upon their minds, as they could
easily believe how delightful it would be so to
wander about in such beautiful scenery. To
make it perfect, they said, there should be a
Valerie de Ventadour, and an Ernest Maltravers
to re-people each scene for her with the heroes
and legends of old, to unroll before her the lore
of the ancient historians and poets, and thus to
light it up again with a light once its own.
And Flora laughingly added—

"Now, Mr. Blake, you will be obliged to play
Ernest Maltravers to one of us."

"Indeed, young lady! and do you mean to
imply that 're-peopling some lonely scene for
you, with the heroes and legends of old, unrolling
before you the lore of the ancients, and thus
lighting it up with a light once its own,' would
be at all the same thing done by a rough, grey-
headed old man, as by an Ernest Maltravers? If
so, I am afraid I must say that you are a sad

deceiver. Now, I'll lay a wager on it you are thinking of some one who could play Ernest Maltravers to your Valerie de Ventadour, very much to your satisfaction?"

Mr. Blake chuckled with delight as he saw Flora get red and turn away her head.

Thus the day passed quickly away, and about five in the evening they arrived at Civitta Castellana, where they were to sleep on the first night of their journey.

It took them about six days to travel from Rome to Florence by this route. Were we to follow them step by step, we should be writing a guide-book and not a story. Nevertheless, we cannot pass by in silence two such spots as the Falls of Terni and Assisi. Byron says that the view of the falls either from above or below is worth that of all the cascades and torrents of Switzerland put together. The Staubach, Reichenfels, are rills in comparative appearance. Who could forget his description of the contrast between the "giant element leaping from rock to rock with delicious bound," and the lovely smiling valley by which the falls are surrounded? It is indeed

"Love, watching madness with unutterable mien."

Then the church of Assisi, with all its wealth

of interest! To the lover of the picturesque, of art, or of religion, it has special attractions. Dante sings the loveliness of its site; Cimabue and Giotto's works adorn its walls, and mark the progress of painting; and Saint Francis throws over it a halo which dims the glory of poet and artist, and makes Assisi—for those who know and love his life—another holy land. Such is the creative power of charity or love. Centuries ago, Saint Francis died in self-imposed poverty and privation, barely covered with the cloak of another; yet hardly had the grave closed over him, when a structure, matchless even in Italy, was built in his honour, and the precious germs of love and self-sacrifice which he planted in the hearts of his spiritual children went on fructifying until his Order spread itself throughout Christendom, and now blesses the world almost in spite of itself.

Our friends thought that if this route could boast of Assisi alone, it would have been almost unrivalled; but Assisi was only its crowning point. It traverses a track of country, for upwards of two hundred miles, where beauty, history, and poetry combine to give a charm to all around. The vale of Clitumnus and its stream—

"Haunt of river nymph!"

the lake of Thrasimene, where Hannibal and his

swarthy hosts revelled in their sanguinary victory over the brave Flaminius; the towns perched on mountain-tops, and surrounded by deep romantic ravines, where still stand a ruined arch or pier to tell of the massive bridges which once spanned them—the colossal works of the mighty Romans.

It was altogether so delightful a journey, that to some at least of our party it caused a feeling of regret when about six o'clock on Sunday evening they reached the top of the hill of San Donato, and for the first time looked upon *Firenze la bella*, and the beautiful view over the valley of the Arno. They quickly descended to the Porta san Nicolo, by which they entered the city— crossed the Ponte alle Grazie, drove along the Lung' Arno, passing the arcades of the Uffizi, and the Piazza di Santa Trinita, and drew up at one of the hotels which face the river. And here, in beautiful Florence, let us leave them to repose.

CHAPTER IX.

On the morning after their arrival our travellers
—the younger ones especially—were all impatience to see something of the fair city of
Florence, so famed, moreover, for the beauty of
its position; and the scene, as they looked from
the windows of the hotel, inclined them to join in
singing its praises.

The fine quay of the Lung' Arno; the river
itself flowing along calmly, and glittering beneath
the sun's bright rays; the hill on the opposite side
with its olive-trees and gardens, relieved here and
there by an imposing building, were all beautiful
seen from a distance. The narrow dusty roads
between high walls, the faded and dried-up
appearance of all around, are then hidden; but a
closer view raises a sigh for the lovely lanes with
their flowery hedges, and the fresh green verdure
of our own dear country, or even of the neighbourhood of Rome, where the dampness of the climate
counteracts the effect of the scorching sun, and

prevents, in some degree, the washed-out look which is so striking everywhere about Florence. When our friends come to explore that which looks so pretty from the hotel windows, they may, perhaps, be tempted to think that the beauty of the country round Florence has been overrated, and, were it not rash to say so, even to prefer the charms of some of the other towns which they passed through on their way from Rome. They must, however, visit the "lions" within the gates before they extend their excursions beyond them; and although it is very possible that they may be slightly disappointed with the latter, they certainly cannot be with the former. With such treasures as those which adorn her galleries of the Uffizi, the Pitti, and the Belle Arti, surely Florence could afford to be surnamed *la brutta* instead of *la bella!* Yes, she might well dispense with all exterior loveliness, and pointing to the long line of celebrated men to whom she has given birth, say, in the words of the mother of the Gracchi, "Here are my jewels!" As it is, Nature too has been bountiful to Florence, for she has undoubtedly given her a large share of beauty in addition to all the rest.

Their first visit was to the Uffizi, and in the far-famed tribune they saw, with wondering eyes, Mr. and Mrs. Penton, and her brother, Mr.

Barkley. As they shook hands with Mrs. Penton, and expressed some surprise at seeing them there, since they supposed them to be in Naples, she replied, "We did go to Naples on the evening after Mrs. Elton's ball, and we spent a week there; then Edmund"—looking towards Mr. Barkley, who was in another part of the room—"came to us from Sicily; we sailed direct to Leghorn, and arrived here yesterday."

"You certainly have lost no time," said Mrs. Adair; "for we came straight from Rome, and yet we only arrived yesterday. We travelled however by the Perugia route, which is a long one, but oh, how beautiful!"

"So every one says. We were, however, pressed for time, and therefore we had to get over the ground as quickly as possible; but how we shall ever tear Edmund away from Florence is more than I can say. You know my brother, do you not?"

"Yes,—that is, Flora and I know him, but the Blakes have never met him; he would, I am sure, find Mr. Blake a delightful companion; he knows Florence so well, and is quite an enthusiastic admirer of its works of art; in fact, he is a most desirable guide to them."

"Then please to ask him if I may introduce my brother; to make his acquaintance would be quite

a *trouvaille* for Edmund." Mrs. Penton was one
of those who like to introduce French words into
their conversation. "Gerald and I, not being
such worshippers of painting, should be quite
exhausted if we attempted to keep pace with him;
it is so fatiguing to look up at pictures for any
length of time. We have been here more than
an hour already, and I do not want to be tired
before the afternoon, when we intend to drive in
the Cascine to see the *beau monde* of Florence; so
it will be an excellent thing if we can get Edmund
and Mr. Blake together, and then I can make
Gerald take me home."

Accordingly Mrs. Adair turned to Mr. Blake,
who was near to them, examining a picture, and
said that Mrs. Penton wished to introduce him to
her brother; and Mrs. Penton added, "Edmund
will have a double pleasure in making your
acquaintance, as Mrs. Adair tells me you are a
connaisseur here."

"It is indeed true that I am a warm admirer of
the great treasures which Florence contains, but I
have no claim to the title of *connaisseur*. I shall
be most happy, however, to be introduced to
your brother, and to give him any information
I possess about the Florentine galleries,—they are
old acquaintances of mine, but strangers, I
suppose, to him."

" Yes, it is our first visit to Florence; we only arrived yesterday. Let us go to Edmund ! "

They crossed to Mr. Barkley, and his sister— laying her hand upon his shoulder—said, " Edmund, I have just met Mrs. Adair, her daughter, and some friends of theirs, whom I had the pleasure of meeting in Rome. Mr. Blake knows Florence à cœur, I believe, and he kindly says that this knowledge is at your service: Mr. Blake—my brother, Mr. Barkley."

They bowed, and Mr. Barkley said, " I am most grateful for your kind offer, Mr. Blake, and shall gladly avail myself of it."

After a few moments of conversation Mrs. Penton said, " You must speak to the Adairs, Edmund ; but first tell me, where is Gerald ? "

" I think he went into that room," pointing to the door on the left side of the tribune.

" Will you then take me to my husband, Mr. Blake, while Edmund goes to the Adairs?"

Mrs. Penton made this request in the manner and tone of voice of one who feels certain that any man—even an old one—would be pleased at being asked to walk with her.

Mr. Barkley was like Mrs. Penton, but hand-somer, and, apparently, of superior intelligence. His complexion was dark—if black hair, eyebrows, and moustache, with grey eyes and a pale face,

constitute the dark style; his well-formed forehead was almost ivory-like in its whiteness, his
nose straight and finely cut, and his mouth small
and sufficiently expressive, without, however, being
very remarkable for that distinctive quality.   He
was just the sort of man that the greatest number
of women rave about,—quite a *héros de roman*, with
his tall, straight figure, and air of refinement.
Nevertheless there was something wanting; it was
not a face which gave one the idea that its possessor was a man of courage—we mean *moral*
courage, or fortitude; nor did his fair and deli-
cately-moulded hands redeem his face : they were
not hands formed for a firm grasp, or to hold on
steadfastly through time and difficulty.   He was,
however, generally considered to be quite an
Adonis, a lady-killer.   Of this he was fully conscious, but he had far too keen a sense of what is
really worthy to be admired ever to betray this
consciousness in his manner or conversation; and
towards women he was almost chivalrous in his
courtesy and deference,—another reason, doubtless, why he was so great a favourite with them.

Meanwhile he went to speak to the Adairs, and
was introduced to Mrs. Blake, Mina, and Marie.

Mrs. Penton returned in a few moments with
her husband and Mr. Blake, and, addressing her
brother, she said, "Edmund, Gerald and I are

going; but I suppose you will not come with us?"

"Nay; here is something more attractive," answered Mr. Barkley, with a smile and a bow towards the three girls who were standing together.

"But you will come to drive in the Cascine, will you not? There will, I suppose, be plenty of attraction for you there, in the youth and beauty of Florence."

"Then you may depend upon me."

Did Mrs. Penton divine what her brother's wishes were? For she turned to Mrs. Adair, and said, "We shall have a vacant seat in the carriage; will you allow one of your young ladies to accompany us?"

"With pleasure."

"Then I will call at a little after four. But which of them am I to have the honour of chaperoning?"

"Marie," replied Flora, quickly. "Mina and I are great walkers, and shall probably go for a walk in the country with Mr. Blake."

Mr. and Mrs. Penton left the tribune, but the rest of the party remained. Mr. Blake and Mr. Barkley agreed to go on the following day to the Accademia delle belle Arti and also to San Marco. "I know a good little Padre there," said Mr. Blake, "who will show us everything. He and I are the best of friends, although I cannot help regretting his blindness in matters of faith. And I dare say he has the same sort of feeling towards me."

" No doubt he has," replied Mr. Barkley, laughingly ; " and I, as you probably know, side with the Padre."

" Oh, yes,—I know that you do; so I must be upon my guard, as you will be two to one. But the ladies have gone on; we had better follow them."

They left the tribune, and went into the small rooms on the right-hand side of it, and there they found the ladies. Marie and Flora were standing together,—the former talking eagerly of the goodness of Flora in wishing her to drive with the Pentons instead of herself. To all of which Flora answered—

" I deserve no praise whatever, for I really do not care to go. I shall be quite as much pleased to have a nice long walk, which would only tire you. You don't know, Mignonne, how often an appearance of goodness may spring from indifference. You may indeed enjoy your drive without imagining that I have made any sacrifice whatsoever in not going."

Just then Mr. Barkley joined them, and asked what they were talking about so earnestly ?

"My share in the conversation," said Flora, "consisted in trying to persuade Marie that I am not making any sacrifice in giving her my place for the drive this afternoon,—indeed, as I have already told her, I shall prefer a walk to driving up and down a public promenade, with nothing but fashion to look at."

It is probable that an Adonis like Mr. Barkley found it rather difficult to believe that any girl should prefer a walk with other ladies, or, at least, with an old gentleman, to a drive in *his* society; and he said, with a smile, "It is fortunate for our vanity that at least one of you wishes to come out with us. We shall do everything in our power to make it an agreeable drive to Mademoiselle——I have not caught her name."

"Arbi," replied Flora.

"Thank you;" then turning to Marie, he continued—"Then, Mademoiselle Arbi, we may expect to have the pleasure of your company this afternoon?"

"*Oui, Monsieur,*" replied Marie, blushing. Whenever she was eager about anything, or particularly shy, as she was at that moment, she spoke French.

Flora now moved on after the others, who had gone into the next room, and Marie followed her as closely as possible, in terror at the thought of having to keep up a *tête-à-tête* talk with Mr. Barkley.

The conversation now became general, and naturally turned upon painting ; so, between talking of, and admiring, the many beautiful works contained in the Uffizi, the hours sped on until past two o'clock. It was then decided that they should go home for luncheon, and take a rest before the fatigues of the afternoon began.

After leaving the gallery, they stopped to *flâner* a little in the Arcades. Mr. Barkley had succeeded very fairly in dispelling Marie's shyness of him. He made her laugh merrily at his account of some of his adventures in Sicily, and his ridiculous mistakes in the language, which he then knew but slightly. His French, however, was perfect ; and this was to Marie a great boon. He purposely lingered at one of the stalls, explaining something which he had pointed out to her, until the others had got into the Piazza della Signoria ; and having thus managed that she should walk home with him, he exclaimed, " I declare they are half way across the Piazza ! What a hurry they are in ! But do not tire yourself; we shall easily keep them in sight, and that is all we require. But that we *must* do, or we should not find our way to our hotels."

He took care, however, not to overtake them

before they reached the hotel, at the door of which they had to wait a minute or two for Marie. When she and her cavalier did come up, Mr. Blake said, " Can you find the road to your abode, Mr. Barkley ; or shall I accompany you?"

"Thank you, it is so near that I cannot mistake my way. Good morning."

CHAPTER X

At breakfast on Tuesday morning the plans for the day were talked over. Mr. Blake began by saying, "I suppose you know, ladies, that I am engaged to go with Mr. Barkley to the Accademia at eleven; but in the afternoon I shall be at your service."

"Which is a polite intimation, uncle," said Mina, "that our company is not wished for in the morning."

"Really, I never thought about your coming with us, for after we have been to the Accademia we are to go to San Marco; and you know that ladies are not permitted to pass the outer cloister. There's one of your pretty Roman rules for you!"

"Not badly turned, uncle. I suppose that closing observation was intended to excite our indignation, and so make us forget the truth that you do not want us to go with you. But don't be afraid,—we shall have no design upon you;

indeed, before we came down we had agreed to go to the Pitti."

"Then the morning is disposed of; and what do you mean to do in the afternoon?"

"Mamma and Marie are going to drive with the Pentons," answered Flora, "and as for the rest of us, we have not thought about what we shall do."

"Then you two girls had better come with me to San Miniato. The church is well worth a visit, and the walk round the hill upon which it stands is most lovely. Will you come also, Agatha?"

"Perhaps," replied his sister-in-law; "if I am not very tired after the Pitti. *My* going, however, is not a matter of any importance; the girls can go with you whether I do or not."

"Well then, young ladies, I shall be ready for you at any time after three; and now, adieu for the present."

The ladies remained some time longer at the breakfast table laughing at Marie's animated description of the people whom she saw on the Cascine on the day before, and at the theatre in the evening. She was most enthusiastic in her praise of Mrs. Penton and her brother's kindness, and asked naively if Englishmen—meaning natives of the United Kingdom—were generally as hand-

some and as charming as Mr. Barkley, adding that
there were not any so nice at Mrs. Elton's ball.

"You think so, Mignonne, do you?" said
Flora. "Well, I should say that, had he been at
Mrs. Elton's, he would not have been unrivalled,
or perhaps unsurpassed."

"But who den, Flore, was so seducing (*séduisant*)
as he?"

"Oh! *I* should say *this* person; somebody else
would say *that* person; it is all an affair of taste,
you know," answered Flora, smiling at the question itself, and also at the *very* literal translation
of *séduisant,* as she stood up and went to look out
of the window. Marie jumped up and followed
her, put her arm round her waist, and leaning
her little curly head upon Flora's shoulder, she
looked up coaxingly at her and said, "Flore, will
you not tell your Mignonne who it is dat you
have found better than Mr. Barkley *chez* Madame
Elton?"

"What a little goose you are, Marie. I did
not speak of any one in particular. I only said
that he would not have been unrivalled. You
know—as I also said—that it is all a matter of
taste. Helena Elton, I dare say, would prefer
Mr. Caulfield."

"Mr. Caulfield! But you are not of her advice,
Flore?"

" *Opinion* you mean, Mignonne, and not *advice*, which is the English for *conseil*. For your satisfaction I am glad to be able to say that I do not agree with Helena ; and as you are going again to enjoy this afternoon the society of the person who suits *your* taste best, I consider that you are a most enviable little being. But see, they are all gone,—we must go also."

Marie held up her fair face for a kiss, which was cordially given, and then they left the room.

The difference in their characters, as shown in their manner, was most striking. Marie was shy in the simple acceptation of the word, but she was not reserved. She knew nothing of Flora's bugbear—that dread of importuning or wearying others. As soon as Marie had got over the childish timidity which she always felt on a first acquaintance, she was demonstratively affectionate. It never crossed her simple little mind that her caresses might bore any one ; so that whilst Flora would stand at a distance from those whom she liked, longing to be near them, yet afraid to go to them without a word or look which seemed to call her, Marie would at once run to *her* favourites, throw her arms round their necks, and tell them how much she loved them, without stopping to think whether they wanted her or not.

How Flora envied this simplicity, and wished

that she had a little more of it. It would have saved her so much pain; but it is one of those things which cannot be acquired, at least by a person like Flora, who could not summon up sufficient courage even to touch the hand of any one whom she liked extremely, unless she were unmistakably made to feel that it would give pleasure. Flora had said after reading Marie's history, "We shall be such contrasts!" and so they were; but this difference of disposition only seemed to make them greater friends.

But it is time for us to leave the ladies, and follow the two gentlemen to the Accademia. As it was Mr. Barkley's first visit to Florence, he had still most of Beato Angelico's masterpieces to see. He had indeed seen his works, on the day before, at the Uffizi, and the " Crowning of the Blessed Virgin," in the Louvre, was an old familiar friend to him; but another treat was now in store for him, for Beato Angelico was his master-painter.

On their way they talked of the different subjects from his pencil which they were about to see, and especially of the "Descent from the Cross" and the "Last Judgment." Mr. Barkley said that he meant to keep these for a *bonne bouche*, and begged to be taken straight to il Beato's "poem in painting," the "Life of our Lord."

Mr. Blake could not help rallying his friend a little about his desperate enthusiasm for the *Frate*, which he thought somewhat extravagant.

"But here we are," he exclaimed, "so you will soon be gratified. I shall, as you wish, take you straight to the 'Life of our Lord,' and then leave you to your ecstasies for a time. When I come back, be pleased to impart some of them to me."

Accordingly Mr. Blake left him to the contemplation of this august history, and did not join him again for a considerable time, which he spent in paying long visits to his favourite pictures. He was not at a loss for occupation during this time, as a most varied experience and a fair share of study had rendered him capable of really enjoying fine paintings.

When he did at length return to Mr. Barkley, he found him at the closing subject—the "Last Judgment;" not the great picture on that subject, but an older one, and asked, "Well?"

"Well!" echoed Mr. Barkley, "this *is* art indeed! Here we see that the painter had a higher aim in view than that of displaying his own talent in originality of design, or even correctness of outline. These indeed have not been neglected, but they have been used only as means to a great end, and that end was to teach a sub-

lime lesson. Each of these thirty-eight compart-
ments is a study in itself, a study in which the
mind of the angelic painter speaks to us through
his works, causing us to know, and by knowing, to
love something of ' the splendour of unity'—the
Beautiful itself. To produce this—you will agree
with me—is the highest triumph of art. Where
this is not, what do we see but the works of copy-
ists, who portray, more or less well, what they
see with their mortal eyes ?"

" I quite agree with you that we cannot rightly
call anything a work of real art which is not in
some degree a creation, and a teacher, whose purpose it is to draw us from the lower and material
world to the contemplation of higher things.
But we must have a standard of truth, and
therefore I cannot altogether share in your admiration of Angelico's ' History of our Lord,' as
there are many things represented in it for which
we have no authority, and in some places the
meaning is obscure and unintelligible. Much of
it seems to be inspired rather by the mystic imagination of a pious monk than by the grand and
simple written record of our Saviour's life upon
earth, the beauty of which these paintings ought
only to illustrate. When your favourite keeps to
this he is truly great, as in the ' Descent from the
Cross,' for instance."

"Ah, true! Will you forgive me if I say that you can hardly seize *all* the speaking beauty depicted in this great history? I do not say this, as you will believe, in any way to depreciate your judgment, but in regard only to the *extent* of your belief."

"I do not quite catch your meaning. Have we not an unerring standard to direct us here?"

"The *letter* of Scripture, no doubt? . . . Yes, you have *that*, but you have it surely without the spirit. Moreover, you have, so to say, dislocated yourselves from the family traditions of Christianity—from the memory of Christendom; and having lost this, and therewith all traditional intercourse with the past, you hopelessly seize upon our first written records, and in them alone have you any knowledge or faith. The living voice which from age to age has handed down every detail of the glory of Christ and His saints, is silent for you. You are strangers here, and these family records, which to us are so precious, are the objects of your suspicion, are even rejected by you as unworthy of belief; it is thus, I mean, that you are unable to seize *all* the speaking beauty depicted here."

"Would you have us then to accept as truth the wild fantasies of individual painters? . . . It is far too much."

"Most assuredly not; that would, I should say, be to fall into another snare like the very one which has already caught you. When I said that you can hardly seize *all* the beauty of il Beato's poem on our Lord, my meaning was, that having rejected the recognised sources of sacred Tradition, you can receive nothing but what is written; although, by the way, even there it is said that 'there are also many other things which Jesus did, the which if they were written the whole world itself could not contain the books that should be written.' Think for a moment: if you so confine the works of art to the text of Scripture, how greatly you limit and narrow their field, and how many great pictures, which through ages Christendom has honoured as its family heirlooms, you will be forced to condemn as false. You object to the touching scene of Saint Veronica—to this exquisite painting of Jesus carrying His Cross and meeting His blessed Mother on her way to Calvary. Scripture does not say that He *did* meet her; therefore, to you it appears to be a deviation from truth; but these facts are household words in Christendom, resting upon the highest of all moral certainty—Christian Tradition. The spoken testimony of His chosen companions and the dogmas of our faith, in harmony with the loving memory of Christendom,

hand down these family records to us with holy
and unerring care. You would hardly believe
how jealous we are of any mutilation of them.
Numberless, however, would be the great pictures
which must thus seem to you to be false or unintelligible, whilst to us they are rich in truth and
supernatural meaning. I love Saint Paul's cry, '*Be
ye enlarged!*' You know not how much you
lose even of Scripture itself;—the very parables
of our Lord, which, you will remember, are not so
to those 'to whom it is given to know,' are
parables indeed, or at very best but beautiful
histories, to *you*."

"You are too hard upon us. I grant you that
the principle of limitation, in our sense, fully
admitted and carried into practice, would go far
to strip our galleries of their treasures, and leave
us without connection with the past. I am a
sincere lover of art, and I am old enough to have
the courage to confess to you that the conse-
quences of the proper application of such a principle terrify me. I frankly acknowledge that it
would hardly leave a monument standing of more
than a few centuries old, and how few, I fear even
to say. I comfort myself by the hope that the
great storm has already past, and there I rest,
with the principle still in my belief, that you
must not venture into the work of God—Scripture

itself,—there all is holy, because all is Divine. The parables are far more to us—believe me—than beautiful histories."

"Let me explain what I have expressed with, I hope, pardonable enthusiasm. It is not a question, as you seem to suppose, of *criticising* the divine work, but of *appreciating* it in a greater or lesser degree. You will grant us, I think, the larger comprehension of what was intended to be, to some, simply parables or riddles. In the parable of the prodigal son, for instance, *we* learn how God receives repentant sinners. The young man leaves his father's house, and, in a far country, wastes his substance in wrong-doing; he soon feels the want of the *spiritual life* which he has squandered away, and of which there is a famine in that country. Still he cleaves to one of the chief citizens there, who sends him to feed swine; but his hunger is unappeased. At last he resolves to return to his father and confess his error and his sin. His father runs to meet him while he is yet a great way off, and falls upon his neck and kisses him. Then He says *to His servants,* 'Clothe him quickly with the robe of innocence, put the ring of adoption upon his finger, the shoes of safe direction upon his feet, offer the Holy Sacrifice, and feed him with the food of life, for this my son was dead and is alive again, he was lost and is found!' Here, we have Dogma, Tradition, and Scripture, harmoniously illustrating this, as indeed all the other parables. To us they are neither riddles nor beautiful histories, but sublime declarations and proofs of the divinity of our faith, since to us—by our Divine teaching—'it is given to know the mysteries of the kingdom of God.' Now how would one of your painters portray this? Were he merely to represent it as Scripture relates it, it would be simply a riddle; or did he attempt a higher meaning, there would be evident discrepancy between the truth of Scripture and your belief and practice. So that should he aim at anything beyond drawing graceful figures and giving dramatic effect to his picture, he would be forced to abandon the subject altogether, or turn to us for its true illustration. So it is, and it is a very momentous fact that no country fallen away from Christian unity ever produces real artists; it may even outstrip all the rest in material discoveries and progress—'the children of this world,' you know, 'are wiser *in their generation* than the children of light'—but it has lost the Divine power of creation. Like Mirabeau to Barnave, we may indeed say to each of them,

'There is no divinity in thee!' You may find painters who can copy a dog to a hair, a blade of grass, a battle, anything that the eye of man can see and measure; but you will never find an Angelico where 'the evidence, the light, the splendour of unity' is no longer intact."

"I have listened to you with all the admiration of an artist, although with some patience, since I cannot admit your starting-point—namely, that you have an unerring source of tradition and knowledge. There are few subjects, however, in which I feel so wide an interest: so let us return to it again on another occasion. We have forgotten time: it is already one o'clock, and we ought to be with the Padre in half-an-hour, as that is the best time for seeing the convent; and I suppose you would not be willing to leave this gallery without having a look at the two pictures which you said you would keep for a ' *bonne bouche?* ' "

"Certainly not. I must have a look, as you say—if nothing more. Let us go to them."

If Mr. Barkley was pleased with the " Last Judgment," which closes the " Life of our Lord," what must have been his delight with that later one, and with the " Descent from the Cross ? "

After a little time spent in admiring these two masterpieces, our friends proceeded to San Marco, and found the Padre at home. He received them most graciously, and took them over the convent, sparing no trouble in showing Mr. Barkley everything of interest, and especially the matchless frescoes of il Beato.

When they had made the tour of the convent, they were shown the relics of Savonarola, the church, and its exquisitely illuminated choir books. Having now seen all San Marco's treasures, they thanked the good Padre for the great pleasure he had afforded them, and took an affectionate leave of him.

As they walked home, Mr. Blake said—

"You will confess, I suppose, that the relics of Savonarola rightly belong to us; that soaring spirit, who could not submit to injustice and tyranny in the person of Alexander VI., and so became the forerunner of the great emancipation of mind which was brought about a century later. Savonarola is truly one of our most illustrious forerunners and martyrs."

"His brother—our kind friend, the Padre—would not like to hear you so slander him! The whole life of our great Dominican,—all his teaching,—his public acknowledgment of the supremacy of the Pope, accepting his absolution on the way to death,—all will rise up against you. We have no lack of reformers of morals; but we have

no reformers of Divine dogmas amongst us. The
life of the illustrious Savonarola has yet to be
written ; but if you will read one, published not
long ago by Villari, and which is already in
English, you will hardly have the courage to talk
of Savonarola as one of your 'forerunners and
martyrs.' He died as he lived, in the unity of
the Christian faith."

Mr. Blake looked at his watch, and exclaimed—

"I declare it is three o'clock! and I promised
to be at home by that time. I had no idea it was
so late!"

"Nor had I. So it seems that all our battling
only made the time fly?"

"Indeed it did. I have seldom spent a shorter
or a pleasanter morning."

"Thanks. Then I hope you will feel inclined
to spend another in the same way very soon."

"Shall it be to-morrow?"

"Most willingly! At the same time as to-
day?"

"If you please. And now I must say good-
bye, and hasten home to keep my appointment
with the young ladies."

"With many thanks."

CHAPTER XI

LOITERING amidst the artistic haunts of *Firenze la bella*, we seem to have forgotten some of our Roman acquaintances, who, when leaving the Eternal City, took the southern instead of the northern direction.

We know already that Naples, or its neighbourhood, was the Eltons' destination; it was also that of the three gentlemen who played so prominent a part at their ball. How strange it is that such a *trio* should have fixed on going to the same place, each moved by motives so unlike those of the others!

Mr. Earnscliffe went there because he wanted change of scene, and thought Naples the most interesting;—Mr. Lyne, because it was a part of his plan to visit the south of Italy before returning to France; had Flora Adair accepted him, he would have done so with her, as his bride; now he would do so alone, for he was far too methodical to allow a disappointment to interfere with any of his arrangements ;—Mr. Caulfield's motive was to meet the Eltons, and he wished to get there before them, in order that the "dragoness" might not be able to say he had followed them.

Mr. Earnscliffe chose Capri. He liked boating excessively, and would sometimes spend hours alone in his little craft, accompanied by a poor fisherman called Paolo, whom he had engaged as his boatman, and who interested him greatly by his free and amusing tattle. Mr. Earnscliffe was fond of mixing in this way with the people in foreign countries. Thereby he learned their habits and thoughts ; and although among his equals he was considered as haughty and proud, such thoughts were never entertained of him by his inferiors. With them his generosity and readiness to help any one in real distress, combined with an evident determination not to let himself be imposed upon, caused him to be truly liked and respected. He thought about difference of position and inequality of fortune just in the same way as he did of the creation around him—namely, that all was full of inexplicable mystery. Reason told him that when he and Paolo came into the world there was no real distinction between them ; it appeared unaccountable why the one was born in a wretched hovel and was only to have rags to cover him, whilst the other first saw light in a luxurious chamber, and servants waiting ready to serve him. He would often sit looking at Paolo, as he lolled with careless grace in some part of the boat, singing or reciting something with all the characteristic animation of his country, and wondered what each would have been had their conditions been reversed,—had Paolo been the highly-born rich man, and he the poor lowly fisherman. This train of thought would often lead him to ask, "Why do these inexplicable contrasts exist?" Then, with a gesture of impatience, he would begin sometimes to row vigorously, much to the wonder of the indolent Italian, who saw no cause for this sudden display of energy.

Mr. Earnscliffe's equals in the social scale were not unjust when they called him haughty and overbearing; so he was, to them: an open scoffer, indeed, at many of their opinions, and even at their faith; but to the poor he was all gentleness, he respected their religion, and even their superstitions he refrained from ridiculing. Intolerance towards persons of his own rank, or above it, was a marked feature in his character; if one of these had not cultivated his mind—if he were not all that *he* thought a man ought to be, he looked upon him with contempt, and considered himself. merely obliged to treat him with cold politeness. To the poor, on the contrary, he was most indulgent, because he felt that fortune had denied to them all the advantages which she had given to the rich. The poor are forced to toil incessantly to gain their daily bread, they have scarcely any means of acquiring knowledge, of seeing and knowing what is good and true, and therefore it was that he, who in his own sphere would turn into ridicule the most solemn observances of Christianity, never even smiled at any practices, or cast a shadow of ridicule towards the feelings, of these poor Capri fisherpeople.

One day an acquaintance of his came to Capri, and he proposed that they should go out in his boat. As they got to the shore they found Paolo there playing with a beautiful little girl of about nine years old, who, as soon as she saw them coming, ran towards Mr. Earnscliffe. He caught her up in his arms, seated her on his shoulder, and carried her back to Paolo, who, with a gratified look, said, "*Come è buono sua eccellenza!*" and then turned to get the boat ready.

"You will come with us, Paolo," said Mr. Earnscliffe.

"*Bene, signore;* but would their excellencies wait a moment while I take *la ragazzina* to her mother; she is so precious!"

" Certainly," answered Mr. Earnscliffe, " I would not for worlds expose my little Anina to any danger." He bent down and kissed her, saying, "*Addio, carina !*"

As Paolo and Anina turned away, Mr. Earnscliffe's companion, Mr. Elliot, said, "Well, you do appear in a new character here, Earnscliffe ! "

" I was not aware that you did me the honour of studying my character so well as to know what is old or new in it," was the reply, with a haughty look ; " but is not Anina a beautiful little creature ? "

" Yes, very much so indeed ; but what did the man mean by saying, 'She is so precious,' and at the same time looking up to heaven in that strange manner."

"Ask Paolo to tell you ; the story will sound far better from his lips than from mine."

Paolo returned, and they all got into the boat. Soon after they were fairly afloat, Mr. Earnscliffe said, " Paolo, my friend wants to know why you said that Anina was so precious—will you tell him ? "

" With pleasure, *illustrissimo*," and his eyes looked the pleasure which his words expressed, for he was always happy and proud to talk of Anina ; " but," he added, "perhaps it will weary his excellency, as he knows it all so well."

"Not at all—I never tire of hearing about her."

The father's face lit up with pleasure as he said, "The *signor* must know, then, that last year there was great distress in our poor island—so much so that the poorer fishermen, like myself, were hardly able to live. In the month of April our great trial fell upon us: our eldest child, a boy about a year older than Anina, sickened and died. Our little Anina herself began to fade too; she grew weaker and weaker, and lay in the sun all day hardly moving or speaking. One day the doctor happened to pass, and my wife asked him for charity's sake to examine *la poverina*. He did so, and said, 'She is sinking from weakness, and I fear in this time of distress there is but little hope for her.'

"That evening, as we sat outside looking at the child's little pale face and closed eyes, lying as she was in her mother's arms, we shuddered to think how soon those eyes might be closed, like our other darling's, never, alas! to open again. All at once Maria, my wife, exclaimed, 'Take me to Sorrento to-morrow, Paolo, that we may go to the shrine there and pray to the Madonna to save our child.'

"' *Via!* Maria, *via!* Have I not already prayed to the Madonna and the saints, as only a

despairing father could pray, and all in vain,'
was my answer.

"'Hush! *marito mio*,' she cried, 'if thou
speakest so we are lost—only take me to Sorrento,
and thou shalt see what the Madonna will do for
us. She *must* hear me. Take me, Paolo! Oh
take me!'

"I could not refuse poor Maria, although I
thought it all fruitless—*Santissima Madre di Dio
mi perdoni.*"

Paolo took off his cap and crossed himself; but
he did not see Mr. Elliot's smile, and he continued—

"Accordingly we started for Sorrento the next
morning. A neighbour had promised to look
after the child, so we were not uneasy at leaving
her for the time.

"As we went up to the church my wife was
full of hope, but I was gloomy and dejected. We
heard Mass, and then I said to Maria, 'I am going
into the town, but I will come back for thee.'

"I had determined to try to get a small loan
from some of those to whom I was in the habit of
selling fish, but they all talked of the bad times,
and bestowed only their pity upon me.

"I went back for my wife, and we returned to
the boat; then I exclaimed, 'Fine things thy
Madonna has done for us! I have been to every

one whom I know in the town, and I have not got a carlino.'

" Maria answered me gently that she was sure the Madonna would not fail us if I would only have trust and patience. I heard it all in silence. When we reached the shore I did not follow her out of the boat. She turned and asked, 'Paolo, art thou not coming? The little one will miss her father—*il babbo.*'

"' Why should I go?' I retorted. 'To see the child die? I'd rather trust to the waves than to thy Madonna. I'll put out to sea.'

"' If she is to die, then must I see her die all alone? Art thou going to desert me, Paolo?'

" Poor Maria! These words made me feel how cruel I had been to her; and jumping out of the boat, I joined her, saying, ' Come then, we will watch her together.'

" When we got near to the house, we saw our good neighbour leaning over *la bambina,* and clasping her hands. I grasped my wife's arm, and exclaimed, ' *è morta!*'

" With a cry, Maria darted forward, calling, ' *Maddalena, Maddalena, dica di grazia non è morta mia bambina!*'

"' *Morta!* No. See what the Madonna has given her!' And Maddalena held up two gold pieces.

"Maria gave me one look of joy and triumph ; then she knelt down by her child and covered her with kisses. As for me, no words could express my remorse. I fell upon my knees and asked forgiveness of *Iddio e Sua Santissima Madre.*

"After a little time, and when we had all become a little calm again, Anina told us that a beautiful lady with golden hair came to her and asked her what was the matter with her? She answered that she had long been ill, and was dying like her little brother, because her parents were too poor to get what was necessary for her ; and they had gone to Sorrento to pray to the Madonna that she might get well again. The lady kissed her, and, putting the two gold pieces into her hand, said, ' Tell *il babbo e la madre* that the Madonna sent these to them.' And then she went away. ' I felt so happy,' added the little one, ' because I knew then that it was the Madonna herself who had been with me !'

" You will not be surprised to hear, *eccellenza,* that we all wept for joy over the precious child whom the Madonna had visited and saved to us !"

Mr. Elliot laughed, and said, "That is an exceedingly well made up story, my good man ; but you don't expect me to believe——"

"Stop," interrupted Mr. Earnscliffe, in a tone of indignation ; "it is the action of a coward to laugh at a man who neither in words nor action has the power to answer you!"

"Earnscliffe, you insult me!"

"If I do, I am ready to answer for it. All that, however, is not for the present time; now, the least you can do is to allow me to explain away, as well as I can, your ill-timed merriment. Shall I do so?"

Mr. Elliot quailed before his haughty gaze, and muttered, "As you like; the fellow is not worth so many words between gentlemen."

"The 'fellow,' as you call him, is, perhaps, the superior of the two gentlemen;" his lips did not say "of one of them, certainly," but his eyes looked it; and without giving Mr. Elliot time to make any rejoinder, he turned to Paolo, and said—

"This gentleman wished to test the truth of what you have related by appearing to ridicule it. But I have explained to him how undoubtedly true it is, and he begs that you will finish the story."

The conversation between the two gentlemen had been carried on in English; but Paolo had watched their faces, and had rightly interpreted their different expressions. So he answered, " *Come piace a sua eccellenza,*" looking pointedly at Mr. Earnscliffe, and laying a strong emphasis on the singular pronoun. He then went on to relate Anina's story.

"The child quickly recovered with the good things we were able to obtain for her. The first time that she followed me down to the boat, as she used to do when her poor brother and I were going out to fish, I felt beside myself with happiness; and you may be sure, *illustrissimo*, that a morning or evening never passes without my returning thanks to the *Santissima Madonna*, who has been so good to us, and that after the wicked things which I had said of her.

"A year went by, and the eve of the day in which our *bambina* had that blessed vision, Maria said to me, 'Paolo, thou must take us to Sorrento to-morrow.'

"'With all my heart,' I answered; for had I not learned to have as much trust in our blessed Patroness as my wife? The winter had been hard again, and we were very poor; but the child was well, and how could we complain? God knows what is best for us! So the next morning we set out for Sorrento with our little favoured one; and who shall be able to say how happy we were, as we thought of our trouble there on the same day a year before!

"After our return, on the evening of that same day, about the Ave Maria, my wife and I were sitting outside our door, and the child had wandered away among the rocks, when suddenly we heard her voice, and, looking up, we saw her in the arms of *sua eccellenza*. He gave her to my wife, and said that as he walked along, he heard a sound of crying, and saw at a little distance a child seated on a rock, and holding one foot in her hand. He asked her what ailed her, and she answered by taking away her hand from her foot; and he saw that it was cut, and bleeding fast. She had slipped, and fallen on a sharp piece of rock! God reward *sua eccellenza!* He bound up her wounded foot, and carried her, while she pointed out the way, to my cottage. *Sua eccellenza* then turned to me, and asked if I knew any one from whom he could hire a boat, and said that he also wanted a boatman to manage and take care of it for him. I replied that he could not do a greater act of charity than to take me, and that he could have my boat, too, only it was rather old and weather-beaten for *un gran signore* like him. He said that the boat being old did not signify, as he would probably buy one if he remained at Capri; and that he would take me on trial. And he has been graciously pleased to keep me in his service ever since. *O santissima Madre di Dio!* how much do we owe thee! When our precious *bambina* was dying from want, you came from heaven and gave her the gold which saved her life, and on the anniversary of that happy day you sent us a good angel, *sua eccellenza!*"

Paolo ceased speaking; but, with all the impetuosity of an Italian, he seized one of Mr. Earnscliffe's hands and pressed it to his lips. Mr. Earnscliffe flushed. He *felt* that Mr. Elliot was laughing at this scene ; and one of his weak points was a horror of ridicule even from those whom he despised. Yet he would not hurt Paolo by showing that his demonstrative gratitude annoyed him ; so he said gently, "*Grazie, amico, ritorneremo adesso!*"

Mr. Elliot exclaimed in a bantering tone, "Why, you are the eighth wonder of the world, Earnscliffe ; and what a fool I was to be angry with you just now, when you were so ready to strangle me for laughing at that wretched fisherman's absurd story about the *Madonna.* You must confess, however, that you are about the last person whom one could have expected to act so. I myself have heard you hold up to scorn the worship of idols before dignitaries of the Romish Church,—before men whose position, one might have thought, would have prevented you from attempting to ridicule their creed in their presence. Yet you were ready to fight with me for venturing to laugh at the same thing in this fisherman!"

An expression of unutterable contempt was visible in Mr. Earnscliffe's face as he replied—

" Can you not understand that one should laugh at anything so false and absurd as this species of idolatry in those who ought to know better, and yet respect it, yes, religiously, in a man to whom has been denied the means of knowing what is and what is not true? If you cannot, I pity you; but it is vain to answer you. All I can say is that I would rather have died than have acted as you have done to-day."

" Upon my word, Earnscliffe, if ever any man had a right to quarrel with another, I have that right now."

" Then use it by all means, if you like, although I cannot see what you would gain by it."

" I believe you are right there, and you are so strange a mortal that one may as well let you alone. I declare it would not astonish me to hear you say that you considered that fellow there to be a more respectable personage than Monseigneur N——, brother to an English Earl, and covered with honours and distinctions!"

" Of course I do,—*one* of them is respectable, because he is true; the *other* is not, because he is a hypocrite."

Here appeared Mr. Earnscliffe's ill-formed intolerance. He could not understand that men of education and great intelligence could sincerely believe what appeared to him to be folly, and therefore it was hypocrisy. In the world around him he saw so much falseness and self-interestedness, that he became a harsh judge of his fellows. Had he exercised towards them only a small portion of the indulgence which he extended to the untaught and to the poor, he would have seen many virtues which in his sweeping severity he overlooked.

When they reached the shore they saw a party from Sorrento disembarking, and Mr. Elliot recognised some intimate friends of his. They begged him to join them, but he pleaded his engagement to dine with his friend Earnscliffe.

"Even so," they answered; "could you not stroll with us a little before you dine?"

"Excuse me for a moment then;" and turning to Mr. Earnscliffe he said, "I believe my absence would be more agreeable to you than my company until dinner time, and, perhaps, even then you would rather dispense with it!"

"Nay," he rejoined, laughing, "I am not quite so bad as that. I do not ask people to dine with me and then wish to get rid of them. My invited guest shall always find a welcome at my table if

he chooses to accept it. Do we say *adieu* then, or
au revoir?"

" *Au revoir,—se piace a sua eccellenza,*" and with
a gay glance at Paolo he turned and followed his
friends.

The dinner had been ordered for two, but Mr.
Earnscliffe now determined to add another guest
in the person of the resident doctor, with whom
he had a slight acquaintance.

A little before the time appointed Mr. Elliot
returned from his walk in high spirits, and was
introduced to Doctor Molini, who spoke English;
so they conversed generally in that language.

As they sipped their coffee and had lighted
their cigars after dinner, Mr. Earnscliffe alluded
to the story which they had heard in the
morning, and said that Dr. Molini was the
gentleman of whom Paolo had spoken as having
seen the child in her illness; upon which Mr.
Elliot exclaimed, "Then, Dr. Molini, perhaps,
you can tell us the truth as to how they got that
money, instead of the story that Paolo related
about a beautiful golden-haired lady, dressed in
white, appearing to the child and giving it to
her?"

" Signore, I can only confirm what he said; it is
all perfectly true."

" You surely cannot mean to tell me that the

Madonna brought down the gold pieces from heaven!"

"De facts are, as I said before, all true, but not de inference which dese poor people draw, dat it was de Madonna who appeared to Anina. I happened to walk dat way; I saw a beautiful lady in white and wid golden hair speak to de child, kiss her, den go away. I was curious,—I did follow her until I saw her run to a *signore* and lean upon his shoulder, as he sat on a rock drawing. I knew dey were English, and raising de hat, I said dat I hoped *il signore et la signora* were pleased wid our poor island. *Il signore* said, 'Yes, very much.' Den *la signora* asked if I could tell her anything about a lovely little child she had just seen. I said I was de doctor of Capri and knew de child, but dat I feared she would die from weakness, her parents being very poor, and de bad time had made it hard for dem to live. *La signora* said she was glad to learn it, and as I was a doctor, perhaps, I would look at de child sometimes and see her cared for, and she put money into my hand. It was not wonderful for de child to call her de Madonna, she was so beautiful; her hat and cloak were on a rock by de *signore*, and her hair sparkled like bright gold in de sun. I suppose she was his bride,—I tink so. He told me dey must return to Naples, and wished me

buon giorno, and *la signora* said, 'Please not to
forget de pretty child, and I shall be grateful to
you.' I answered, putting my hand on my heart,
dat it was a happiness to me .to serve so gracious
a lady. *Il signore* looked impatient, and as if
he did not want me to stay, so I left dem, but I
have never forgotten her or de charge she left to
my care."

Mr. Elliot laughed at this specimen of foreign
forwardness and English reserve as he answered,
" Well, we shall not quarrel with you for having
been a little curious, as it has procured us the
pleasure of learning the truth about the story,
which is really a most interesting and remarkable
one. But "—turning to Mr. Earnscliffe—" I must
leave you now, for, as you know, my time is running close."

" Stay a moment, I will get my hat and walk
down to the shore with you; perhaps Dr. Molini
will accompany us? "

" I should like it very much but I have a call
to make, so I must wish you *felice notte* now."

The good little doctor took his departure after
much bowing, and Mr. Earnscliffe and his friend
set out on their walk. After some desultory chat
the former asked, " Are there many English at
Sorrento now? "

" Yes," replied the other, " the hotels are said

to be very full;—by the way, there were two acquaintances of yours staying at my hotel in Naples, which I only left the day before yesterday,—Mr. Caulfield and Mr. Lyne."

"Mr. Lyne! Is it possible that he is in Naples? Are you quite sure of it?"

"Very possible indeed, my dear friend. I saw him there two days ago."

"You amaze me: but is he not going back to Rome? Is he not going to be married?"

"Married! I should say not; and he certainly is not returning to Rome, since he starts in a few days for Sicily."

They had reached the shore, and Mr. Elliot added—

"Do you wish to know if there is any probability of his being married; he seems to interest you so much?"

"Thank you, no; he does not interest me in the least. I was merely astonished to hear of his being in Naples, for in Rome he was said to be on the eve of marriage with an English lady there."

"*Addio* then. Come and see me at Sorrento some day,—it will be a change for you."

"You are very kind, but I do not want change; I like my island solitude. Good-bye." And Mr. Earnscliffe turned immediately away as the boatman pushed off.

CHAPTER XII.

THE next morning found Mr. Earnscliffe still wondering how it was that Mr. Lyne came to be in Naples, and what had become of Flora Adair. Was it possible that she had refused Mr. Lyne? He felt a little startled at finding how much these thoughts occupied his mind; but, as he had often done before, he tried to persuade himself that he was quite indifferent to her proceedings *personally*, and that it was merely for the sake of the possible good of human nature in woman that he wished to know if she had been true and high-minded enough to reject this offer. What delicious self-deception! Had Mr. Earnscliffe said to himself, "If Mary Elton, instead of Flora Adair, were in question, should I be so interested in the possible good of human nature in woman, and care so very much to discover how she had acted?" But he asked himself no such question. It would have been an unsatisfactory way of putting the case; whereas, by placing it under the head of a laudable desire to acquire knowledge of human nature, it was quite another matter, and in that light he felt himself free to dwell upon it, and even actively to endeavour to unravel the mystery. Yet he could not succeed in finding a clear starting point for his investigations.

He wandered about without any settled object, or sat upon a rock with a book in his hand; but its pages remained unturned, and not even Anina, who well knew his favourite rocky perch, and seldom failed to join him there, could win from him now anything more than an absent smile; and having exhausted all her pretty little wiles to attract his attention, she at last went and stood beside him and asked, " Is *il caro signore* ill ?"

The child's question roused him, and, drawing her to him, he said, " No, *carina*, I am not ill, I was only thinking."

"Thinking, *signore*," repeated Anina slowly, as if that word gave her the idea of a very mystic operation indeed.

" Yes, thinking, little lady; and would she like to know about what ? "

" *Di grazie, signore.*"

" Well, then, I was thinking of going to Napoli."

" *A Napoli ?* but *il mio caro signore* will return ; he is not going away ?"

" No, *carissima,* I am not going away ; I will take *il babbo* with me, and we shall be back again to-night if possible. Will your *eccellenzina* give me leave to go ? "

" Yes," she answered, laughing merrily at the new title which he gave her ; " *il signore* may go, as he says he will be home to-night, and "—like a true child, in Italy or elsewhere—" perhaps he will bring Anina something pretty from Napoli."

"It is *not* impossible that he might do so. What would her *eccellenzina* be pleased to wish for ? "

" There are beautiful *Madonne* at Napoli, *signore,*" she said timidly, "and the one I have is *bruttissima,*—unworthy of the Madonna who has done so much for me."

Mr. Earnscliffe pretended to be very intent on the examination of a flower which was growing at a little distance from him. He did not know how to answer the child. He felt that it was too much, not only to tolerate superstition, but actually to encourage it by giving Anina an image: and yet he did not like to disappoint her. He raised his eyes, and they met her soft liquid ones, so earnestly and pleadingly fixed on his face, that he could not bear to pain her, and he said, " You shall have your Madonna, *carissima.*"

She threw her arms round his neck, declaring

that never was anybody so good as he was, and
" was he not also very fond of the Madonna ?"

This was going from bad to worse, and he
thought that the only thing to be done was to put
an end to the conversation, so, without answering
her question, he said, " Come, *carina*, we must go
and tell *il babbo* to get ready."

" But is not *il signore* very fond of the Madonna ?" she repeated with childish persistence.
. . . How constantly he was tempted to tell her that
all this was false, and try to teach her something
nearer to truth, but he was always stopped by the
thought that he himself could not explain clearly
to her what truth was, and that when he left
Capri he would only have rendered her unhappy,
and different from all her own people ; thus her
faith in the Madonna and the Saints remained un-
tarnished. Surely his good angel must have
been whispering in his ear when he refrained
from saying a disparaging word upon a subject
which naturally irritated him, and which was so
often brought before him by Anina in her lively
affection for the Madonna. After a few moments'
hesitation he replied, " We must ever love all
that is good and beautiful, just as one loves you,
carina, as long as you are such a dear, good little
child. . . ."

" But *il signore* will go away some day, and

then he will forget Anina," she said, looking up gravely at him.

" Ah, *carina,* you will be more likely to forget than I shall. You will have other and dearer ones to love you, while I——," he stopped suddenly, and muttered in English, " What a fool I am making of myself!" Letting go Anina's hand, he walked on quickly, saying, " Here is *il babbo.*" She stood still for a moment looking at him with a puzzled air, then away she ran to tell her mother that *il signore* had promised to bring her a beautiful Madonna from Napoli.

Mr. Earnscliffe told Paolo to have the boat ready in about half an hour, as he wished to go to Naples, and as the wind was so fair he preferred to sail rather than to take the steamer.

In this visit to Naples he had no fixed plan of action ; he had not even determined whether he would call on any of his acquaintances there, yet he had a vague notion that in some way or other he would see Mr. Lyne, although at the same time he had not the slightest idea of how he was to gain any information from him. He could not ask him a single question about what was uppermost within him, yet he could not rest without making an effort in that direction. Suddenly it occurred to him that the Eltons might know something about it. He recalled the day at the

Catacombs, thought of Mary Elton's eagerness to
tell him that Flora was going to be married to
Mr. Lyne; perhaps she might now be equally
ready to tell him why the marriage had not taken
place. It was possible that she might not know,
but it was a chance, and so he would try to find
out their address and call upon them.

As soon as he arrived in Naples he went to the
Hotel de la Grande Bretagne, and asked if Mr.
Caulfield and Mr. Lyne were staying there.

"Yes," answered the waiter, "but they are
out. Will the *signore* leave a card?"

"It is unnecessary," replied Mr. Earnscliffe, "as
I shall probably meet them; but perhaps you can
give me some information about an English
family of the name of Elton, who have been in
Naples for the last two or three weeks?"

The waiter repeated the name with tolerable
correctness, and after thinking for a few moments
he said, *una signora e due signorine* had stopped
there for a few days, and had afterwards taken a
villa in the neighbourhood,—did the *signore* think
that these were his friends?

Mr. Earnscliffe remembered having heard that
Charles Elton was obliged to return to his regi-
ment when his mother and sisters were going
to Naples, therefore it most probably was Mrs.
Elton and the two young ladies of whom the

waiter spoke; so he asked to see the visitors' book, and found that his supposition was correct. The address of their present residence was written after their names; and, having gained all the information he required, he rewarded the waiter's services, and desired him to call a carriage, in which he then drove to the villa.

Having reached the gate, Mr. Earnscliffe alighted, saying that he would walk up; and discharging the man, he entered.

The villa was situated about half way up one of the hills which rise behind Naples, and which command so lovely a view. Our friend stood still for a moment gazing upon it; as he did so he thought he heard a sound of voices, and looked round in the direction whence the sound seemed to come. He saw nothing, however, but a thick hedge; but on approaching it he discovered that it bordered a pretty secluded walk, which it shaded effectually from the sun. It looked very inviting, and he followed it, until he came to a spot where the hedge formed a sort of bow, and there, sitting on a stone bench, he saw Mary Elton. There was a table before her, and she leaned upon it with crossed arms and her head bent upon them. By her side knelt Helena, who had thrown one arm round her sister's waist, and with the other hand she tried to draw away the crossed arms which hid her face.

Did Mary hear Mr. Earnscliffe's step, or did she *feel* that *he* was looking at her? However that may be, she raised her head suddenly and saw him standing before her. Starting to her feet, the blood rushed to her face, crimsoning it all over; but it receded as quickly, and left her as pale almost as marble as she exclaimed, "Mr. Earnscliffe!" and then stood looking at him in silent amazement.

He smiled, and putting out his hand to her he said, "I came to call upon Mrs. Elton, but as I entered the gate I thought I heard voices in this direction, and that the sound of my own name caught my ear, so I took this walk instead of going direct to the house. I hope I have not intruded."

"Surely you need not fear to be looked upon as an intruder here," answered Mary, with a slightly faltering voice; "mamma will be delighted to see you."

"Of course she will," added Helena, shaking hands with him; "but where have you come from, Mr. Earnscliffe? I declare you appeared before us in so ghost-like a manner that Mary and I have not yet recovered from the shock."

"I see that I have startled Miss Elton very much," he replied, looking fixedly at Mary, who was still very pale; "yet I should have thought that she was less afraid of ghostly apparitions than you. But on this occasion you have shown more courage."

"Nevertheless," answered Mary, quietly, "I am less afraid of such things than Helena, and at all events, as I need scarcely say, I did not look upon your sudden appearance as supernatural; but I have been suffering from a nervous headache all day, and anything unexpected would have startled me for the moment."

"Then I regret having given you a start," he said, still looking inquiringly at her, as if he did not think that the effect was quite justified by the cause assigned.

"Pray do not say a word more about it, now that it is over. I dare say the start may do me good—as an electric shock. Let us go to the house."

"But all this time, Mr. Earnscliffe," interposed Helena, "you have not answered my question as to where you came from. To me it seemed as if you had dropped from the clouds."

"I did not drop from the clouds, but a friendly wind wafted me across the sea, and a chariot bore me through the air to the gate of your villa."

" Why you must be a demi-god, to have winds and chariots in attendance to bear you where you will. Are you a magician, Mr. Earnscliffe ?"

" Neither, Miss Helena ; but surely this is no more wonderful than dropping from the clouds as you suggested, and, as in politeness bound, I answered you in your own language."

" What a provoking man you are ! You always manage to make it appear that you are right whether you are or not. But now please to answer me rationally."

" Well, then, I came from Capri, where I have been staying since I left Rome, intending to spend an afternoon in Naples. I heard that you were residing in the neighbourhood, and asked at the *Hotel de la Grande Bretagne* if they knew your address, and as you may judge by seeing me here, my question was answered in the affirmative."

Mary turned aside her head in order to hide the flush of pleasure which she could not keep down at hearing this proof of his anxiety to see them, and Helena said, " How wonderfully condescending it was of you to take the trouble to seek us out !"

" Nay, I could not well spend a day in Naples and not call upon you, for I had not time to do so in Rome after your ball."

" There is more of your provokingness. You

will never allow one to imagine that you pay a compliment."

"Surely the Misses Elton must be surfeited with compliments, and therefore could not care for, or expect any, from a half-hermit like myself."

"Oh! a compliment is always acceptable when one can flatter one's self that it is true, and *you*, I suppose, would not deign to say anything which was not strictly so."

"Certainly not." He turned to Mary and said somewhat abruptly, "I hear that Mr. Lyne is here. Was it then a groundless *on dit* that he was going to marry Miss Adair?"

Poor Mary! What a blow this was to all her rising hopes, founded on the fact of his having shown anxiety to find them out. This question revealed to her the true motive of his visit. The revulsion of feeling was too great to allow her to speak at once, and Helena said, "Oh no, but Flora would not——"

"Helena!" interrupted Mary, sharply; "you are treading on my dress," and she laid her hand heavily on her sister's arm. Helena looked astonished, but remained silent, and Mr. Earnscliffe said—

"You were saying, Miss Helena, that Miss Adair ' would not——' Pray finish the sentence."

"Helena ought to have said," returned Mary, without giving her sister time to speak, "that Flora could not have *afforded* to refuse such an offer as Mr. Lyne's; so perhaps she is engaged to him."

"That is not very probable, Miss Elton, as they have gone in contrary directions," answered Mr. Earnscliffe, drily; whilst he said to himself, "There is some motive here for trying to make me believe in this marriage, and it is evident I am not to be allowed to hear the truth about it, or why was the sister hindered from speaking? But I *will* know what the mystery is." His face assumed so stern and determined an expression that Helena· exclaimed, "Why, Mr. Earnscliffe, you look as if you were struggling with some imaginary enemy, whom you are resolved to conquer!"

"It must, indeed, have been an imaginary one," he answered, smiling, but the smile was not a pleasant one, "as in reality I am walking with two young ladies, neither of whom could be supposed to be my enemy, or the enemy of anybody, I suppose; but you are right in thinking that were there any such struggle, I should be resolved to conquer. I am not so easily turned aside from any purpose, whatsoever it may be" —and his eyes rested for an instant on Mary.

She felt uneasy under the scrutiny; but fortunately for her they had reached the steps, and running up, she threw open both sides of the glass-door, saying, in imitation of Helen's gay, mocking manner—

"Welcome to Bel Vedere, O mighty conqueror !"

"That is a bad edition of me, Mary," said Helena, "and does not suit you at all,—does it, Mr. Earnscliffe ?"

"We are unaccustomed to it in Miss Elton," he replied; "while in you it appears as if it could not be otherwise."

"*You* think so, of course. In your estimation I know that I am a mere butterfly, and incapable of any deeper feeling than the amusement of the moment."

"Such *you* say is my opinion; I cannot be so rude as to contradict you, however. I certainly never said or implied anything of the kind. But we are keeping Miss Elton waiting."

They had remained standing at the foot of the steps during this little skirmish of words; then they followed Mary into the deliciously cool stone-paved hall, and from it into the drawing-room. There, too, it was equally cool, for the floor was of marble; the furniture was of a pale amber, so that the light which pierced through the closely-shut *persiennes* was tinged with a soft golden hue ; bouquets of roses gave a delicate perfume to the air; and through the open windows there came every now and then a slight breeze, laden with the scent of orange flowers.

Even Mr. Earnscliffe felt the charm of that room creeping over him. How strongly at that moment did he feel the refining power of woman's presence !—And involuntarily he sighed.

Mrs. Elton came down quickly. She seemed delighted to see him, and begged that he would partake of their four-o'clock refreshments, which were about to be served, and drive with them afterwards on the Riviera, and hear the band in the Villa Reale.

"Thank you. I shall be very happy to do so," he replied, thinking that he might chance to see Mr. Lyne there.

Shortly afterwards came coffee, cakes, fruit, creams, and light wines ; and as soon as they had partaken of these, the ladies went to get ready for their drive.

CHAPTER XIII.

WE left Mr. Earnscliffe alone in the drawing-room waiting for the return of the ladies, and during their absence that unfinished sentence of Helena's — "Flora would not—" occupied his thoughts. "Did she mean to say that Flora Adair would not accept Mr. Lyne?" His heart beat strangely fast as the conviction that it was so began to dawn upon him, and again he felt startled at his own feelings. But he would not stop to examine them now: he must first discover the whole truth. And once again he thought, "What can Mary Elton's motive be in not letting her sister speak?" He remembered her extraordinary agitation upon seeing him, and wondered what could have caused it. It was not possible to suppose that Mary wanted him as a desirable match for herself, as with her beauty and ample fortune he knew that a suitable marriage could be no difficulty for her. Why, then, should she waste her energies in trying to catch him? . . . .

Evidently it could not be that; yet he could think of no other reason for her extraordinary conduct. He was not a vain man : so it never occurred to him that the cause of all this was love for himself; besides, he hardly believed that women ever acted from any but interested motives,—thus he missed the solution of the riddle.

His musings were interrupted by the entry into the room of the subject of them. Mary came in and threw herself into an armchair, and as she lay back in it she looked so weary that Mr. Earnscliffe said—

"You look tired, Miss Elton."

"Tired? Yes. Tell me—you who are said to be a philosopher—have you found life to be so pleasant a thing that you have never been tired of it?" She did not give him time to answer, but went on hurriedly, "Is it not, on the contrary, made up of struggles which wear one out; —of vain efforts to win some longed-for object? And how great is the weariness which follows these struggles, when one sees that object slipping from one's grasp, and about to fall into the hands of one who has, perhaps, never fought for it!"

He looked at her in amazement as he exclaimed—

"You speak almost with the bitterness of experience, Miss Elton!"

" I speak of life in general. Is it not what I have said ? "

" Yes, perhaps it is so,—at least, until we have learned that there is nothing in it worth struggling for ! "

" But I do not think it true that there is nothing in life worth struggling for; nor in reality do *you*. Ay, there are things worth struggling for, and at this very moment you feel that there are ! "

" Miss Elton ! "

" I know that I astonish you greatly. You cannot understand that I should speak thus,—I, who am generally so calm and quiet. But there are times when one forgets conventionality, and everything else ;—times when life becomes a burden, and one envies the Pagans, who saw no crime in laying it down voluntarily. We are given too much or too little light and faith—enough to prevent us from choosing between life and death, as they did, but not enough to prevent us from longing that we, too, had the power so to choose. . . . Ah! if one did not believe in eternal happiness or misery ! "

At this moment, Mrs. Elton and Helena came in, and there would have been an awkward pause, had not Mary continued, with perfect coolness—

" Yes, as I was saying, happiness and misery— or rather, prosperity and misery—come into such

close contact in Italy ;—the palace and the hovel
lean one against the other; the lady in costly
velvets and the beggar-woman in rags walk side
by side. Indeed, it is in southern lands alone that
you see them thus face to face."

"That is quite true," observed Mrs. Elton.
"In England the proper distinction of classes is
admirably well marked."

"The carriage, ma'am," announced Thomas,
opening the door.

"What a strange girl that is!" thought Mr.
Earnscliffe, as he looked at Mary, who was seated
opposite to him in the carriage. "She was speaking with all the earnestness of excited feeling when
her mother entered the room, and at once she
changed her tone and manner so completely, that
one could scarcely believe it to be the same person
who, a moment before, was talking bitterly and
eagerly, with flashing eyes and hands twitching
nervously. . . ."

When they reached the Riviera they found it
already crowded with gay equipages. No sooner,
however, had they taken their place among the
other carriages than Helena exclaimed, "How I
should like to get out and walk in the Villa Reale;
then I could see the programme of the music, and
one enjoys listening to a band so much more when
one knows what it is playing."

"And why do you not gratify your desire? I need scarcely say that I should be most happy tŏ escort you," said Mr. Earnscliffe.

"Thank you! Thomas, open the door."

"I will go with you," said Mary.

"But," interposed Mrs. Elton, "you surely will not leave me quite alone; you may as well stay with me now, Mary, and when Helena comes back you can take a turn, if Mr. Earnscliffe should not be tired of handing young ladies about."

"On the contrary, Miss Elton may count upon my being ready to accompany her."

Mary felt that she could not persist, so she reseated herself, saying, "Thank you, but I dare say that by the time Helena returns I may not feel inclined to trespass upon your readiness to oblige. You know that it is a woman's privilege to change her mind as often as she likes, and we have so few privileges that it would be unwise not to avail ourselves of them."

He merely smiled as he handed Helena out of the carriage, and offering her his arm, he led her into the Villa in order to see the programme, which was posted up close to where the band was playing. Mary soon lost sight of them amidst the crowd. Before they had come out she had given Helena a lecture upon her thoughtless way of speaking, and cited as an example of this what she was about to say on that very morning about Mr. Lyne and Flora Adair, declaring that even if she positively knew—which she could not—that Flora had refused Mr. Lyne, it was not right of her to speak of it.

"You are mistaken, Mary," answered Helena, "in saying that I could not know it. I *do* know it, for Harry's answers were so confused and contradictory when I asked him about his friend, that it was just as plain to me that he had been refused as if Harry had admitted it in so many words. Poor Harry! he thinks that it would be betraying his friend to tell even me; but with all his determination he has 'let the cat out of the bag'—he would have done much better to have told me in confidence; I should then be bound in honour not to divulge it."

"It matters not—you ought not to speak of it. What would Mr. Lyne think if he should hear it said that Flora Adair had refused him, and that the Misses Elton had said so? So please, Lena, to be more cautious in future."

"I will not speak of it, Mary, because it would, I see, annoy you; but why not have said candidly, 'Do not tell *Mr. Earnscliffe*,' for you know that it is not my saying generally that Mr. Lyne has been rejected which displeases you."

"What possible advantage could it be to me,

Helena, that Mr. Earnscliffe should not know this? Do you suppose that it would make him like me any better? Absurd! But we must not get the character of being *mauvaises langues*. You said you would not speak of it again, and therefore I am sure you will not." So saying she left the room.

Even to Helena she could not bring herself to acknowledge to what meanness she could descend in order to keep Mr. Earnscliffe away from Flora Adair, and it was after this conversation that she went into the drawing-room looking so weary.

As she saw Mr. Earnscliffe and Helena leave the carriage together she thought, " What Lena said of Mr. Caulfield—that his very determination not to speak betrayed the secret—will be her own case now. She will mean to keep her word, yet Mr. Earnscliffe will know it, for he is determined to know as much as possible."

She was right: Mr. Earnscliffe was determined to find out the truth, yet he felt awkward about asking Helena; so by way of introduction he led the conversation back to Rome, and their ball, and chance favoured him. Helena inadvertently disclosed all that he wished to know. He exerted all his power to be agreeable in order to amuse her, and drew such laughable caricatures of the different people there that Helena forgot all

restraint, and yielding to her natural delight in
ridicule, she added many an absurd feature to
Mr. Earnscliffe's pictures, until, carried away by
the subject, she exclaimed, " But the hero of the
night was Mr. Lyne. His air of confidence and
triumph as he danced that last quadrille before
the cotillon with Flora was delicious; then afterwards the poor rejected creature looked so crest-
fallen as he sneaked away that I could not help
laughing at him. I met him near the door, and
was so tempted to cut off his retreat and make
him dance with me for the fun of teazing him ;
but I took pity upon him and let him escape."

"Then he did propose for Flo——, for Miss
Adair, and she refused him?" said Mr. Earnscliffe,
in a low thrilling tone.

" I said nothing about Mr. Lyne's proposing to
Flora Adair," retorted Helena eagerly, and blushing deeply as she felt how imprudent she had
been—that she had told the very thing which she
had been desired not to tell.

" It is quite needless to make any explanations
about it, Miss Elton. I am aware that you did
not *say* that Mr. Lyne had been refused by Miss
Adair," he answered, smiling.

Helena grew still more flushed as she cried out •
hotly, " You are unkind, ungenerous, man——"
she was going to say manœuvring, but she stopped

suddenly, feeling that getting angry about it was only betraying herself still further.

"How many more evil qualities have I displayed, Miss Elton?" he replied, with a slight laugh. "But here are two friends of yours."

She looked up and saw Mr. Lyne and Mr. Caulfield standing before her, the latter gazing at her with somewhat of a displeased air. A lover is not often particularly well pleased to see his beloved walking alone with another, and that a handsome, man! Helena understood it all at a glance; it quite restored her gaiety, and for the time being made her forget her vexation with herself and Mr. Earnscliffe. As she shook hands with the new-comers she thought to herself, "So you are jealous, Master Harry, are you?—then I shall have grand fun in teazing you." She had drawn her arm from Mr. Earnscliffe's, and stood with downcast eyes before Mr. Caulfield. Mr. Earnscliffe proposed that they should return to the carriage, but Helen objected, saying, "Surely it is pleasanter to walk about a little longer; and now that these gentlemen have joined us, one of them I dare say will allow me to walk with him, so that you, Mr. Earnscliffe, will be freed from the wearisome task of *making me talk.*" She emphasised the latter words, and again an expression of annoyance passed over her features.

"It was not a wearisome task I assure you, Miss Elton,—very far from it; your conversation was most interesting to me."

"True, I suppose you did find it interesting for once." She turned away impatiently, and said in a low tone to Mr. Caulfield, "Come."

He required no second summons to join her, and they walked on together, Mr. Lyne and Mr. Earnscliffe following.

From what Helena had said Mr. Earnscliffe felt certain that Flora had refused Mr. Lyne, yet he wanted to have assurance made doubly sure; he longed to hear Mr. Lyne himself confirm it, for he found it very difficult to believe that a woman had acted so disinterestedly, and at the same time he wished ardently to be compelled to believe that *Flora Adair* had done so. But the difficulty was to make Mr. Lyne speak—how indirectly soever it might be—on the subject. . . . Again chance favoured him.

An Italian lady with her two daughters passed them and bowed to Mr. Lyne. Turning to his companion, he said, "Did you observe the plainer of those two girls? She has just returned from a convent for her month of probation before she enters as a nun."

"Indeed! poor girl! so she is to be a victim to this horrible custom in your Catholic countries of sending plain or portionless girls into a convent! Yet, after all, I don't know that it is a great deal worse than our own system of selling women in marriage, save inasmuch as that we use no force. But then—alas that it should be so!—it is not necessary for us to use force,—our women are only too ready to be sold if the bidding be but high enough, too ready to become the property of any man who can give them wealth or position, with or without love on their sides. To me, this appears to be the lowest of all degradation, and the sanction which the world's rules gives to it can make no real difference. It is merely *legitimatized* degradation, yet I half believe that *all* women are capable of submitting to it."

"Surely you are mistaken," answered Mr. Lyne earnestly; "there are many women far above anything of that kind. You must not forget that, on principle, many persons disapprove of ardent love as an ill-regulated feeling; therefore women often marry without what is called *love*, but they would not for worlds accept one whom they did not respect and look up to; and these surely are not to be condemned. There are others again whom no possible advantage would induce to marry without that intense love of which they dream."

"This is all very well in theory, but does not

experience teach us the contrary? Could we name one woman out of all those whom we know who would really act so? Lives there the girl who, without an independence of her own, ever refused a rich man merely because she did not love him intensely? You know you could not point out one."

"Pardon me, I could."

"Really? truly?"—exclaimed Mr. Earnscliffe, laying his hand upon Mr. Lyne's arm.

"As really, as truly, as that I am walking with you."

"Thank you, Lyne, you don't know how much good you have done me; you have restored my belief in the truth and beauty of woman's nature, for even one true woman is sufficient to redeem the sex from general contempt. . . . Yet God knows I had reason to distrust them."

"Still you ought not to distrust all because some are unworthy."

"I feel that you are right, and again I thank you for having given back to me one of the old feelings of my youth."

To Mr. Lyne's calm, passionless temperament this lively gratitude seemed uncalled for, and he made no answer. After a few moments' silence Mr. Earnscliffe said, "We must return to the carriage. Mrs. Elton will think I have eloped with her daughter." Quickening his pace, he joined Mr. Caulfield and Helena, saying, "Miss Elton, I regret to break in upon a conversation which seems to engross you so much, but I really think we ought to return to Mrs. Elton."

" Very well," answered Helena in an impatient tone.

Mr. Earnscliffe fell back to his place by Mr. Lyne, but before they got within sight of the carriage Helena and her cavalier stopped apparently to examine a flower, and when the others came up she said, "Mr Lyne, I believe you are a good botanist, so come and tell me the name of this flower ; and I also want to hear about your proposed tour in Sicily."

It was easy to see that the object of all this was to change the order of the procession, accordingly Mr. Earnscliffe walked on with Mr. Caulfield, while Helena and Mr. Lyne were occupied with the flower.

When they reached the carriage neither Mrs. Elton nor Mary seemed pleased at the addition to their party in the persons of Mr. Caulfield and Mr. Lyne. The two gentlemen, however, appeared not to observe it, and went up and shook hands with them. Mr. Earnscliffe handed Helena into the carriage, then said to Mary, "Now, Miss Elton, shall we have our walk ? "

"Thank you, not now; I do not feel inclined to walk; but if you will return to dinner with us we can have a stroll in the evening."

"You are very kind," he replied, "and I shall be delighted to do so, if you will permit me to say adieu for the present. I must see my boatman and tell him at what hour to be ready for me."

"Could not Thomas do that?"

"No. I must go myself, for I promised to buy a present for my boatman's little daughter."

"Well then, *au revoir!* We dine at half-past six to-day, on account of some national fête to which our cook wants to go, so you have not too much time to spare."

"Nevertheless I shall be punctual—adieu."

Mrs. Elton turned to Mary and asked, "Is Mr. Earnscliffe gone?"

"For the present, yes; but he will return to dinner."

"Oh, that is all right," answered Mrs. Elton, without taking the trouble of lowering her voice so as to prevent the other gentlemen from hearing that Mr. Earnscliffe was going to dine with her; indeed she was rather glad to make Mr. Caulfield feel that he was in the way; had it not been for him she would have asked Mr. Lyne to dine, but, as it was, she could not ask him and leave his friend uninvited; it would have been *too* much.

At six the band went away, and the Eltons immediately afterwards. . . . When they reached home Mrs. Elton told Thomas that Mr. Earnscliffe was coming to dinner, and desired that as soon as he arrived he should be shown into a dressing-room. The ladies then disappeared.

Helena dreaded the dressing beyond measure, for she was sure that Mary would at once ask her about her walk, and what could she answer? In fear and trembling she entered her own and her sister's room; but Mary asked no questions: the mischief, she instinctively felt, had been done, and it was useless to reproach Helena. She dressed herself in silence; but her varying colour, and the trembling of her hands, showed how excited she was. Helena looked on with dismay. She found this silence worse than any scolding could have been, yet she was afraid to break it. To her great relief the bell rang for dinner, and she hastened downstairs. Mary followed her in a few moments, but went direct to the dining-room, and there she found the rest of the party.

It is said that "drowning people will catch at straws." Mary caught at the shred of a hope that, perhaps, after all, Mr. Earnscliffe was not quite lost to her, since he had accepted *her* invitation to dinner; especially as he had, no doubt, gained all the information he required; and, moreover, as he generally disliked society so much, there must be some motive for his staying. . . . It was a straw, indeed!

What would she have said if she had known that Mr. Earnscliffe only stayed from curiosity as to what her motive could be in trying to conceal from him the truth about Flora, as he thought it possible that during the evening something might occur to throw light upon it?

After dinner the girls proposed going out, to which their guest gladly assented. Mrs. Elton said she would remain in the house, as she felt a little tired. At the foot of the steps they met a peasant girl with bouquets, and Helena stopped to speak to her, as she had a shrewd suspicion that the bouquet girl did not come unsent. Mr. Earnscliffe and Mary went on and strolled into the alley where they had met in the morning.

Mary looked very handsome. The blue opera cloak which she had thrown round her shoulders showed off to advantage her brilliantly fair skin and auburn hair; and she could not help thinking, as she looked at herself in a glass on passing out, "How strange that *he* should prefer Flora Adair to me! . . . I am far more beautiful than she is. What *can* I do to keep him from her?"

With this question ringing in her ears she went out as we have said. She broke the silence after they entered the alley by saying "Are you going to remain at Capri?"

"I think not—I shall probably start in a day or two."

"And where do you intend to go?"

"I have not fixed upon any place as yet, but southern Italy is becoming too hot."

"And Venice, I suppose, will be cooler!" she answered, bitterly.

"I did not say that I was going to Venice?"

"Of course you did not—you did not wish to acknowledge that you were going to meet the *Adairs!*"

"Really, Miss Elton, for the third time to-day you astound me more than I can say; but as you *have* named the Adairs, will you tell me why you took such trouble to make me believe that Mr. Lyne was to be married to Miss Adair,—and, of course, you knew as well as your sister that she had refused him?"

"Are you blind, that you do not see what has urged me to this?"—She had evidently lost all self-control, as she stopped walking, and stood opposite to him with her flashing eyes fixed on his face. What more she might have said or done, had not the sound of an approaching step caught her ear, it would be difficult to tell. She added hurriedly, "Go now to Flora Adair, and

win her love if you can ; but in the hour when
you feel most sure of her, or when you only wait
for religious rites to make her yours for ever, may
she be torn from you—more, may *she* play you
false—may her hand strike the blow which shall
crush your heart, even as mine has been crushed
to-day ! Now go ! " She seized his hand, and
for an instant her fingers closed upon it like a
vice ; then she let it go with a start as if it had
burned her, and, turning away, she darted down
a side walk.

Mr. Earnscliffe stood like one transfixed, until
the step which had been heard in the distance
now sounded close to him. Looking round, he
saw Helena Elton, who exclaimed, in a frightened
tone, " Mr. Earnscliffe ! what does all this mean ?
Where is Mary ? "

" Go to her as quickly as you can," was his
answer,—" she left me in a state of fearful
agitation ; but believe me that, intentionally, I
would not have caused her a moment's pain." He
put out his hand absently : Helena understood
that he meant to take leave of her, and placing
hers in it, she said, " I do believe it, Mr. Earnscliffe, and do not judge poor Mary harshly ; *you*
at least should be indulgent towards her."

" Fear not, Miss Elton ; as you say, *I* at least
can never use her harshly." He pressed Helena's

hand and left her. She went to seek her sister,
while he walked slowly back to the house.

That day had been a day of revelations to him,
and pain and pleasure were so strangely mingled
in those revelations, that he preserved his calm
ness only with a strong effort. He entered the
drawing-room to say good-bye to Mrs. Elton, but
she was not there ; then he rang for the servant,
and said, " Will you be so good as to tell Mrs.
Elton that I came in to say good-night to her
as I am obliged to go at once ; but as she is not
downstairs I do not wish to disturb her."

" Please, sir, let me tell Mrs. Elton that you
are going."

" Thank you, no, I cannot wait." So saying,
he walked into the hall. Thomas opened the
door, and as it closed behind him, he felt that he
had crossed the Eltons' threshold for the last
time.

The carriage was at the gate, and he drove
direct to the shore.

CHAPTER XIV.

The stars were crowding fast into the clear sky, and the moon was shedding forth her pale rays, when Mr. Earnscliffe reached the boat. Such a scene must be witnessed to be understood. To those who have seen the Bay of Naples on such a night memory will hold up her mirror, and they will see again the dim outline of the gracefully-curving shore, Vesuvia's dark and awe-inspiring shadow, and the deep blue waters upon which the moonbeams glance like silvery darts; and to those who have not seen it imagination will paint a no less vivid picture—but to them is unknown the balmy air, the charm, the beauty of an Italian night, and nowhere, perhaps, as well as in Naples and Venice, is it so completely seen and felt in all its unrivalled beauty. It is lovely, too, in its inland scenes: how lovely those can truly say who have known what it is to stand upon a balcony at "the witching hour," and look down upon a woody dell with myriads of busy fire-flies gleaming through the dark foliage, every branch, every twig covered with those brilliant and living lamps,—'tis nature's illumination, and in what does she not excel?

O Italy! thy beauty, thy poetry, thy loving memories are surely more than adequate to counterbalance the many great but material disadvantages which one meets with in thee. . . .

But we have drifted away from the subject of our chapter, and deserted Mr. Earnscliffe, to whom we must now return.

He got into the boat—the sails were filling, for with the fall of day the wind had veered round, and promised them a quiet and favourable passage —threw himself upon the cushions, and took off his hat, as if he felt that he could more thoroughly enjoy the lovely night when there was nothing between him and the starry world above. Paolo saw that he looked strangely pale, and asked the same question which his little daughter had done in the morning, " Is *sua eccellenza* ill?"

"*Grazie, amico, sto benissimo,*" told a different tale from the listless abstracted one with which he replied to Anina. That smile, and a certain softness in the tone of Mr. Earnscliffe's voice, made Paolo feel that *sua eccellenza* came back a happier man than when he set out for Naples. And so he was, although pain and pleasure were closely mingled in his sensations; but, at least, the future was no longer quite a blank to him; there was something to hope for—something, as Mary Elton had said to him, worth struggling for. He did not consider himself in love with Flora Adair, but he felt that she *did* occupy his thoughts almost exclusively, that everything connected with her interested him deeply, and he could not help smiling as he remembered all the ingenious arguments which he made use of to account to himself for that interest. Then, too, came the remembrance of the delight which he felt when he heard that she had refused Mr. Lyne, and he murmured to himself, "Yes, I will go to Venice, try to meet the Adairs, and if——" Ah! what visions rose after that if? . . . They were like mental lullabies, and under their soft influence he fell asleep and dreamed.

He dreamed of winning Flora's love, of the happy life which was to begin for him with her at his side; . . . . but suddenly a change came over the picture—Mary Elton seemed to stand between him and Flora, with a countenance full of passionate anger and yet of triumph, as she cried out, "I warned you!" . . . . He made a movement to clasp Flora, but she seemed to shrink away from him and fall. This startled and awoke him, but so real was the impression which the dream left upon his mind that he exclaimed in Italian, " Catch her, Paolo—she will be drowned!"

" What does *sua eccellenza* mean? There is nobody drowning."

" Thank God!" he muttered, with a long-drawn breath of relief as he reseated himself. Then he said to Paolo, " You see I have been dreaming, *amico.*"

" But not *un sogno sinistro, eccellenza?* that would be a bad omen indeed, at this hour of the night, and by moonlight too," answered Paolo, eagerly.

" It was probably the sleeping with the moon shining full upon my face which caused me to dream," he replied, without saying whether the dream was a sinister one or not. Paolo did not seem to be satisfied with this answer, and said gravely, " Oh *eccellenza*, it is very unlucky! . . . May you be preserved from all evil!"

Mr. Earnscliffe smiled, but he would have pre-ferred that Paolo had dwelt less upon his fears about the dream; for although not generally superstitious, he could not shake off the gloomy impression which it left upon him. All his bright visions had vanished, and in their place came painful reminiscences of poor Mary Elton. He would have given much to have been able to feel sure that she would forget him and be happy again; but something whispered to him that it would not be so—that, whether in good or evil, she was not one likely to change, and she had given proof of how strong a woman's feelings can be. Perhaps, also, there was mixed up in his pity for her a latent, almost a superstitious dread of her as he had seen her in his dream. Then he thought of Anina—of how he was to tell her that he intended to leave Capri immediately, and the thought of the child's grief made him shrink from facing it; yet he felt that it would be cruel in him to go away without telling her: no, that could not be—and then it was that he felt *how* fond he had become of the beautiful child.

Beauty in women had naturally a most powerful attraction for him, yet for years he had been shut out from the enjoyment of it by his blighting belief in their falseness. This, in his estimation, overclouded all their loveliness. " Beauty in a woman," he would say, " being so overclouded, is less worthy of admiration in her than in a statue; in this, at least, there is no deception—we find here all that we can expect, namely, regularity of outline and one fixed expression." But in Anina he saw living beauty combined with perfect artlessness, and it won his heart at once; then, too, her ardent affection for himself and desire to be with him had its own charm for the lonely rich man. She had been quite a companion to him in his wanderings about the island; he had taught her to read, and with a feeling of sadness he recalled the pretty lighting-up of her expressive face whenever he praised her; and again, how charmingly penitent she used to look when he chid her for inattention. And he had to tell her that there must be an end to all this, and doubted that even the beautiful present which he was going to give her would console her for his departure. He felt that her grief would probably not be of very long duration, but he feared that it would be sharp and violent, and it pained him to think that he was to be the cause of it. All this brought him to the conclusion that the sooner the leave-taking was over the better; so he resolved to go the next day.

It was very late when they touched Capri. As Mr. Earnscliffe wished Paolo good-night, he desired him to come to the hotel in the morning at six, and to bring Anina with him.

But two hours remained before sunrise, yet even for that short time Mr. Earnscliffe could not rest; his head was tossing about upon his pillow until about four, when he got up—no unusual hour in Italy during the fine season—and ordering his coffee at half-past five, he went out and bathed.

Soon after his return, and by the time he had finished his light breakfast, Paolo and Anina had arrived—he had learned from his master that anti-Italian virtue, punctuality.

Mr. Earnscliffe told Paolo that he wanted to speak with him ; as the child left the room, he said, " Paolo, I asked you to come to me this morning in order to tell you that I mean to give you my boat——"

Paolo looked delighted and exclaimed, " *Sua eccellenza è troppo buono.*"

But Mr. Earnscliffe went on without noticing the interruption—" And if you will name any means by which you can be permanently advanced in your trade, it shall be done; but for this, perhaps, you would like a little time for consideration —if so you can speak to Dr. Molini, and he will communicate with me. . . . I am obliged to leave Capri to-day."

"*O eccellenza, questo maladetto sogno*—I knew it was the sign of coming misfortune."

" Not so, *amico;* the dream has nothing to do with my going away, and it shall not be a misfortune to you—you shall not lose by it."

" It is not that, *eccellenza,* which I meant by misfortune. It was the Blessed Madonna herself who sent you to us; and now that you are going, we shall feel as if she were taking something

precious from us; besides, what could ever be the
same to me as being in your service? You have
treated me—the poorest fisherman in Capri—
almost as your equal; and that day when the
signore laughed at my story bound me to you for
ever. I felt that I could die for you, *eccellenza.
Dio*, how shall I tell *la moglie e la bambina?*"

Mr. Earnscliffe, with an Englishman's dislike
to any show of feeling, turned away his head to
hide any traces of emotion which might have
been seen on his countenance, for he was deeply
touched by Paolo's sorrow. After a few moments'
silence he said, "Believe me, Paolo, I value your
affection more than I can say, and I would do
anything to make you happy."

"Then, *signore*," interrupted Paolo eagerly,
"let us go and live near you in Napoli?"—poor
Paolo never thought of anything beyond Naples—
"and I can be your boatman still."

"But, *amico*, I am not going to live in Naples;
I am going to travel." Paolo's head drooped,
and Mr. Earnscliffe continued kindly, "But I
promise you that you shall see me again if I live.
And now, Paolo, go to Maria and consult with her
about what you would wish me to do for you."

"Ah! *signore*, we could not consult about anything to-day; we can only think that the Madonna
is taking one of her best blessings away from us."

"Well, as I said before, you can speak to Dr. Molini after I am gone, and he will write to me."

Paolo saw that Mr. Earnscliffe meant this to terminate the interview, and he asked at what hour *sua eccellenza* would want the boat; but Mr. Earnscliffe answered that he would not require it, as he was going by the steamer.

"Then I shall never row *sua eccellenza* again," exclaimed Paolo, giving way to violent demonstrations of grief. . . . This was all extremely painful to Mr. Earnscliffe, and so contrary to all his natural, or, rather, national, notions of what grief ought to be ; yet he could not be *brusque* to Paolo, for he saw that, although it appeared most unseemly to him, it was real and natural in the excitable Italian, but he said gravely—

"Paolo, it is a man's part to be strong, and not to give way to feeling as women do, and for my sake you must subdue all this. Think how you grieve me by making me thus feel that I give you pain. Now *addio*, I must go to the *bambina*."

"But I shall see *sua eccellenza* again, surely ? He will come to say *addio* to Maria ?"

"Yes, but I shall expect you both to be very calm,—*al rivedersi dunque!*"

Mr. Earnscliffe gently turned away, and taking the case which contained the statue for Anina, he left the room. Paolo slowly followed him

At the hall door they met the child, and taking her by the hand Mr. Earnscliffe drew her on quickly so that she might not see her father's emotion.

After a short walk along a pretty rocky path they came to a kind of creek formed by the rocks, so as to be completely shaded from the sun ; here he sat down and opened the box, displaying to Anina's longing eyes a little white temple; the roof was arched and supported by four columns, round which ran scrolls of lilies painted on a blue ground and bordered with gold ; inside, on a pedestal, was a small, but, for its size, beautiful figure of the Madonna, draped in a blue cloak starred with gold.

Mr. Earnscliffe looked upon the Madonna as being nothing more than a good woman to whom superstition had given an undue and almost a Divine celebrity; but, in imagination, no one could form a more poetical idea than he did of the purity and beauty surrounding the mother of an incarnate God ; therefore, he had chosen the best representation of this idea that he could find.

Anina's delight was unbounded. She literally danced round it, repeating, " *Come è bella, bellissima !* " Then throwing her arms round Mr. Earnscliffe, she half smothered him with her gratitude.

"Listen to me, *carina*," he said, gently unfolding her arms from his neck. His grave tone made her look up wonderingly at him, and he went on. "I want you to give me a reward for having brought you the Madonna. Will my little one give it to me?"

"Oh, *signore!*" and her little face was nestled on his shoulder.

"Then you *will* give it to me, *carina*. But I am going to ask a great deal. It is to promise that you will not fret very much if I tell you that something you love dearly is to be taken from you."

"But what is it, *signore*, that you are going to take from me? Not the Madonna?"

"Not the Madonna, certainly; but you have not given me the promise. Will you not be very good, and not cry too much?"

"*Si, signore.*"

"Then, *carissima*, you must remember that promise when I tell you that I am going away to day."

Alas for promises! Anina's answer was to burst out crying as though her little heart would break, and then through her sobs she murmured, "*No, no, non va via il caro signore;* he told me so yesterday?"

"Yes, *carina*, but afterwards I heard some-

thing which obliges me to go. This is not keeping your promise, my child. I hoped that your
beautiful Madonna would console you, and I will
come back some day, *Anina mia, sia buona.*"

He put his arm round her waist and kissed her,
but she hid her face on his shoulder, and sobbed
so violently that he saw it was vain to attempt to
quiet her now, and that all he could do was to
take her home and leave her; time he knew
would calm this violence of childish grief. With
his disengaged hand he put the little temple into
the box, and said, "Come, my child, take your
Madonna, and let us go home." But Anina
made no movement to take it, and he said, "Then
you do not care for her. I may throw her into
the sea."

"Oh, give her to me, *signore,*" she cried,
stretching out her hand for it. "I will pray to
her every day for you, and perhaps she will send
you back to me."

He had not told her before, and now he could
not tell her, how worse than useless he thought
those prayers; yet her affection for himself,
mingled as it was with her devotion for the
Madonna, touched him almost in spite of himself,
and giving her the box silently, he took her by
the hand and led her home.

It was the same path down which he had

carried her when first he saw her; and her
parents, too, were sitting at the door as on that
evening; but now sorrow, instead of joy, was to
be seen in their faces as they rose to receive him.
Maria threw herself at his feet, crying and
muttering a great deal, in which *la Madonna* and
dolore were the only words that could be distinctly
heard.

"Maria," exclaimed Mr. Earnscliffe, "you
are surely not going to give *la bambina* such
a bad example!" and, turning to Anina, he
added, "Show your Madonna to *la madre*, my
child."

The trembling little hands began to undo the
lid, and Mr. Earnscliffe said in a low tone, " I
must wish you *addio* now, *amici, siate felici.*"
He pressed a hand of each; then bent down and
gave Anina a hurried kiss, and said, " Take her,
Paolo." He turned and walked away as fast as
he could.

Paolo held Anina, who struggled to get free
and run after Mr. Earnscliffe, whilst Maria knelt
down, and in an excited tone called on the
Santissima Madre di Dio to guard and protect
him in life, and after death to lead him to her
Divine Son in the bright heavens above.

Mr. Earnscliffe heard it, and for the moment
their lively faith in the influence of a mother,

even over a Divine Son, appeared to him to be
strangely beautiful.   That scene often recurred to
his memory, and he scoffed not at it, but his heart
yearned towards the poor superstitious Capri
fisher-people.

Two hours later the steamer was bearing him
swiftly away from their island. . . .

CHAPTER XV

To the Piazza San Marco, in all its beauty and grandeur,—the richest jewel of the Adriatic's bride,—we must now turn. It is about nine at night; and beneath the long lines of arcades the gay shops and *caffès* are brilliantly lighted up. Their illumination—for, indeed, it is like one— contrasts well with the darkness of the great Piazza upon which they give; for, although from the centre of every arch—and there are in all nearly a hundred—there juts out a gracefully- curved branch, bearing a lighted lamp, they are but as faint glimmers in that vast space, making mysterious solemn shade of all around, especially, as now, when there is no moon to be seen in the deep blue and star-spangled vault above. The dark mass of San Marco's basilica, the *campanile*, the adjoining Piazzetta, with the Ducal Palace, the two columns of oriental marble, surmounted by the bronze lion of St. Mark and the statue of St. George, still guarding that port where, in days of old, so many proud galleys sailed in triumph; and opposite, across the Grand Canal's dark watery road, rising as if from the water's midst, the dim outlines of San Giorgio in Maggiore and Santa Maria di Salute:—it is, indeed, a combination unrivalled in the world!

In the centre of the Piazza an Austrian band is playing; and round the *caffès* are seated crowds of people sipping coffee or eating ices. Among them are Mrs. Adair, Flora, and Marie Arbi.

When last we saw them they were in Florence with the Blakes and Pentons; but now they are alone, and their friends far on their way towards England.

During the time they spent there, Mr. Barkley was much attracted by Marie, and was constantly at her side; that is, as constantly as he could be without rendering his attentions marked. He invariably tried to keep either with her or with Flora, on the principle, it may be supposed, that if one cannot be with the especial favourite, the next best thing is to be with her intimate friend; at all events, it prevented observations being made. Had there appeared to be anything serious in his manner, Mrs. Adair would naturally have considered herself obliged to interfere, as Marie must be given up to the de St. Severans free from any entanglement; but Mr. Barkley

managed so well that it would have been difficult
to say which he liked best, Flora or Marie,
although they were nearly three weeks in
Florence, and met almost every day.

But what were Mr. Barkley's real feelings?
Was he only amusing himself, or was it something deeper? Yes, it was something deeper; he
loved Marie as he had never loved before or would
ever love again, even though he should not marry
her, which was very probable, as there would be
many difficulties in the way, and he was one who
was more likely to succumb to difficulties than to
bear up against and conquer them.

He was the only son of an Irish nobleman, who
—as unfortunately so many do in the sister
island—had lived beyond his income, got his
property deeply into debt, and trusted to his
son's making a rich marriage in order to clear it.
Edmund Barkley himself, in a vague way, gave
in to this idea. He thought that fortune would
be a most desirable addition to the charms of the
future lady of his choice ; but, being fastidious to
a fault, he had hitherto found all the heiresses
of his acquaintance unattractive, and answered
the parental urgings to his marrying quickly
with, "Time enough, father; the right heiress
has not appeared yet. And if she should not
appear at all,—well, I suppose, as a *pis aller*, I

must take one of those whom you have named; but to make up my mind to that will require a good long run of freedom." So he kept his liberty, and went from flower to flower until he met Marie, and—never imagining that the little unsophisticated African girl could really touch his world-proved heart—he dashed into a brisk general flirtation with her; when, one day, to his great dismay, a sad truth dawned upon him. He caught himself dreaming day-dreams of Marie presiding in his ancestral halls, and charming everybody around her with her *naïve* grace, and her sweet, wild voice warbling her simple ballads, which she sang with such feeling that all who love music rather as the highest expression of language than of harmonised and learned combinations—as speaking to the heart rather than the judgment—would prefer her singing to that of the finished pupil of a fashionable London master. Marie's history, too, had taken a strong hold of his imagination; and even more,—although, perhaps, unknown to himself,—there was a feeling that this little creature, so unequal to himself in intelligence and education, had acted with a degree of strength and heroism of which he was incapable; so that, almost involuntarily, he looked up to her as something above him, loving her at the same time with the pro-

tecting love of a man for gentleness and innocence.

This discovery set him thinking :—"Marie has
no position, and of course not much fortune ; she
is not even St. Severan's child, so he may not
give her anything. . . . It will never do for me ;
I must think no more about her in this way.
Adieu, then, sweet Marie ; would that it could be
otherwise, but it cannot. So, once more adieu,
my bright little fairy !"

After these musings he took up a novel which
lay on the table ; but Marie would not be dismissed from his thoughts in this summary manner.
He saw her face multiplied in the pages of the
book instead of its printed characters. He closed
it and thought he would try a little music. He
went into the saloon, where there was a piano,
and began to play some of his favourite reveries ;
but insensibly he glided into the melodies which
Marie used to sing, and which he knew so well.
Then the sound of her soft voice began to ring
in his ear ; and he ceased to play that he might
better listen to those clear young tones which were
sounding, not on his ear, but in his heart. . . .
"Devil take it !" he exclaimed aloud, and starting
up from the piano ; "I have never allowed myself
to be really caught by this little wilding ! Yet
it looks horribly like it. . . . I see I must keep
away from her !"

He shut down the piano, and went back to his own room ; then he took up the novel again, muttering, "Novels must certainly be gone to the bad when they can't amuse a man for half-an-hour ! I remember the time when I could sit for hours over them." Mr. Barkley did not seem to remember that he, perhaps, was changed rather than the novels.

There came a knock at the door. He lazily drawled out, "*Entrate.*" In came his sister with her cloak on, and, seeing him lying in an arm-chair in his dressing-gown, with a novel in his hand, she exclaimed—

" What are you about, Edmund ? Are you not coming ? "

" Where, may I ask ? "

" You cannot have forgotten that the Adair and Blake party have got permission to see San Donato—Demidoff's Villa—and have asked us to go with them ? We are to call for one of the girls at eleven. You know, the laying out of the grounds is said to be very beautiful, and the house itself gorgeous. There are collections of paintings, statues, and I know not what, to say nothing of the charms of *living statues*, Master Edmund—eh ? "

Here was a test for his newly-formed resolution of avoiding Marie. What a pleasant vista his sister's words had called up, of wandering in the grounds of San Donato with Marie—getting purposely separated from the others, and only finding them after a needlessly long search; but it was just what he ought to keep clear of; and he felt irritated with Mrs. Penton for thus putting the temptation before him. However, he would be strong — he would sternly resist it—and in accordance with this determination he answered gruffly—

"I can't go and expose myself to such a sun as this. I have a headache."

Mrs. Penton turned round from the survey which she had been making of herself in the glass, and looked at him laughingly as she said—

"What's up now, Edmund? Have the little African's charms palled already?"

"Damn it!" he muttered, with uncontrollable irritation.

"Damn what, Edmund?" asked his sister, laughing more than ever. "San Donato or me? or perhaps the little African?"

"How tiresome you are, Maria! I told you that I could not go because I had a headache, and the sun is so awfully strong to-day."

"Of which I believe as much as you do. You were quite well an hour ago. The headache is nothing but a sham. Perhaps you have got some

new *innamorata;* but come: the little African is
not so bad after all. She will do once in a way;
and you know at first you certainly were a little
épris in that quarter."

"For pity's sake, Maria, go to San Donato, and
leave me in peace ! How teasing women can be !
What a happy fellow I am not to have a wife !"

"It strikes me, my dear sir, that you are anything but a *happy* fellow this morning. Now I
am going; but tell me first, what has made you
so bearish ?"

"If I am bearish, I think the best thing you
can do is to get out of my way at once."

"I quite agree with you. You might tear me
to pieces if I remained much longer in your den;
but I daresay, when this fit has passed over, you
will regret that you did not come with us. Indeed, I should not be astonished if you were to
follow us, if only for the pleasure such a vain
creature would take in seeing the little African's
bright eyes look brighter still when you appear."

Mrs. Penton retreated after this sally, but
called out from the door—

"Good-bye, dear ! I hope some kind fairy
will soon transform you back to a man ! Shall
I send the little African to you ? and then you
and she could play 'Beauty and the Beast' over
again ?'

She closed the door as Mr. Barkley dashed his book into the opposite corner of the room, and began to walk up and down in a state of laughable irritation, declaring that women were the plagues of a man's life, and that he wished they were all kept locked up and out of the way, as in the East. Having given utterance to this charitable wish towards the fair sex, he threw off his dressing-gown, dragged on a coat, and, seizing his hat, he went out and walked to the Belle Arti, quite forgetful of his asserted headache and dread of the sun. Beato Angelico, at least, could not fail to absord his attention.

Alas for il Beato! His pictures could teach no grand lessons to his admirer to-day. His beautiful angels, lovingly leading the enfranchised spirits of their earthly charges over flower-clad meadows to the heavenly Jerusalem, only suggested to Mr. Barkley how delightful it would be to be wandering thus in the shady alleys of San Donato with Marie; and he felt more than half inclined to curse his folly in having refused to go. . . . At last, tired even of Beato Angelico, he left the Accademia; and as he walked home, he began to think seriously that he had behaved like a fool. "After all," said he to himself, "St. Severan might give her a fortune, and then I don't see why I should not marry her! Why

should not an African chief be as good as an
Irish one? and that's all my father is, I suppose.
In any case, the birth question would easily be
got over, if it were not for that damned money;
and if it were not for my father, I would marry
her, fortune or no fortune. But that is all for the
future: there is no good in making one's self
miserable about it now. 'Sufficient for the day
is the evil thereof.' . . . If I thought that Maria
would not tease me unmercifully, I declare I
would do as she said—follow them to San Donato.
By-the-bye, though, the sun has got all clouded
over, and dread of its heat was my excuse for not
going; now that it has disappeared, I can go
without any sacrifice of dignity, and I am glad to
see that Maria does not think I really care for
little Marie; if she did, she would try to keep me
away from her, instead of laughing at me about
her. . . . And so here goes for a pleasant day."
He called a carriage, and drove to San Donato.

Thus ended Mr. Barkley's resolution to avoid
Marie, and thenceforth he struggled no more
against the stream, but let himself float gently
down, enjoying the present, and, as far as possible, shutting out all thought of the future. The
spoiled child of his family and of the world, he
was too much accustomed to self-indulgence to
refrain from pleasing himself because of the pos-

sible pain which he might inflict on others,—in fact, he never thought about it. Intentionally, he would not render any one unhappy,—how much less Marie; yet he was in a very fair way of so doing by this thoughtless gratification of his own wishes. . . .

At length arrived the last evening of their stay in Florence. The Adairs and the Blakes spent it at the Pentons'. Marie, as usual, sang a good deal; but she remained seated at the piano after she had ceased singing, until Flora went over to say that it was time to go away, when the latter saw to her astonishment that Marie's eyes were full of tears, and Mr. Barkley—he had been standing by her all the time trifling with the music—was looking down at her with a very unmistakable expression of intense interest. He tried to say something light about the pain of leave-taking in general; but as Flora raised her eyes from the tearful Marie, and looked earnestly at him, he coloured, and exclaimed in a low tone—

"Forgive me, Miss Adair! I know that I ought to have kept away, and I tried—indeed, I did!—but it was too strong for me!"

. "I do not know what all this means, Mr. Barkley," answered Flora, gravely; "but it appears to me difficult to explain satisfactorily.

Mignonne, dry up those tell-tale tears, we are
going now."

"Oh, Flore!"—and Marie leaned her head
against Flora as she pressed her handkerchief to
her eyes.

"For your own sake, Marie, try not to let it
be seen that this leave-taking affects you so
much," whispered Flora, and, turning to Mr.
Barkley, she spoke to him for a few moments on
some indifferent subject, so as to give Marie time
to recover herself; then, seeing that she had
dried up the tears and only looked pale and
dejected, she said, "Come now, Mignonne," and
they joined the others who were wishing the
Pentons good-bye.

Mr. Barkley said he would walk home with
them, and took care to get Flora to himself. He
then told her that he had yielded to the temptation of being with Marie, persuading himself that
perhaps he might be able to marry her after all;
and as a salve to his conscience, he had determined
not to utter one word of love to her. The last
evening, however, had been too much for him,
he forgot all but his love and his yearning desire
to know if it were returned. He now bitterly
blamed himself for not having had the strength
to go away at first, and, more than all, for his
conduct on that evening.

"It was particularly reprehensible in you, Mr. Barkley," answered Flora, " to speak to Marie as you have done, knowing that she is not with her own friends."

" I know it, Miss Adair, and, until this evening, I assure you that I scrupulously avoided "—and this was literally true—"anything like love-making."

" Even so, Mr. Barkley, your determination not to *speak* of love to her was only a splitting of hairs; you felt that you loved her, and were not without hope that she might respond to that feeling ; nevertheless, although you know that you could—*would* is perhaps the more fitting word— not ask her to marry you now, you continued to seek her society. Was it honourable ? "

"I can only say again, I know but too well how much I am to blame, but will you make no excuse for the power of temptation ? . . . Believe me, I would give worlds to marry her."

" You would give worlds to marry her," replied Flora, with a bitter smile, " yet there is no real impediment; surely there is a strange inconsistency in this ? God knows how far *I* would go in excusing any yielding to strong temptation, but I *cannot* excuse any one for inflicting pain on another when it only requires a resolute act of his will to avoid it."

" By heavens, Miss Adair, it is true that I would give worlds to marry Marie—I beg your pardon —Miss Arbi ; and I would do so, fortune or no fortune, were I my own master, but my father would disinherit me if I married in opposition to his wishes ; he has already told me so, and I could not ask any one to marry me on nothing."

"I don't believe that your father would disinherit you, Mr. Barkley, you, his only son, his idol, and the future lord. But pray do not imagine that I want you to marry Marie. I only speak thus because it is laughable to hear a *man* say that he cannot ask one whom he professes to love, to marry him unless she has a certain number of thousands, because, forsooth, his father will disinherit him ! But as far as regards Marie, I would greatly prefer that you did not marry her, unless it be that her affections are very deeply engaged, and this I hope there is no great fear of. You have not treated her well, Mr. Barkley, and I do not think that you are suited to each other. I doubt if your happiness would be of very long duration."

" Oh, Miss Adair ! "

"Spare me a lover's rhapsody, please, and take a word of advice from me : try to forget Marie, as I trust and believe she will forget you ;—but here we are at the hotel, so good-bye."

" You are dreadfully hard upon me, Miss Adair, but it is no use to talk of forgetting. I love Marie, and shall ever love her, truly ! "

. " Then act like a man gifted with a free will," answered Flora, as she entered the hotel.

Flora and Marie slept in the same room, so, before going to bed, the former heard a tearful confession of love and sorrow from poor gentle little Marie. The wretched weakness of her lover's conduct seemed to have no effect upon her, although to Flora it appeared despicable, and she thought to herself, " Such an one would not do for me; he whom I shall love must be strong and great, even in his faults. He must be one of whom I could say

'He was a man, take him for all in all,
We shall not look upon his like again.'

However, it must be my work now to comfort poor Mignonne."

She endeavoured to rouse her by talking of her dear papa, Monsieur de St. Severan ; of how grieved he would be if she were to return to him after so many years, looking pale and melancholy, when he expected to see her in the bloom of youth and happiness ; and urged her, for his sake —and for all their sakes—to struggle against this, her first experience of love's trials.

At length Marie said—speaking French, as

she invariably did when very earnest, but we will give the substance in the vernacular—" Yes, Flora, I know it is very wrong to grieve so, to repine at what I suppose God sees is good for me. I know that I ought to be content to be unhappy if He wills it, but it is very hard at first, Flora. . ."

" Hard ? Oh how hard, first or last ! But you bear it like a saint, Mignonne ! *I* could not bear it as you do; it would be a hard struggle with me to submit to the power which deprived me of the person I loved best, even before I had known the bliss of being his companion."

" Ah ! It is very nice to be happy," murmured Marie through her tears, " but, if *le bon Dieu* sees that it is better for us not to be so, we ought to be satisfied, ought we not ? "

" Ay, and it is comparatively easy for a little angel like you to be so, but for me it would be a fierce battle. . . ." Were Flora's words prophetic ? " However, that has nothing to do with the present hour, the duty of which is for you to go to bed, dearest."

Marie's tears broke out afresh, but she allowed Flora to unfasten her gown and help to undress her. When she was in bed Flora kissed her and said good-night. Marie clasped her arms round her, and drawing her face down to her own, murmured, " Flore, what should I do without you ? "

"Better, perhaps, than with me, Mignonne," answered Flora, somewhat brusquely, in order to hide the inclination which she herself felt to cry. Marie's gentleness in her sorrow was so plaintive. "I am not saint enough to know how to console you with religion as another might do, I can only feel for and with you, darling, so good-night again."

At last Marie sobbed herself to sleep like a tired child, and next morning the hurry and fuss of departure prevented her sad face and red eyes from being observed. It was not a pleasant morning to Flora; she was losing her friend Maria Blake, and she knew that she should miss her sadly. On Marie she looked as one does on a pretty, loving child, but she could not make a companion of her as of Mina,—and how great is the loss of one with whom we can talk on the different subjects that most occupy our thoughts,—one with whom we can really have an interchange of ideas! . . . This Marie certainly could not be to Flora, for she did not think much on any subject, or read much except of light literature. She had no lack of intelligence and quickness, but she was by nature averse to application; she worked beautifully and was very fond of it,—it did not hinder her from giving vent to all her innocent gaiety of disposition in chattering about all sorts of little nothings. These were the things which made Flora think that Marie was not suited to Mr. Barkley; she would be to him a little attendant, loving, laughing sprite, ready to work for him, to do anything for him, in short, but to be a real companion to him; and Flora feared that when the first charm of Marie's beauty and caressing manner had become familiar to him, he would tire of living without one who could interest herself in, and, as it were, take part in, his pursuits, and that by degrees he would begin to leave her alone, and seek elsewhere that interchange of ideas which he could not have with her.

Thus, after they left Florence, it was rather a gloomy time for both girls, but the various sights of Bologna, Parma, Milan, and Padua—in each of which towns they made a short stay on their way to Venice—were good distractions, and Marie's light, buoyant nature was not one to which the absence of a loved one rendered every-thing sunless, so that sometimes she would be as gay as possible, although at others large tears might have been seen rolling slowly down her cheeks, as on the lovely night when she sat in the Piazza San Marco.

The band was playing a beautiful though somewhat sad serenade,—all conduced to a soft

melancholy which was deeply felt by Flora as
well as Marie; but her own name—" Miss Adair!"
—pronounced by a voice whose music she loved,
perhaps, too well, sent the blood flushing to her
cheeks, and made her eyes sparkle . as she
exclaimed, " Mr. Earnscliffe ! "

How inexpressibly sweet she thought his smile
was as he shook hands with her. Then he turned
to speak to Mrs. Adair and Marie. She felt too
astonished, yet delighted, to speak, but Mrs.
Adair said, " Well, this *is* a surprise! We thought
you were in Naples."

" So I was, but as I have not any ties to any
one, or to any place, my movements are often
sudden and changeable. I began to find it rather
hot, so I determined not to spend the summer in
Italy, but I wished, before leaving it, to have
another look at Venice,—it is so beautiful. Is it
not, Miss Adair ? "

" Yes, this Piazza alone contains a world of
beauty and interest."

" Quite true, it has indeed been the scene of
stirring deeds. We have but to look upon that
gorgeous Ducal Palace to recall them, and with a
shudder we think of the fearful dungeons with
which it is connected by the fatal Bridge of Sighs,
and half expect to see the terrible state barge
gliding swiftly and noiselessly to the dark

Lagunes where some poor wretch is about to be consigned to a watery grave. . . . Oh, Venice is one vast romance!"

He looked at Flora as if he expected that she would continue the conversation; but she did not want to speak, she only wanted to be allowed to sit there and silently enjoy the luxury of listening to him. Finding that she did not answer, he said, "How strange it was that on the very night of my arrival I should chance to see you!"

These words recalled to her the night when she had last seen him, and she replied with a smile, "I wonder that you stopped to speak to us, as we are all ladies. Do you remember the harsh condemnation which you pronounced upon women in general at Mrs. Elton's ball? And I have not seen you since!"

"So, Miss Adair, you have not then forgotten my unfortunate speech to you?"

"I could not forget it, it was so sweeping and severe upon us."

"I fear I was very rude. Will you forgive me?"

"Personally, I have nothing to forgive, but as one of the sex, I must repeat, you were very unjust to us."

I believe so *now*, sincerely; at least I know that

there are exceptions to what I then said, as
you"—his voice was lowered so that there should
be no possibility of its reaching any other ears
than hers—"proved on that very night; therefore,
you, personally, have a great deal to forgive."

Flora blushed deeply as she looked up at him
in wonder. "What can he have heard?" she
asked herself. . . . Just then the band stopped
playing and went away, so that this *sotto voce*
conversation could not be continued.

The loiterers in the Piazza now began to dis-
perse. Mrs. Adair stood up as if she wished to
go home, but Flora said, "How I should like to
see the Lagunes at night!"

"Then let us go now," said Mr. Earnscliffe;
"there could not be a better night for seeing
them than this dark and starry one, and my
gondola is at the steps of the Piazzetta. Shall it
be so, Mrs. Adair?"

"The girls would like it," answered Mrs.
Adair, "so I suppose we must go."

. . . What a happy closing to the evening did
Flora find in that row in the gondola! How
vividly did Mr. Earnscliffe's language call up
the past,—the far-famed Doges of other days;
the hapless Marino Faliero, the father of the
Foscari; great "blind old Dondolo." . . . .
Byron and Shakespeare lent their aid; Shylock

and Antonio seemed to walk again on the Rialto;
. . . bravos lurked behind dark buttresses for the
coming of their victims; . . . lovers fled in the
close-curtained *gondole* from cruel guardians to
some freer shore. . . . Mr. Earnscliffe did indeed
make Venice "one vast romance" to Flora, the
spell of which was hardly broken by his taking
leave of them on the steps of the Hotel Zucchese.

CHAPTER XVI.

WHAT a delightful yet wakeful night did Flora spend in thinking over the events of the evening! . . . When Mr. Earnscliffe's voice fell upon her ear she was musing sadly on the weariness of life, and the emptiness of its ordinary pleasures. And if perchance one did get a glimpse of something like real enjoyment, it came, she thought, only to vanish. But the vibration of that voice put to flight all her blue devils, or rather transformed them into bright airy spirits with rosy wings. . . . And now as she lay awake in bed, she kept repeating over to herself all that she could remember of that last hour's conversation, It was a habit of hers this repeating over to herself conversations which had given her great pleasure : it recalled the tones and look which accompanied the words ; it was a clinging to, and an effort to reproduce that which had filled her heart with delight.

Unfortunately for Flora, she did not love religion so as to find in it a centre round which all her thoughts and actions could revolve; and without such a centre—as we have seen—she found existence wearisome. For a while, indeed, her faith had been a little tottering; but, happily, this momentary wavering had been conquered. From the time when she first began to think upon such subjects, she felt that there could be no medium between mere Rationalism and Faith in a Divine teaching authority upon earth, or Christianity in all its fulness. . . . She thought and read, until reason itself—aided by God's grace —showed her that the Authority which had existed and grown with the growth of mankind— like all life, of which God alone can be the author —must necessarily be Divine; . . . that Religion —or the tie which re-unites fallen man to God— had been revealed by God from the beginning; . . . that it is the same yesterday, to-day, and for ever; . . . that this Divine Word, spoken to the Patriarchs—written by Moses—in the fulness of time became Incarnate, and left the Spirit of Truth itself to lead that Divine teaching Authority into all Truth, and will so lead it until the end of time. . . . In this faith she now believed with unshaken firmness, yet she had none of the practical piety of Marie.

Most applicable to Flora are Lady Georgiana Fullerton's beautiful words in "Lady Bird." . . . Speaking of characters in whom a craving for excitement is a disease, she says—"There is but one cure for it, call it what you will : self-education, not for this world, but for the next. The work of life understood ; perfection conceived and resolutely aimed at ; the dream of human happiness resigned, and in the same hour its substance regained ; the capital paid into the other world, and the daily unlooked-for interest received in this." . . . . But to "resign the dream of human happiness" is just what Flora finds it so hard to do, especially on that night when lying with unclosed eyelids, and a happy smile hovering about her lips, she whispered over the words which had been such music to her during the evening, and then added, "How nice it would be if I could die now before this brightness has faded out of my life, as it will do so soon ! . . . What a mercy it would be not to have to go back to the old, weary, objectless life again ! "

You see, reader, how faulty a character our heroine is : she could toil patiently for anything which she prized highly, and at no self-denial would she hesitate in order to attain the goal ; but passive submission to suffering, or even to the

absence of happiness, tried her sorely. Byron
says strongly, but truly—

" Quiet to quick bosoms is a hell ;"

and so, indeed, did Flora find it, although as yet
she only knows what the " absence of happiness "
is ; . . . the suffering has yet to come.

By half-past nine the next morning she and
Marie were walking up and down the terrace
walk which gives on the Grand Canal. They
were talking eagerly, and the subject was an
interesting one, to Marie at least. . . . Flora was
sorry to find that Marie loved Mr. Barkley more
deeply than she at first imagined; for although
she believed that if Marie were never to see him
again she would bear it patiently, be apparently
contented, and perhaps even marry any one whom
the de St. Severans chose, yet she felt that all
the bright joyousness of her youth and character
would be gone—buried in the grave of her first
love. Flora was sorry for it—very sorry; but as
it was so, she thought it would be cruel, as well
as unwise, not to let her talk of him : it would do
her less harm than to brood silently over the past.
Then, in speaking of him—of his tastes and inclinations—Flora found an opportunity of naming
books upon different subjects which interested
him ; and because they were connected with him,

Marie would listen to what Flora said of them,
ask questions, and generally end by declaring that
she would read them. . . . They had been talking
in this way to-day, when suddenly, and looking
up inquiringly, Marie said—

"You do not think me good enough—clever
enough—for Mr. Barkley, Flore?"

"You not *good* enough for him, Mignonne!"
answered Flora, smiling. "Why, you are a little
angel, and he is a very weak mortal; and you
could be *clever* enough for him, too, if you chose
to exert yourself a little. I know that study does
not suit my Mignonne's African indolence, or
French *esprit volage*. Nevertheless, everything
is comparatively easy when done for those whom
we like. But remember, Marie, there is scarcely
any hope that you and he will ever come together;
so, for the sake of your own peace, try not to
think so much of him : study, because it will be
an occupation to you and a *resource*, rather than
to please one who may never be more to you than
he is now. You know how it pains me to say
these things to you, dearest ; but it is to save you,
if possible, from any more suffering.

"I *do* know it, Flore, and I will try to do as
you say, and not think too much of him ; but——"
she broke off with a sigh, and added in a different
tone—"There is the gondola."

"Then I must go to tell mamma. I hope she
is ready!"

And away flew Flora. What would she not
rather lose than one of the precious moments
which awaited her at the Belle Arti? for they
were to meet Mr. Earnscliffe there.

Scarcely had they started from the hotel steps
when Flora descried a gondola coming from the
opposite direction; and although the features of
its occupant were not distinguishable as he re-
clined beneath the awning, she knew from the
first that it was Mr. Earnscliffe as well as when
he got out at the Accademia, and waited to hand
them on shore.

"At what time shall we desire the gondola to
come for us?" asked Mrs. Adair.

"Do not desire it to come at all, Mrs. Adair,"
said Mr. Earnscliffe, before Flora had time to
answer. "Allow me to take you home in mine,
and my gondolier shall sing for you: he has a
very fine voice."

"Thank you," rejoined Mrs. Adair, and she
dismissed their gondola.

This was not a first visit to the Accademia for
any of the party; and to Mr. Earnscliffe it was
as familiar as such a little world of paintings
could be to any one who did not habitually live
in its vicinity. This gallery is perhaps richer

than that of any other city in Italy in the works
of Titian, Domenichino, Jacobo Tintoretto, and
the two Palmas; and besides these, it is enriched
by the productions of many of the most celebrated
names in the history of painting, belonging to
foreign schools, as well as to Italy's own. So our
friends spent a most agreeable time there, and
only regretted that it was a farewell visit.

When they came out, Mr. Earnscliffe said—

"Do you wish to go back at once to your
hotel, Mrs. Adair? or shall we row to the Lido
and bid the Adriatic adieu? It is such a lovely
day, and your last in Venice, that it would be a
pity not to spend as much of it as you can in
these delightful *gondole.*"

The proposal was accepted. Flora wondered
what could have come over Mr. Earnscliffe to
make him thus seek to be with them. She
thought of the last time that they had looked at
pictures together,—it was at the Farnese Palace.
How disappointed she had been on that day, a
now, how more than realised were all her dreams
of the pleasure of visiting such places with one
like him.

"Must you really go to-morrow, Mrs. Adair?"
he asked.

"Yes, it is all arranged; we go to-morrow to
Verona, thence to Botzen; we shall spend a little

time at Meran, and then cross the Brenner to Innsbruck."

"And how will you cross? Will you take a carriage?"

"That would be the most agreeable way, but as we are three ladies, without even a courier, I suppose it would not do; . . . we must take the *coupé* of the public conveyance,—there is always protection in numbers, you know."

"If it is only the want of an escort which prevents your enjoying the convenience of travelling by a private carriage," said Mr. Earnscliffe, after a moment's hesitation, "I can supply that deficiency, if you will permit me to join you."

"It is very kind of you, indeed, to offer to hamper yourself with us, particularly as— according to what Flora says—you have such a sovereign contempt for women, without exception."

"*Without exception!* Does Miss Adair say so?" he asked, looking intently at her.

"Could I think or speak otherwise of your sentiments towards us, after that night at Mrs. Elton's?" she replied, blushing.

"Perhaps not, but will you never forget that night? . . . Can I make *you* no sufficient atonement, Miss Adair?"

" You *have* made more than sufficient atonement by offering to travel with three of us; it is
really quite heroic and saint-like, thus voluntarily
to impose such a penance upon yourself; I
declare, notwithstanding all your hatred to Rome,
you would make an excellent Catholic."

" If *such* were the only penances practised by
your saints, and the only objection to Rome, I
admit I should make an excellent Catholic."

" Well, perhaps you may some day."

" I should say not, Miss Adair. . . . No doubt
an hour sometimes works wonderful revolutions,
breaks down even the convictions of years; but,
unless you can make me believe that black is
white, I see no possibility of such a change as
that."

" Alas! I am not an enchantress, but if I were
one I should only have to touch your mental
vision with a wand to make 'the scales fall' from
it, and instead of making you believe that ' black
is white '—which would be false—you would be
enabled to see the snowy white of the mountain
above you, whose very brilliancy before had
dazzled you so that you called it black !"

" This is all very pretty and poetic, Miss Adair;
more so, I fear, than true," he answered with a
smile. Then turning to Mrs. Adair, he said,

"But we have not arranged about the journey—where shall we meet?"

"Ah!" thought Flora, "I see he is determined to have as little of us as possible; he will not come *with* us now, but only meet us and see us across the pass; it is a sort of reparation for his speech at Mrs. Elton's; and yet, at times, he almost makes me think that it is something more, that he really likes to be with *me;* but of course it is not so, he merely prefers talking to me instead of to Marie, whom he considers a child. However, be his motive what it may, I should be content if the present could only last." She was so occupied with these thoughts that she scarcely heard her mother's answer: "Then if you will come and spend the evening with us, we can make all our plans comfortably."

"With pleasure," replied Mr. Earnscliffe; "and now would you like to have some singing? Although Byron says—

'In Venice Tasso's echoes are no more,
And songless rows the silent gondolier,'

memory is not quite dead; there are some who still love and remember those echoes."

They all expressed the great pleasure which they would have in hearing the songs, and Mr. Earnscliffe said to the foremost man, "Paolo,—

Jacobo, I mean,—will you sing something for the ladies?" Then he added, "I am always calling him Paolo; it was the name of my favourite boatman at Capri. There is quite a story about his little child,—I must tell it to you some day, Miss Adair."

Notwithstanding all Flora's sage reasoning about his merely preferring to talk to her rather than to Marie, she felt a glow of pleasure steal over her as she observed that he almost always addressed her. "Thank you," she rejoined, "I shall be so glad to hear about Naples and its neighbourhood, particularly as I never expect to see it."

"*Chi lo sa?* Miss Adair, . . . and you would admire Capri so much! . . . But I see that Jacobo is waiting for us to be silent."

Jacobo sang of the past glories of Venice, his countenance changing with every varying feeling as he kept time to the melody with his oar and the easy graceful motion of his body; now and then his companion joined in, and the two voices seemed to blend together and float away over the waters—the rich swelling tones of Jacobo's tenor and the deep bass notes of the other.

Reader, have you ever known what it is to recline in a gondola, shaded from the sun by its

curtained roof, and the gentle motion, and the
soft sound of the oars as they rise and fall, lulling
you into dreamland? If at the same time you
have heard rich voices poured forth in song whilst
you basked in the presence of one dear to you, you
have known a luxury of enjoyment! . . . How
feeble are words to tell what its delight to Flora
was. More than once she felt that Mr. Earnscliffe's
eyes rested upon her, although she did not look
up; she dreaded that even a movement might
break the spell, and so she sat there immovably
with half-closed eyes, drinking in all the sweetness of the hour. . . .

Jacobo sang song after song until they reached
the mouth of the Adriatic, and then he asked if
they would like to go out upon the open sea.
Flora—who only thought of how she could pro-
long the time—answered eagerly in the affirmative, and complimented Jacobo on his singing,—
said that they were really delighted with it.

After they had gone a short way on the
Adriatic and enjoyed the fresh breeze which then
blew over it, Mrs. Adair proposed that they
should return, saying that it would be tolerably
advanced in the afternoon before they got home,
and they had all their preparations to make for
to-morrow's journey.

At their hotel stairs Mr. Earnscliffe wished

them good-bye until the evening, and as his
gondola sped down the canal, the girls stood
watching it as they leaned over the balustrade,
till Mrs. Adair said—

"Well, young ladies, are you going to stand
there, not star—but, water-gazing all day? At
this rate we shall have packed but little before
evening."

She entered the hotel, followed by the girls;
and now we shall leave them to that most interesting of occupations—packing, but revisit them
with Mr. Earnscliffe in the evening.

About eight o'clock, then, as they sat in one of
the arbours, where they had ordered tea to be
served, they heard the sound of a serenade.

"It is Jacobo's voice!" exclaimed Flora, and
she walked quickly to the railing to look for the
expected gondola. In a few minutes more Mr.
Earnscliffe stood beside her, and she said—
"What a sweet serenade! It is certainly a
very poetic way of announcing one's approach to
friends!"

"Yes," he answered, smiling, "although in
olden days—and above all, in Italy—it was
scarcely to *friends* that one's approach was so
announced."

It struck Flora forcibly at this moment how
much pleasanter it would be to stand there talk-

ing to Mr. Earnscliffe about the poetry of sere-
nades, than to join the others and take tea; but
she knew that it could not be, and so, with a half-
smothered sigh, she said—

"You see mamma and Marie in the arbour,
Mr. Earnscliffe? Will you go to them whilst I
desire tea to be brought up?"

"Cannot I spare you that trouble? I can
order it."

"Thank you. I think I had better go myself.
The hotel people do not know you. Please to go
to the arbour."

"I obey," he rejoined, as he smilingly raised
his hat, and went towards the arbour.

Flora was not a second absent, and as soon as
tea, and the ices by which it was followed, were
finished, the travelling plans were discussed. The
Adairs expected to get to Meran about the fourth
day after they left Venice; and it was agreed
that Mr. Earnscliffe should meet them there, at
the Post Hotel, and then they could engage the
carriage for crossing the Brenner.

By the time that all this was settled it was
past nine. Marie complained of having a headache, and went to bed, and Mr. Earnscliffe
said—

"How beautiful the scene is from the terrace
on such a night as this, Miss Adair."

" Yes; it is most lovely," she replied, rising, and going towards the walk spoken of. He followed her, and they leaned over the balustrade as he named to her the different buildings by which they were surrounded, and which she, being less familiar with Venice than he was, failed to recognise, shrouded as they now were in the dark hues of night.

He ceased speaking, and for a few moments they remained silent, until Flora said, " Now, Mr. Earnscliffe, tell me about Capri and your favourite boatman there."

They walked up and down, as he described to her Capri, its rocky heights, its views, and the celebrated Blue Grotto. Then he told her Anina's story. He passed lightly over the episode with Mr. Elliot in the morning, but detailed fully the good doctor's history after dinner. He dwelt upon the picture of the Englishman sitting on the rocks sketching, and the young wife leaning her little hands on his shoulders, and looking down so fondly at him, that even the old man envied him. Mr. Earnscliffe stopped, and Flora felt that *he* was now looking down on her; she did not dare to believe that it was " fondly;" nevertheless, there crept over her a delicious sensation of happiness. It was not a picture that a girl could well contemplate unmoved, when held

up to her by the man whom she loved, as she
walked by his side in the starlight ; and now, if
never before, Flora admitted to herself that she
did love Mr. Earnscliffe.

After a momentary pause he continued, describing Anina's asking for the Madonna, her delight
with the statue, then her passionate grief at his
departure.   Suddenly he changed the subject,
and said, "I have not told you that I saw your
friends, the Eltons, at Naples ; indeed, I dined
with them the day before I left Capri. I also
saw another friend of *yours* at Naples—Mr.
Lyne !"

How grateful she felt to the night whose darkness hid the bright blush which this name called
up ; and she wondered if Mr. Earnscliffe could have
heard that she had refused him, and if that could
in any way be the cause of the great change in
his manner to her. His words on the night of
his arrival, about the individual injustice to her
of which he had been guilty, seemed to imply
something of the kind. Ah ! if this were the
case, she had, indeed, cause to hope ! She found
it somewhat difficult to steady her voice, as
she answered, "Indeed !   And how are the
Eltons ?"

"Quite well, I believe," he rejoined hurriedly ;
for at that moment there recurred to him the

memory of Mary Elton, as she stood before him
that evening in the shrubbery, with flashing eyes,
and also as she appeared to him afterwards in
his dream ; and he quite shuddered.

"Are you cold, Mr. Earnscliffe?" asked Flora,
in a tone of surprise.

"No. It was one of those unaccountable
shudders which sometimes come over one. . . But
I am keeping you and Mrs. Adair up ; it must be
nearly ten, and of course you would like to go to
bed early to-night. I will go and wish Mrs.
Adair good-night."

He left her ; and again she leaned over the
balustrade, and thought that going to bed was
the last thing in the world that she would like to
do. His voice, sounding close beside her, startled
her, as he said, " Good-bye, Miss Adair! Will
you believe it? it is half-past ten. How uncon-
scionably I have kept you up."

"No, indeed, you have not. It is my last
night in Venice, and I would not have had it
shortened for anything. . . . Good-bye."

He took her hand and held it in his, as he
said, "This is better than the night at Mrs.
Elton's."

"That it is," she returned heartily. "That
night was not a pleasant one to me ; nor was
your parting speech a pleasant one to hear."

"I am sorry that I annoyed you; did I *really* do so?"

"Of course you did; you were so unjust, as I have said before."

"I was horribly so, to *you*. And so, once more, Miss Adair, I ask you to forgive me." . . . He let go her hand, sprang down the stairs and into his gondola, in which he stood waving his hat to her as Jacobo pushed off, and again sang a serenade.

As the sound of the voice came fainter and fainter over the water, and at last died away, Flora murmured, "Venice! . . . now indeed art thou to me 'as a fairy city of the heart.'"

Flora went to the arbour, where Mrs. Adair was putting up her work; and they both returned to their rooms. . . . Here was another wakeful night for Flora. She could not sleep; for a soft voice seemed to whisper every now and then the words, "He loves you." But Flora was determined to be wise, and not believe so flattering a whisper; and she said to herself, "What nonsense all this is. The proud, clever Mr. Earnscliffe love me, indeed! I know too well that I have no beauty, no brilliancy in conversation, no liveliness,— nothing, in short, which could win the love of such a man. I always felt that it would be so; that one whom I could love would be so superior to me that he could not care for me. . . . He is the world,—life,—everything to me ; and what could I be to him? Nothing, of course." . . . But the voice whispered on, and, listening to it, she at last fell asleep. By two o'clock the next day they were standing in the Amphitheatre of Verona, and Flora finally silenced the whisper with—"If it were anything of love he would be here now, and not in Venice."

END OF VOL. I.

VIRTUE AND CO., PRINTERS, CITY ROAD, LONDON.

www.ingramcontent.com/pod-product-compliance
Lightning Source LLC
Chambersburg PA
CBHW060535030726
47498CB00004B/1203